A medium-sized gravestone is c[...] graced with a bulging, moss-cove[...] the middle. I sit in front of it, slic[...] bag and digging inside for a paintbrush I bought at the dollar store. I gently brush off the moss until the stone is clean and dry. Then I take a smaller brush to weed out the cracks, sending dirt and bugs and little moss boogers flying everywhere.

I pause by the owner's name: Jace Hawkins, b. 1917, d. 1934.

Seventeen. Just like me. Seventeen forever. Just like me. Jace. Boy or girl? That name could go either way. Jace. It sounds so Civil War, so Southern.

I picture Jace in overalls, barefooted, fishing in a stream, a bowl haircut, a freckled nose. Then again, Jace could have been one of those frilly Southern belles. Sheesh, back then, they married you off at 15 or 16. Jace could have had a kid! What did him/her in?

I let these thoughts fill my mind as I gently tape a poster board–sized sheet of onion skin across Jace's gravestone, using strips of gray duct tape to fold the edges around the side and keep them secure.

I grip a piece of fresh charcoal and gently, gently rub the gargoyle from Jace's headstone onto the onion skin. The charcoal rasps against the paper, revealing an ornate forehead, then lonely eyes, a sharp nose, and fanged teeth.

Then I go and ruin it, pressing too hard. The thin paper tears, and I have to start again. It's after I'm through taping the crinkly paper back to the headstone that I hear the footsteps.

Dane.

But no. The footsteps are too heavy, and there's one pair too many. And they sound ugly.

ZOMBIES
Don't Forgive

Rusty Fischer

Book 2 in the
Living Dead Love Story Series

MEDALLION
P R E S S

Medallion Press, Inc.
Printed in USA

ZOMBIES
Don't Forgive

Book 2 in the
Living Dead Love Story Series

Rusty Fischer

Dedication

To Martha, as always, who taught me how to
believe in my dreams, even if they shuffled along
and ate brains for breakfast!

Published 2013 by Medallion Press, Inc.

The MEDALLION PRESS LOGO
is a registered trademark of Medallion Press, Inc.

Copyright © 2013 by Rusty Fischer
Cover design by James Tampa
Edited by Emily Steele

Typeset in Adobe Garamond Pro

Printed in the United States of America

ISBN# 978-160542636-5

10 9 8 7 6 5 4 3 2 1

First Edition

Acknowledgments

This book would not have been possible without the support of the many, many (surprisingly many, actually) bloggers, reviewers, librarians, teens, and fellow authors out there who spread the word as its predecessor, *Zombies Don't Cry*, was birthed into this world in April of 2011.

I have been constantly, utterly, and gratefully amazed by the support and enthusiasm of you fine folks and wanted to thank you all—you know who you are—for asking for a sequel.

You know what they say: Be careful what you wish for!

Contents

Prologue
Making Up Is Hard to Do

The monster creeps toward me, bony white arms extended, long cracked nails painted black to match his soulless eyes.

I strain against the ancient leather straps that bind my throat, my wrists, my ankles. I clutch a short piece of wire I've stripped from the rusty bedsprings poking into my back.

The monster groans as it shuffles in giant shoes and short pants, its hideous white ankles draped in drooping black dress socks: the Living Dead Businessman from Hell.

He peers not into my eyes but at my throat: raw, exposed, and long-since dead.

I squirm, fiddling with the stiff wire until it slides into the rusty padlock at my side and, with a quiet click, announces my freedom.

With my hands loose, I quickly unlock the bonds at my throat and ankles. I slide off the creaking mattress just as Frankenstein Jr. reaches me. He growls, louder now, swinging his long arms, licking his headstone-yellow teeth.

I laugh as I inch toward the front door. Its frosted window says Laboratory backward in peeling big block letters.

I easily pick the old-fashioned brass lock and swing the door open just in time to feel hands around my neck. I stumble back, escaping the weak grasp. Now what?

In the room are two shuffling creatures. One is tall and looming. The other is my height but hulky. Both are hell-bent on my ultimate destruction.

Frantically I search the shelves and tables lining the back wall of the ancient lab. All I find are rows and rows of dusty, odd-shaped beakers and flasks locked away. I need some type of weapon.

Meanwhile two pairs of giant feet straggle in my direction. I peer back to see the pursuers' mouths agape. Their teeth are broken. Their hands are outstretched.

I hold up my quivering piece of rusty wire. It's pitiful in the light of day. It's harmless, except to this 100-year-old padlock in front of me. The lock clatters down, and I reach for the nearest beaker, dropping it. I pivot on one bare foot and watch it shatter to the floor. The liquid hisses and spits smoke. I'm engulfed in a whirl of thick fog and . . .

END SCENE.

The lights go up, the small midday crowd roars its approval, and on either side of me Stamp and Dane doff their ghoulish Frankenstein Jr. masks. The guys bow dramatically and wink at the family of chubby English tourists sitting in the front row.

The ushers hand out our cheesy black-and-white head shots, and we autograph a few. The three of us in costume mug for the cameras.

The last of the crowd file out of the small, musty auditorium and into the bright Florida sunlight.

I shove Stamp playfully as he tugs off his latex monster gloves. "Maybe you can break both my feet next show. I could use a week or two off."

He smiles, shouldering me as we head toward the tiny dressing room just off the wooden stage to the left. "Maybe you should mind your marks"—he gives me that toothy grin—"and your toes will stay out of trouble."

"You were both off your marks," Dane growls as he slumps into the scarred wooden chair in front of his vanity mirror. With a tissue he swipes the grease paint from around his eyes. He carefully folds the blackened sheet and sets it on the trash overflowing from the can at his feet.

"Sorry, De Niro." Stamp leaves on his heavy black

eye shadow for effect 'cause that's how he rolls these days. "It's kind of hard to see with a 10-pound mask on your head, but I guess it's easier for you since you have no hair to weigh you down."

Dane sneers, but Stamp is already up and putting on a gray hoodie to hide most of his pale face. He steps into the suede slippers he'll wear until he has to get back into his giant Frankenstein shoes for our next show in less than an hour.

He zips up the hoodie, and I marvel at how he's taken to the Afterlife so quickly. Not that I'm much older among the undead, but still. It's been four months since the Fall Formal that killed him, and he hardly looks a day older. But then, I suppose that's the point of being undead; you never actually get any older.

Sure, his skin's a little grayer, his eyes a little darker, his teeth vaguely yellow—but apart from that, he could be the hot guy with a (really) bad cold at any high school in the country. His little trademark Superman curl is gone, but he's still got all his hair. He mousses it messy, finger combing it over his broad, unlined forehead. "To look younger," as he puts it.

In the mirror I see him fiddling with the hoodie's zipper, his long, pale fingers fluttering while he sneaks a peek at my back. I resist a wink, partly because Dane is there but partly because, let's face it, I've never been very good at winking.

Stamp looks toward the employee exit.

4

"Is Greta on break already?" Dane's chair is facing mine. Clearly he's been watching me watch Stamp. "I thought the puppet show didn't get off until one."

"Greta's training the new girl this week," Stamp says abruptly, probably eager to get to his new squeeze or just away from us, "so her schedule's a little more flexible." He walks toward the door.

Dane nods and says for the thousandth time, "Be careful. Just because we didn't check in with the Elders and just because the Sentinels haven't found us yet doesn't mean we don't have to follow the laws."

"Thanks, Dad." Stamp walks out the backstage door.

The early afternoon sunlight streams in and reflects in 100 different directions off our vanity mirrors.

The door swings shut, and I turn to Dane with a wicked smile. "How long do you give this one?" I dab at the last of the stage makeup with my towelette, not that it makes much difference but it does make me feel all *Inside the Actors Studio.*

"One week longer than the last." Dane cracks his neck. He's removed his bulky Frankenstein jacket, the dusty gray one with shoulder pads, as well as the tear-away monster pants. He's handsome in his tight white T-shirt and those gray sweatpants that hug his tiny waist, the ones that look like they were cut with kid scissors to make jagged pirate edges. "You know he's playing with fire, right?" he says in that paternal tone he uses whenever Stamp, or pretty much any zombie law topic, comes up. Or our apartment. Or what seasoning to put on our brains. Or what color lipstick I should wear.

"Yeah, Dane, I do, but . . . I'm not his mother, okay?"

"He listens to you." Dane rubs the top of his stubbly head.

"Yeah, not so much anymore." I slip into my worn flats. "Not since we broke up on Valentine's Day," I add unnecessarily.

He sighs but can't hide that crooked smile. "What did you think was going to happen?" He puts on his hoodie and brings up one knee to tie his battered black sneakers. "The guy was a jock through and through. Just because he's a dead jock doesn't mean he forgot his jock ways. They're trapped deep in his DNA, where the Z-disease can't quite penetrate."

I shrug and admire Dane's black eyes and hollow cheeks. How familiar his face is to me, how distant we've become since Stamp and I broke up a few weeks ago. I'd expected Dane to rush into my arms, declare his love, breathe a sigh of relief that we could finally be together, and . . . and . . . so far, nothing.

Of course, he could be punishing me for making it official with Stamp in the first place, but what did he want me to do? I'd gotten the guy killed after all. Should I have spurned his affections, dropped him like a hot—er, cold—potato the minute Barracuda Bay was in our rearview mirror and we landed in our skuzzy apartment in Orlando? I had to date Stamp. He knew that, and you know what? I wanted to date Stamp. Most of the time. Kinda. Sorta.

To this day, despite my schizoid feelings before, during, and after, I don't regret a second with Stamp. He was fun, spontaneous—the exact opposite of Dane. But he was also a kid, a goof, and so much of what made him likeable also made me jealous and bitter.

While Dane and I used our sleepless nights to paint the apartment, troll around town for used furniture or wall art, or exercise to stay limber, Stamp prowled the Orlando club scene, partying all hours and latching onto a new group of friends who didn't mind his cold skin, his stiff limbs, or the dark circles under his eyes.

I warned Stamp he wasn't supposed to pass quite that well with the Normals (i.e. heartbeating human beings), but would he listen? Hell, no. He drifted as a boyfriend, as a friend, as a zombie, until that fateful Valentine's night when he didn't come home at all.

There I sat for hours, waiting for some romantic gesture. You know, something zombie sweet, like a pound of brains in a red velvet heart-shaped box or a can of cat food with brains as the main ingredient with a dusty red bow on top. Anything. Something.

Instead, Stamp stumbled in the next morning, carefree and clutching some blonde bimbo in torn fishnet stockings and a black bra, her obligatory maroon lipstick smeared—most of it all over Stamp's face!

I stormed off, he apologized, Dane took the chick home—but it was over. All of it.

Maybe I was secretly glad Stamp turned into the boyfriend from hell, but I can't say I don't miss him. Then again, we all still live together in a dumpy three-bedroom apartment not far from the theme park, so *miss him* isn't exactly the right phrase.

It would probably be easier to take if he wasn't already on Girlfriend Number 3 since our little breakup. Or is it Number 4?

Or if Dane would give me the time of day. Yeah, he helps me rehearse my lines. He takes me garage saling for his favorite oval mirrors to match the one in the living room. But that's about it.

Right now Dane looks wistful, none too eager to roam the theme park between shows. We will, of course, if only to feel the warm sun on our faces and stretch our legs for awhile, hiding in plain sight among the crowds, but for now he seems content to stare over my shoulder at the stage beyond our tiny dressing room.

"Do you miss her?" I say quietly.

"Who? Chloe?"

When I don't answer, when I don't have to answer, he nods. "Sure. We were partners for a long, long time."

"I miss her too."

"Really?"

I shrug. "Sure. She was there for me too, you know. When it counted. She wasn't quite as tough as she acted."

I picture Chloe now, stomping around school, scowling all the while. The only thing she really did to pass as a living student was to scare everybody out of mentioning how dead she looked. Harsh as she was, she was only trying to protect the sad little life she'd created for herself and Dane.

"I know. She would be tougher on Stamp, though, if she were here now. She wouldn't let him date or socialize so much. She'd have him on lockdown." He gives me that look again, not the smoldering one I see sometimes when he thinks I'm not looking but the regretful one he wears far more often these days. The one that says he wishes I hadn't brought Stamp back after all. Not just for our sakes, maybe, but for Stamp's as well. "I don't know what we're going to do about him."

"What can we do?" I say, scrubbing my brain of the same regret.

"I dunno, but this whole Playboy of the Living Dead act isn't working. We've gotten lucky these last few months, finding a place, landing these jobs, staying under the radar. But now. I don't know. Stamp's getting too comfortable. He's passing too well. If he keeps it up, someone's bound to find out."

My mind, like our lives, is uneasy. Up; down. Happy; sad. Mostly, I'm afraid. Of what's around the next corner, who's in the next audience, who might show up at our door, who Stamp might bring home next.

Who knew that the battle, the bloodshed would be the easy part?

That living in the real world would be the hardest part of all?

1
The Culturally Confused Convenience Store

The bodega across from our apartment complex isn't crowded this time of day. A Spanish love song plays on the radio, and incense burns in the corner shrine where a Buddha sits among oranges and bottled water.

The shelves are lined with dusty cans and exotic fruit drinks in funky bottles. The posters on the wall are these kind of funky ads from the 1960s for sodas that don't even exist anymore, like Raspberry Ripple and Orange Fizzy Bottom and Lovely Lime. They all sound kind of good right about now.

Stamp hates coming to The Culturally Confused Convenience Store, as he calls it. Dane doesn't like it much better, although he's pretty sure there are brains involved in some of the crazier canned items, like the braised beef chunks on Aisle 3 or even in the way, way, way off-brand cat food on Aisle 6.

I grab a soda from the clanking cooler in the back of the store, next to open cardboard boxes filled with onions and dirty potatoes. Gargantuan Grape. That's really its name. It has twice as much sugar as a regular grape soda and not just because it's twice as big.

I take it to the cashier, this thin guy with a sweaty moustache and a fiery boil under one of his ears. He hands me a phone card without even asking, which is one of the reasons I try to never come in here with Dane. I'm afraid the cashier will do that in front of Dane and then? Game over; the jig will be up.

"Ten dollars on the card enough this time?" he says without much of an Asian accent. He's got on crisp new blue jeans and one of those button-down Cuban bowling shirts with a palm tree on the pocket. His black fedora looks heavy on his sweating head.

"That should do it," I say, just like every time. I pay in cash, as always, and drop the coins in the Leave a Penny, Take a Penny cup by the register. If anything, Dane's sense of hearing is better than mine—that's saying something—and he'd get suspicious if I came home jingling a ton of change.

The guy nods and turns back to his hot rod magazine.

I leave the store slowly, hand in pocket, feeling the plastic card there. I look across the street for signs of Dane. I kind of feel like Stamp with one of his girl-friends. What I'm doing isn't exactly illegal, but according to Dane it's not smart either. Still it has to be done, and what Dane doesn't know won't hurt him. I walk to the little ice cream stand on the corner.

It's old school, a little brown building with two windows and a huge plaster cone on top. It's so ancient there are actually pay phones—two of them—in a bank along the side wall. I take the farthest one. There's no door to hide behind, but honestly why would Dane walk by? I dig out the card and dial the code.

I call Dad's office phone, which is county-owned and I figure hard for the Sentinels to trace.

He picks up on the second ring. "Cobia County Coroner's Office," he croaks.

Despite wanting desperately to hear more of his voice, I hang up.

I lean against the wall, crack open my grape soda, and suck down a few gulps.

The soda feels good on my tongue. I can feel the sugar working in my cells, filling them up. Sugar. It's the only human food we can still eat, probably because it's not food. It comes; it goes; that's it. But at least it helps me feel a little more human for the few minutes I sip it.

The phone rings. Finally. It always takes Dad awhile to fumble with one of the throwaway cell phones he buys each month, turn it on, make sure it's charged, and then find a safe spot to call me from.

I put the soda down on the hot black pavement and

answer on the second ring.

Dad gives me his latest cell phone number and hangs up. Yeah, it's tiring, but when you're running from a lethal team of zombie-hunting Sentinels, you have to add a few steps to your routine.

I key in the code again, then Dad's number, and this time we're good.

"Maddy!" he gasps when we're finally connected. "How are you?"

It's only the fourth or fifth time we've talked, and it's still new for us both. "I'm good. How are you?"

"Still human. Last time I checked. And you?"

"Very funny, Dad."

He sounds good. I'm so used to grunting and groaning, it always takes me a few minutes to work harder and sound more alive for Dad. "They working you too hard these days?"

"Oh, you know." He sighs. "No more than usual. We're coming into spring break now, so I'm at the beach a lot. When will kids learn not to go swimming after dark?"

Spring break? God, this time last year it was me swimming after dark, taking a cue from my best friend, Hazel, and trying to fit a little fun in before we went back to school.

"But enough about work. How is my Maddy?"

"She's good. Safe. That's the important thing, right?"

"Yes, yes, it is. Are you sure?"

"As sure as I can be."

"Well, you've got Stamp there, right?"

I smirk. Same Dad. Still on Team Stamp. "Yes, and Dane too, don't forget."

"How could I?"

I don't argue with him. We don't have enough time.

"Hey, I ran into Hazel's mother in the grocery store the other day."

"You did? How'd she look?"

His voice goes down a notch. "Not well, honey."

I frown. That's the worst part of being on the lam. Not the hiding, the low-paying jobs, the never going to college, or the constant fear. It's that I'll never be able to look Hazel's mom in the eye and tell her what really happened. Or at least something that might comfort her.

I don't miss the heartbeat, the blood flow, the sweat. I miss the humanity.

"I brought her a casserole the other night," he says shyly.

"Wow, Dad, that's nice of you." I try to picture him, oven mitt on each hand, walking down the street to Hazel's house, knocking on the door with his knee, painting on a smile when it opened.

"It was just store bought. But I heated it up first."

"Still, I bet she appreciated that." I look at my watch. Six minutes left. "How about Stamp's family? Any word on where they might be now?"

There's a long pause. "I've tried tracking them down as well as I could, dear, but you told me not to arouse suspicion." He sounds frustrated and not just because he can't find Stamp's family.

"I know. You're right. It's better this way, maybe, if Stamp doesn't know where they've gone."

"Don't be so sure. I don't know what I'd do if you didn't call me every month. Sometimes it's all I live for."

"Dad." I try not to sound too stern but fail. "Don't say that. What if . . . what if the Sentinels catch me or the Zerkers? You can't count on this. It's . . . it's a bonus, not a right."

His sigh is gravelly through the receiver of his cheap cell phone. "You start thinking like that and you might as well turn yourself in to the Sentinels tomorrow."

He's right, of course.

But so am I.

"When can I see you, dear?"

"We've been over this. Dane doesn't think it's a good idea."

"Fiddlesticks. When you left, you told me to wait a few months. It's been more than a few. How long?"

"It's still too dangerous. What if the Sentinels follow you? Or the Zerkers? It's not just about me being found. It's about you being . . ."

He knows what I mean. What it means to be on the run from zombies who want to capture you and zombies who want to eat you.

"I can take care of myself, Maddy."

Finally, I chuckle. "I know you can. And speaking of the Sentinels . . ." I hate to ask, but with only a few minutes left, I have to.

"They're still here, dear. They think I can't see them, but I can. Their stupid tan vans. You'd think they'd be more creative after doing this a few hundred years. Maybe they're on a budget. I don't know. But, yes, there's one outside my office right now. And another parked in the front drive at the neighbor's house while they're away on vacation. It's almost as if they *want* me to see them."

"They probably do. And that's what I mean: if you come after me, if I come to see you, they'll know it."

"Okay, okay. I get it. I just . . . feel so helpless. Me here and you there in—see there, I almost said it. I guess I do have a little to learn about life on the lam, don't I?"

"Just a little."

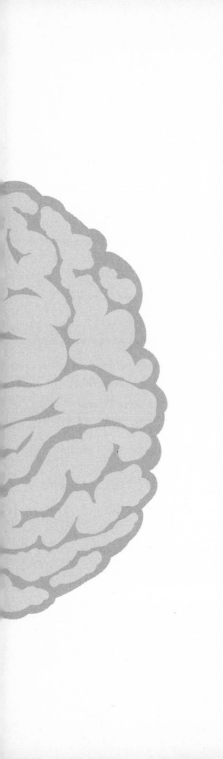

2
Jazz Hands

"Can we please change the music this hour?" I say to Dane while I row my machine in the middle of our large, crowded living room. Hey, some renters have furniture. Zombie renters have a home gym. Deal.

The apartment isn't fancy, but it's big and cheap, and that's just what three relocated zombies need to avoid dismembering each other in our nonsleep.

"What?" He looks genuinely surprised as he pedals his state-of-the art stationary bike. "I thought you liked the smooth jazz station?"

"No," I remind him for the five gazillionth time. "My dad likes smooth jazz. As do, you know, most senior citizens or other folks who've lost their hearing."

"Oh." Dane brushes a large hand over his close-cropped hair. He does that when he's trying to figure out a way to get his way without actually looking like he's trying to get his way. "Well," he finally whines, an un-Dane-like sound, "it's all the way across the room. Can we change it next hour?"

"No, Dane, we can't." I grunt, limping to the iPod dock on the flimsy bookshelf. "Because if I hear another tortured sax solo of 'Careless Whisper,' so help me I'm going to pick up my rowing machine and toss it through the sliding glass doors."

He chuckles halfheartedly as the classic rock station breaks through. It's a smidge more conducive to our nightly workout, although it would be really nice if someone started a station for zombie listeners, you know? I mean, really, all they'd have to do is change the name of their Halloween station. How hard is that?

"Yeah." He smirks as a blistering guitar solo heats up to blast for, oh, I dunno, the next 12 minutes or so. "Much better."

God, I hate it when he's right.

I drop into the rowing machine bucket seat, grab the oars, and get back into it. We've been at it for two hours now, doing our best to fill the middle of the night with something other than reality TV and deepening our butt impressions on the sagging couch.

I'm nearly four months into reanimation, and according to Dane if I don't start good limbering habits now, I'll wind up like all those rheumatic shuffling TV zombies there seem to be so many of these days.

"So," he says, inevitably, his bony knees pumping in his cutoff sweatpants, "where do you think he is tonight?"

I row harder, and it's not to rid my joints of the stiffness that's been building all day. "What do I care?"

"Well, we should both care," he says reasonably, which is totally annoying. "Because every time he stays out this late, meets someone new, or does something stupid, we all get exposed."

And that's it, really. Our entire life, all of it, every day, has come down to this one stupid thing: exposure. Or, more specifically, how to avoid it. From our theme park job playing monsters to working out in our living room instead of a gym, we're all about the down low. Way down low.

I row harder. I guess a lot harder because the next time he speaks, Dane has to shout over the furious clacking.

"You're not jealous, are you?"

I sigh, taking it down a notch. "No. We've talked about this, right?"

"Yeah." He huffs. "A lot."

"Hey, he broke up with me, remember?"

He shakes his head, slowing his legs a bit. "Face it, Maddy. You and Stamp were over long before he brought that skank home for Valentine's Day."

"Okay, well, there are easier ways to break up with

someone, you know. And, technically, he brought her home after Valentine's Day."

"What did you expect him to do? He knows about us."

"Us?" I snort.

"I just—it wouldn't be right to start officially dating so soon after you two broke up."

I bite my lip, trying not to say something I'll regret. "How can Stamp know about us if I don't even know about us?"

He gives me a look that makes me feel stupid, sad, and hopeful all in the same breath. Or nonbreath. Whatever.

"Trust me. He knows."

"So you're saying he's staying out every night because he doesn't want to be around us anymore? Because we're an us?" It's not the first time the thought has crossed my mind. "But Stamp and I made a clean break. He said he was fine with it."

"Maddy, saying it and feeling it are two different—"

A key fumbles at a lock in the front door. I steal a cold glance, and we continue exercising as if it's not Stamp unlocking the three locks, as if it's not 4:00 a.m., as if this isn't about to get really ugly really fast.

"You guys are still up?" Stamp says from the foyer.

"Just like last night." Dane grunts, pedaling harder.

"And the night before," I add, perhaps unnecessarily.

Stamp walks into the living room in his baggy gray cords and striped black-and-white hoodie that hugs his

6'2" frame like a second skin. His hair is spiky tonight, which makes him look even taller and stretches out the hollows of his shadowy cheekbones and dark gray eyes. He smiles softly, thin lips parting to reveal freshly whitened teeth.

Dane and I spend our theme park earnings on exercise equipment; Stamp unloads his on the local cosmetic dentist. What can I say? It works for him.

And whatever nightly activities he's engaging in lately are keeping him plenty limber. It's unfair. I still have to stretch for at least an hour a day just to look like I don't have metal poles in my arms and legs.

"What are you guys doing?" he says, eyes half-lidded and smile fixed on.

"Just keeping it loose," Dane says. "How about you?"

"Me?" He leans against the wall. Ugh. Last time he did that, his greasy blue hair gel seeped into the white gloss paint, and it took me forever to get it out. "Nothing much." He sounds sleepy, which as we all know by now is patently impossible for a zombie.

Dane and I wind down our nightly routine and wait. And wait.

Ninety seconds or so later, Stamp comes out with it. "Hanging with some new friends."

Dane doesn't touch that one.

But I do. "Anyone in particular?"

Stamp focuses on me. "Not really. Why do you ask?"

"Kinda late, don't you think?"

"Not for a zombie."

"Well, I doubt you were hanging with zombies. Right?" Dane sounds like an Elder.

Not that I can blame him. All it's gonna take is Stamp slipping a little of his dead, cold tongue to the wrong semisober Normal, and boom, instant zombie alert.

"Make that hanging with zombie." Stamp looks at me. "Singular."

I roll my eyes and look away, ignoring both of them as the boxy living room suddenly seems claustrophobic, especially with the bluesy, smooth jazz riff currently oozing out of the stereo. (Hey, wait! When did Dane change the station back?) We might as well be the three newest residents of the Orange County Geriatric and Rehabilitative Center for Zombies Who Can't Get Along.

"What is this anyway?" Stamp slouches toward the kitchen in his shiny black high-tops. "The Spanish Imposition?"

Dane shrugs.

Stamp never fesses up when he feels cornered like this. And forget about correcting him. That would really shut him down. Not that I'm not tempted, of course. (Former Normal honor student and all.)

I get back to rowing.

Dane halfheartedly pushes his long, pale legs in slow circles.

Stamp roots around in the fridge for something to drink. Like any self-respecting zombies, we have no food in there. Only sugary sweet, colorful drinks lined in row after row on shelf after shelf after shelf. Soda—the real stuff, never diet. Fruit drinks (not juice). Sports drinks. Anything loaded with sugar, electrolytes, and artificial crap that can boost our energy between bites of fresh brain (currently stored in the freezer, FYI).

Dane and I pretend to ignore Stamp while he rearranges soda bottles on the top shelf. He slams the fridge door, then slumps into a chair at our little table for three. He chugs the blue liquid Sports Slurp (his favorite) from the plastic bottle, doing his familiar little silent treatment.

The good news is he usually comes off with some pretty good info once he's done sulking. The trick is waiting him out long enough.

He sits there about five minutes before speaking. "What do you guys care anyway?" After another minute, he says, "You're not the boss of me."

Seriously? Did he just say that? Out loud? What is he, six? Scratch that. Four?

"No," Dane says, "but, like it or not, we are in this together, so what you do affects us all."

Stamp huffs. "You don't know my friends well, then. They're about as dangerous as a—"

"Are they human?" Dane barks, sliding off his bike and turning off the music to help make his point that *this is a serious discussion*. "Because if they are, then they can't be trusted. Any of them. Ever."

"Yes, they're human. You think I've stumbled onto

25

some huge, secret zombie coven? In downtown Orlando, of all places?"

"Is it called a coven?" I ask seriously, if only to diffuse the tension while Dane paces between the exercise equipment. "I mean, I thought that was for vampires. A vampire's coven. But wait, that doesn't sound right either. Maybe it's witches. Yeah, actually, I think it's witches who—"

"Who was it, Stamp?" Dane walks dangerously close to the table now. His shoulder muscles are flexed, which is never a good sign. "Who was it this time? Angela? Tracy? Lacy? Spacey? Racy? You need to be more discreet. Seriously."

"Val," Stamp says quietly, avoiding our gazes. "Her name is Val."

Dane snorts. "Whatever. The thing is—"

"Not whatever." There is true ugliness in Stamp's voice, in his face, in his deep-set eyes. "Her name is Val. Remember it, Dane."

"Why should I? Is she gonna be around a week from now? Two weeks? Why waste brain cells I don't have on people who don't matter?"

"Because she does matter." Stamp looks from one of us to the other like some teenager trying not to get grounded. "Because she's different."

My heart hurts a little, dead and useless as it is. Because what if she is? What if this Val girl is different? For a while it's been Stamp watching Dane share glances and inside jokes with me. Would I be strong enough, mature enough, zombie enough to trade places and stand by if Stamp was strutting around with some-one . . . serious?

"Yeah, right." Dane sneers.

I guess it's one too many disses for Stamp tonight, because suddenly he's out of his chair, towering over Dane.

"She is."

Neither boy moves an inch.

"Okay, Stamp," I say softly, easing out of the rowing machine and wedging into the four inches of breathing space they've left between their puffed out chests and bad attitudes. "I believe that . . . Val . . . is different. So why not bring her around for dinner some night?"

Dane frowns.

Stamp smiles cagily. "Maybe I will."

Doesn't he know he's sassing the wrong zombie?

"No maybe," Dane presses. "Definitely. You bring her for dinner if she's so special."

God, now we really do sound like parents. What's next? A curfew? Docking his allowance? Taking away his cell phone privileges?

"I will."

"Sunday." I pin down an actual date for once. "You bring Mel over for a nice—"

"Val." He shakes his head at me as if I should know better.

And, of course, I do. "Fine. You bring Val over for

a nice Sunday dinner and show us how special she is."

"Deal," he says, reaching into a pocket to grab his shiny new cell phone. His long thumbs fly across the surface. "Letting her know about it right now." He storms off, texting all the way into his room, where he promptly slams the door and turns on his metal music, just like the surly teenager that he is—that I suppose he always will be.

"You think that's such a good idea?" Dane sits across from me at the table and turns Stamp's Sports Slurp cap over and over in his pale fingers. "I mean, look at this place. You think this looks like a Normal's home?"

I stare at the portable gym on our living room carpet: weight bench, treadmill, rowing machine, exercise bike, medicine ball, jump ropes hanging from the key rack by the door.

"So we'll move the gym into the back bedrooms for one night. Big deal. Besides, you know Stamp. No way will this Val chick still be around by Sunday."

3

The Plot—and the Sauce—Thickens

"God, it's been so long since I've cooked human food I've almost forgotten!"

"Really?" Dane waves a hand in front of his nose as I set the foggy lid on the pot of simmering spaghetti sauce. "I just thought you were a really, really bad cook!"

He zips out of range just as I'm trying to snap him with the damp dish towel that's been draped over my shoulder for the last two hours.

Yes, two hours. For spaghetti. And a salad. And garlic bread. (Good thing I'm a zombie and not a vampire. Hehehe.)

"You take that back, Dane Fields." I put the towel back on my shoulder. "I'll have you know this is my dad's famous recipe for million-dollar spaghetti I'm making here."

He holds his hands up in mock defeat. "You're making

it from memory, I hope." Even now—oven on, the smell of fresh garlic in the air, the table set—and there is still a warning tone in his voice.

"Mostly."

His eyes go big.

"Don't worry. I used a pay phone, way across town, and so did he. It's totally, completely untraceable."

Dane shakes his head.

I finish draining the pasta.

"I thought I said you could talk to your dad once a month."

"It was my one call this month. Trust me. I'm not going to jeopardize what we've worked so hard to build here just to impress Stamp's stupid girlfriend."

He sighs, obviously resigned to the fact that he can't control me any more than he can Stamp. "So how is he this month?"

"He's fine," I offer, distracted with layering the thick, hearty meat sauce through the noodles in the brand-new lasagna pan. All the utensils I'm using are new. We never needed them before.

Dane leans against the kitchen entryway, looking dashing in gray slacks and a purple dress shirt, which has two buttons opened at the top. A thin gray belt winds around his narrow waist. "Sentinels still following him?"

I nod, smoothing hearty tomato sauce over another layer of twisty vermicelli. "He says it's down to two teams now and only every other day. I guess they're still hoping we'll come back and that my house is the first place we'll stop. Dad thinks maybe they're giving up and will go home soon."

Dane shakes his head and looks at me sympathetically. "They'll never go home. Not without us anyway. Get used to that. And tell your dad to get used to it too."

I nod, biting my lip.

"I'm sorry, Maddy. That's just the way it is."

"But it's been four months. I mean, what's the point after all this time?"

"First of all, we're zombies. Time means nothing. And they're Sentinels, so time means even less than nothing. Their entire Afterlife is spent destroying other zombies. And us? Well, we broke the Zerker-Zombie truce and a few dozen zombie laws. We set an entire high school—with the Living Dead bodies of an entire football team, a cheerleading squad, and a dozen teachers— on fire. So we're pretty much the Bin Laden of zombies, you know."

I shake my head, picturing myself in an apron and Dane looking like the cover of *Zombie GQ*. "Can someone tell me how we became the most wanted of the Living Dead? I mean, suddenly we're the baddest zombies around?"

He smirks at last, and all is good in the world again. "No, just the baddest zombies who were also dumb enough to get pulled into an all-out Zerker killathon. That's all. Anyway, tell your dad I said hi. That is, when you talk to him next month."

I chuckle. "Will do."

The scent of Dad's special recipe makes me wistful and homesick, but at least Dad sounded good today: hopeful, happy I was safe and nothing had changed for me, for him.

It was hard leaving him behind without saying goodbye, but we both understood that with the Sentinels on our tail, with the high school burning down, with sirens wailing, there was no way to leave town the right way. Only the fast way. And we barely made it out of Dodge leaving the fast way.

Since then we've settled into a routine, Dad and I. Like fellow spies or something. Communicating is complicated and tiresome, and Dane says we should only talk for 15 minutes at a time, just in case, but we usually stretch it to 20 just because there's so much to catch up on and we miss each other so much. And tonight Dad is with me, if only in meat sauce and oregano and vermicelli.

"How's it looking out there?" I say, hearing Dane setting the table.

"Pretty cramped."

The million-dollar spaghetti needs to bake for 35 minutes, so I wash my hands and join him outside the kitchen.

We've made good on our promise to relocate the exercise equipment, at least temporarily, to our two back bedrooms. We dragged the couch and coffee table from Dane's room and the two chairs from mine into the living room. So now at least the living room looks like a living room and not some triathlete's home gym on steroids.

"No, Dane, place mats for real." On the table, the clearance wicker place mats from Dockside Imports are practically on top of each other, the table's so jam-packed. It's really designed for two people, and none of us ever sit at it at the same time. We usually eat our brains while leaning over the sink, so we've never really run into this problem before. "This just won't work," I say. "It's going to feel enough like an interrogation without all of us actually sitting on top of her."

"Well, what, then?" he whines, holding the brand-new silverware to his chest as if I might yank it away at any minute and set it out myself.

"Well, two of us can sit at the table, and we'll set two places over by the couch on the coffee table."

"But then we won't be together." He mopes but follows my suggestion anyway.

Honestly, I don't know how he can look so tough and still act like such a princess sometimes.

"It's fine, Dane. It's not like this is some great banquet hall and we won't be able to see each other. We'll be 10 feet away, for Pete's sake."

I admire his work as he drifts toward the iPod deck

on the bookshelf. "Smooth jazz, right?" he says hopefully.

I nod because, really? There's no use fighting him on this one. Even if I say no and we argue for 20 minutes about some different station and he actually tunes it in, he'll only change it 5 minutes later when he thinks I'm not looking.

Dude is obsessed with the smooth jazz. It's completely baffling to me. He's all lean and hard, bony elbows, molded biceps, and close-cropped hair. You'd think biker music or something hard-edged or maybe even dubstep, but nope. It's wah-wah guitar solos and tickling ivories all the way. Go figure.

I wonder idly if he and Chloe used to argue about it when they lived together in their trailer back in Barracuda Bay. I can't imagine her putting up with funky fresh beats and smoldering saxophones. Then again, what do I know? I never imagined Dane being the easy listening type either. She could have been into golden oldies for all I know. Doo-wop or malt shop memories.

The music oozes, sticky and sweet and undeniably smooth. I smile because he's smiling and, believe me, there's nothing quite like a Dane smile. This cruddy apartment, the smell of spaghetti I can't eat and a dad I can't hug and a job I can't stand—and it all just melts away the minute Dane gives me that little crooked grin with the left side a smidge higher than the right.

He spies me in my apron, standing midway across

the room, and saunters toward me, that smirk overtaking his entire usually stoic face.

"May I?" He extends a hand.

I'd blush if I could, but I take his hand just the same. It no longer feels cold or strange to me but oddly familiar, like my own. He pulls me close, but not too, and we circle the small living room in time with the music.

He is freshly showered, and we've both been hitting the tanning booth near work for the last few days, if only to cover up some of the deathly pallor. We've grown so accustomed to it, but it can be a shock in intimate settings, like when Normals come over for dinner.

We've hit up Stamp's dentist, too, so our teeth are not quite so yellow. It's funny to see Dane looking mostly mortal, when I've kind of gotten used to us looking undead. It makes me think this is what he must have looked like in his "Before Life," the life he lived previous to his Afterlife.

I can easily picture him dripping wet on some beach somewhere, tanned face beaming, white teeth showing, hard body rippling, long legs extending from black swim shorts. I would have liked that Dane, but it wouldn't be my Dane—the Dane I've come to love.

He kisses me, cold lips gentle as if he can read my thoughts. His long fingers trace my spine until they rest at the small of my back and gently pull me in.

My own fingers circle his waist as we cling to each

other, still gently kissing, knowing there's not enough time to do much more. Not that, you know, we can do much more anyway. But, yeah, that's a whole other book. A science book, not a love story.

Even his small kisses, his quick kisses, are strangely exotic. It's such a new thrill, the sensation of cold lips on cold lips, and it's vaguely addictive. I hardly miss the warmth of human flesh but instead crave the chilly sensation of our mutual touch. It's hard to explain. It's still making out, but now it's special, like making out in the snow while the rest of the family's inside playing checkers around the Christmas tree or something.

"You should have asked me to dance earlier." I sigh, licking my lips, when I finally push him away.

"You were slaving over a hot stove all day." He straightens his shirt where it's tucked into his snug slacks.

"Whatever. It's just . . . I've missed that."

"Me too." He looks into my eyes, his lips a thin gray line now, the stillness surrounding him saying more than words ever could.

"Okay, then," I say. "Well, we should do that more often."

"I agree. We will. I mean, if it's okay?"

I smirk. "We'll see."

I start toward the kitchen, watching him straighten a fork on the coffee table. "You smell good, Dane. You should wear that cologne more often, you know? Not just save it for guests."

I don't wait for a reply, but I know he's smiling behind me.

A key slides in a lock a few minutes later, and I slip off the apron and smooth down the simple black dress I bought yesterday. I slide into my low-slung heels, giving myself a few extra inches, and scurry next to Dane in the living room.

"Why are we so nervous?" Dane whispers as the door swings open. "It's like being a parent on prom night or something."

"Yeah, so what does that make us, some old married couple?"

He frowns. "Would that be so bad?"

The door is opening now, so I don't have time to answer, but I would have said, "Hell, no."

"What's that smell?" Stamp says rudely, antsy and utterly alone.

"It's dinner," I snap, waiting for Val to join him.

"What?" Dane leans over just a smidge to peer out the door. "Did you forget?"

Stamp avoids our gazes and says, unconvincingly, "Uh, yeah. Yeah, it totally slipped my mind." He slams the door.

"No, it didn't." I give him a good once-over. Maybe even a twice-over, dammit. "Look at you. You're as dressed up as we are. New pants, new shirt, and is that? Yes, it is. You even got a haircut. I can tell because now I can actually see your forehead. So what gives?"

His nostrils flare, and I can tell he's about to give me some guff. But then he just kind of deflates, like an old duffel bag once you yank out all the clothes, into one of the chairs I dragged out of my room.

"She just called and canceled at the last minute." He yanks his cell phone out of his pocket and tosses it onto the end table. It slides almost all the way to the end, stopping just before falling over into the magazine rack on the other side.

He looks hurt, like genuinely hurt, and I am suddenly reminded of the old, Normal Stamp and how he always wore his heart on his sleeve. Even just after meeting him, I could tell he was a raw nerve. Happy, sad, scared, angry, relieved—it was all right there on his broad face, hiding just under that cute little Superman curl he used to sport before the limpness of his new, undead hair made that little flourish, that part of him, impossible. The new Stamp tries so hard to be tough, to be zombie, that I haven't shared a single human emotion with him in days, maybe even weeks.

Now he's nothing but emotion.

"Well, what'd she say?" I say softly, sitting next to him while Dane eases onto the couch.

"Just—she said she was having car trouble and couldn't make it, blah-blah. She's really sorry, yeah right. And maybe we could reschedule, yada yada. It's fine. Whatever. We'll do it another night."

All I want is to hold his hand and tell him it's all right. Not in the old way but because he's a friend and maybe it might cheer him up.

Dane says, "What if I call her? Ask her nice? I mean, if it's car trouble, we can go pick her up, right?"

"What?" Stamp snaps, standing to tower over us both. "You think I didn't offer to pick up my own damn girlfriend? What kind of a douche do you think I am? I did offer, but she said AAA was on the way, so . . . whatever. I'm going for a walk. I'm—I'm sorry about dinner, Maddy. And what I said? I didn't mean that. It smells good, actually. You know, if I could eat it."

He storms off, a ball of fire on long legs, before I can thank him or forgive him or, well, I dunno what I'm supposed to be doing for him, exactly.

Dane waits until he hears Stamp lock the door—all three locks—from the other side. (House Rule Number 1: Always triple-lock the door, every time, no exceptions.) Then Dane leaps from the couch and, like some supersecret extrastealthy agent or something, snatches Stamp's phone.

"What the hell?" I say, feeling a little too protective of Stamp's property.

"I'm going to call this Val chick, check her out."

"Dane."

It's no use. He's got that determined look in his eye.

"That's a little much, don't you think?" I say anyway. "If you want to double-check, let Stamp do it."

He's already speed-dialing.

I watch his face kind of with one eye and the door with the other, just in case Stamp barges in to get his phone. Frankly, I can't believe he hasn't already. Dude doesn't go anywhere without it.

"She's got it going straight to voice mail," Dane says, scowling.

I know that look. I've seen that look. He's got Sentinels on the brain. That's what that look is.

He paces, Stamp's sleek phone in hand.

"What's the big deal, Dane? Why are you so intent on meeting this one, out of all of them?"

Dane shrugs, then stops and looks at the phone. "I just don't trust her, is all."

"Why?" I chuckle. "She's just another nightclub skeezer who hasn't complained about Stamp's ice cube fingers yet. So she stood him up. She's not the first. She won't be the last. I just don't see what's so special about—"

"Because it's too easy to think we're out of the woods. To think the Sentinels have given up on tracking us down."

I'm still sitting. He's paused at my feet, peering down at me with his scary flared-nostrils look.

"So what? You think they sent some skanky, super-agent spy chick to seduce Stamp and call in the cavalry once they confirmed his blood pressure was zero over zero?"

He sits in Stamp's old chair. "Yeah, actually, I do."

"Oh." That kind of takes me aback. "Well, I mean, I was just kidding."

"I'm not. Now that you mention it, it sounds like just the kind of thing the Sentinels would do. In fact, I'm surprised they haven't done it sooner. Who knows? Maybe they have. Maybe we've just gotten lucky so far."

I look at him.

He looks at me.

"Pictures," I blurt, reaching for the phone. "Look at the pictures. Maybe he's got one of her in there and we'll be able to see if she looks like a Sentinel or not."

He yanks the phone close before I can reach it. He scrolls through pictures. "This was last month's chick," he says, shaking his head. "I recognize that stupid pink nose ring. God, kids these days. And I already know this one . . ." He's flipping through the images, one by one, until he stops and holds the phone out to me, turning it around so the screen is glowing right in my face. "This one." He points at Stamp and some short blonde chick at a club.

"What one?" I take the phone. "You can barely see her with Stamp's stupid arm in the way."

"Keep going."

So I do that little finger swipe thing so that the screen changes. Suddenly there's another picture, same club, same night, and the petite chick with the spiky blonde hair is kind of purposefully hiding behind Stamp

41

now. Like it's a game. She's smiling all cutesy, but no one's able to get a good picture of her just the same.

I keep going and see spiky, dyed blonde hair in one, a metal bracelet in another, a thick black sock in the next, a bare white belly over a short red skirt after that— but nothing more than flashes of her here and there.

Dane takes the phone, and we look together at another picture, another night, another club: same thing. Someone's taking a picture of them together, arm in arm, and spiky blonde chick is hiding. Even when you can tell it's Stamp taking the picture, she holds something in front of her face: a cocktail napkin, a giant wineglass, or her shiny pink purse. You can see her fingers in one, all over the purse, but the flash is so bright even the purse looks dead, so how can you tell if she is?

"So she's shy," I offer, but the words feel limp on my lips.

Dane's tongue is out, a sure sign he's working something over in his brain. His fingers fly on the phone's keyboard once more.

I sigh, then practically shriek.

The key! In the front door.

"He's back!" I say, as if Dane hasn't heard it himself.

"Sit," he orders.

Like a dog, I obey. But I wasn't even standing! I scoot back in my chair, and so does he on the couch.

"The phone," I gurgle as I hear the key in the third lock and the quick puff of air that happens whenever the door slides open.

Dane grunts, looks at me, then at the doorway, and quickly tosses me the phone. I've never been good at catching things, not even a cold, but here comes this sleek phone and—yes!—somehow I clutch it from the air and slide it onto the same end table we plucked it from only minutes ago. It doesn't glide all the way to the end and hang there like it did for Stamp but stops square in the middle. I doubt he'll notice, but with Stamp you never know.

Stamp still looks surly, maybe even more so, with his hands buried in the pockets of his crisp new slacks and his chin tucked deep in his stiff shirt collar. For the first time, I notice how cheap the black shirt with red stripes looks. Not inexpensive but brassy and flashy. And I wish, for just a moment, he would have asked me to help him pick one out instead of trying to do everything for himself all the time.

"Forget something?" Dane says a little too loudly.

Stamp hardly notices. "My phone," he says, reaching for it in the middle of the end table without further comment.

"Gonna try Val again?" I say, if only to fill the awkward silence.

He looks at me sharply, then softens. "Not really," he says quietly, turning for the door again. "I just feel naked without it, you know?"

Before I can answer, he's disappeared again, shoes scraping the pitted concrete beyond our welcome mat, shutting and triple-locking the door behind him.

I slump in the chair. "Phew, that was close. Who were you texting, anyway?"

"Not texting," Dane says, standing and dragging me into his room with those thin arms I always forget are so strong. "I was sending those pictures to myself so we could study them a little more closely and on a bigger screen."

"Oh," I say, a little disappointed.

I mean, I thought he was dragging me into his bedroom because Stamp was finally gone . . .

4
Monsters on Parade

Growl. Dane chases me across the stage of *The Great Movie Monster Makeover Show*.

Stamp growls even louder, pursues even more aggressively.

I nearly duck his wide, swinging arms. "Hey," I whisper as I hide behind him, the audience laughing as if this is part of the performance. "Take it easy on the over-aggression there, big guy." I shove him, just a little too hard, to let him know I'll only play the victim so long.

He goes flying, tumbling toward the end of the stage.

Just in time, Dane grabs the back of his jacket and keeps him from careening into the third row.

More laughter, spontaneous applause.

Dane looks at me from behind the Frankenstein mask. "Cut it out," he says, using the nervous laughter of the audience as cover.

Stamp stumbles back, waving his arms, making a big production out of it. I think he's smiling, even though I can only see his eyes behind the goofy mask. He chases me around the stage, still growling, and now I can't tell if he's happy or sad or scared or faking it or for real mad at me. I only know there should be two Frankies chasing me and there's only one.

"Hey," I blurt when we pass Dane, who's standing awkwardly at the end of the stage, peering past the house lights at the audience. "What gives?"

He springs to life, grunting and waving and chasing me offstage.

The curtain falls.

I punch Stamp in the arm. "The hell?"

But he's already onstage again, ruffling the curtains and poking out through the middle as he yanks off his mask.

Dane and I join him for our final bows.

It's cheesy, sure, but with these tourists, you wouldn't believe who passes for a celebrity these days. They'd rather get the autograph of some two-bit ham in a rubber Frankenstein mask than go home empty-handed.

Stamp does his thing, bounding down into the audience, still wearing his mask and then finally revealing his cute face.

The girls swoon and rush him with their little copies of the black-and-white photo they got up front. Don't worry. It's not even of us, so no danger of the Sentinels using it to track us down.

I'm next to Stamp, feeling lonely and out of place because nobody ever asks the non-Frankenstein girl for her autograph, not even out of pity. So I'm not as distracted as Stamp is when Dane bounds by in his sweats and a flannel shirt, looking around the audience before slinking through the chairs to the exit.

"Dane?" I follow him. I don't know. There's just something about the urgency in his step, the tension of his shoulders, that screams three-alarm fire.

I look back at Stamp, still playing the ham, growling and mugging for the cameras with the tourists. He doesn't even notice me. I race past the last row. Outside, I get slight waves from folks.

"Hey, hey, lookee there," says some red-faced bloke with an English accent, tipping his madras driver's cap. "It's the lass from the monster show!"

I bow and smile and see Dane's bristly head weaving and bobbing through the crowd beyond. I walk as briskly as possible, legs a little rigid for this kind of cat-and-mouse chase. Folks smile at me as I pass, figuring the stiff-legged walk is all part of the act, and suddenly I remember. I'm still in costume!

It's a pretty big no-no. If my manager, Mr. Frears, were to spot me offstage like this, I'd be fired. But he's not working today, so I'm not too worried about it. I look down at the scrappy dress, the fugly shoes, and the blood splatters on my stockings. I must look a fright, but sometimes it's easier to hide as a monster than it is to pass as a Normal.

"Dane!" I finally catch up, yanking him around more roughly than I wanted to.

He turns around and clutches my hand to drag me along. "Hurry," he says, weaving through the tourists, intent on getting to something or someone in the distance.

"Hurry where?"

He points with his free hand as we narrowly avoid toppling a tour group of Brazilians in matching green-and-yellow sports jerseys. "It's her, Maddy. The girl from Stamp's cell phone."

"Val? How? Where?"

He stops short, pulling me behind a giant green soda machine. "I saw her in the audience at the last show." He peeks around the corner of the machine and quickly looks back. "When you almost pushed Stamp offstage."

I picture her from Stamp's phone, glimpses of spiky blonde hair, pale little face, black fingernails, mesh-covered thigh. "How could you tell?"

"I can't. I just . . . don't ask me to explain. I think, I mean, I know it's her."

"So what are we doing behind this soda machine?"

"She stopped at the caramel corn booth."

I risk a glimpse past his shoulder, although he grimaces like I'm about to get us caught. The midafternoon crowd is thick, but I know the popcorn stand he's talking about. There, in a line of about five people, is a waif with spiky blonde hair. And then she's gone, abandoning her place in line and making for the caricature booth.

"Let's go, Columbo." I snort. "She's on the move. Although, it doesn't look like her."

Then again, as I catch flashes of her in the crowd, it could be. A peek here, past a burly man in a tank top, looks like her. Then, as she coasts through a sea of sticky-fingered field trip kids, she looks nothing like her. Too tall, too short, too broad, too thin.

"Why is she avoiding us, then?" Dane says.

"Have you seen yourself lately?"

"Funny." Then he stops, turning his back to her as I peek under his arm and notice a spiky blonde-headed someone sniffing our way, then turning quickly to disappear into the crowd.

"That little minx!" I'm sure it's her. Kinda, sorta, maybe. I'm dragging Dane along, weaving in and out of tour groups and sweaty, sunburned families until we turn the corner near the cheesy pretzel stand, and—poof! No more Val. Or maybe-Val. Or could-be-Val. Or probably-was-Val.

I start again.

Dane holds me back. "We could do this all day," he says, stretching one arm over my shoulder. "And we've got another show to do in an hour."

It feels good, his arm like that.

People smile at us, two kids obviously on break from some show, not hiding their affection.

"Why would she be here?"

"If it even was her." Dane cocks one beautiful eyebrow.

I slap him playfully on the chest, right between two smears of fake blood on his T-shirt. "You're the one who convinced me it was, remember?"

He sighs, shaking his head. "Maybe I've just been on the run too long."

And I know he means forever, not just now: his whole Afterlife, ever since he was reanimated. This school, that school, before Chloe, after Chloe, and now with Stamp and me. I lean into him, to show him I understand, that I care, and he nuzzles his chin on the top of my head, you know, the way guys do.

It feels good, and I don't want to think it was Val scoping us out. I want to be anonymous, boring. I can't believe undercover Sentinel skanks are watching our every move, like Dane believes they are.

"It probably wasn't her," I say. "We're just being paranoid."

"Yeah, probably."

We're almost back to the front entrance of the theater, all fake spooky with cobwebs in the windows and plastic ivy on the brick facade. A little girl in a Victorian apron and bonnet hands out pictures to our fans.

She nods at us warily, as if she's going to tell our manager about our little between-show excursion.

"Let her," Dane says, reading my mind as we enter the darkness of the theater. "If it was Val, I don't see us being under the radar for too much longer anyway."

"And if it wasn't?" I open the door to backstage.

He pauses on the bottom step below me, shrugs. "Then we tell Mr. Frears we were just hunting down some audience member who forgot her camera."

He smiles as if this is actually what happened.

I smack him again on the shoulder and turn, finding Stamp standing there, still in his stage makeup, tapping one shoe on the floor.

"Where the hell did you guys go?"

"Didn't you hear me? That little girl from the third row dropped her camera," I say, taking Dane's cue.

"So you had to go halfway around the park to catch her?" He's clearly not buying it.

"What can I say?" Dane slides into his cast chair and grabs a makeup remover pad. "She was a lot faster than a couple of zombies."

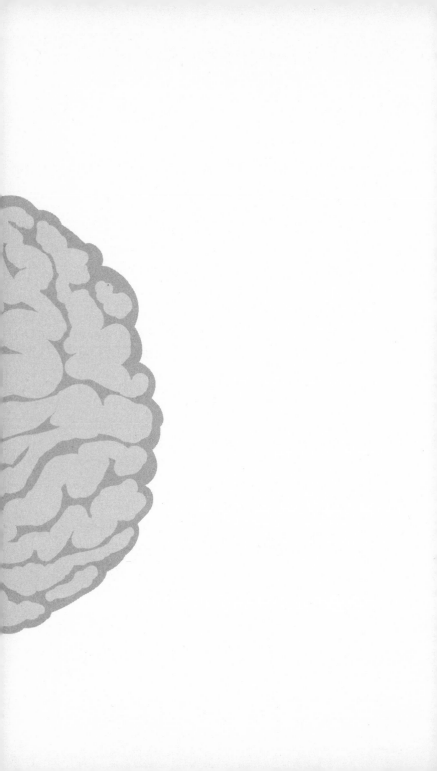

5
Cursed Again

"That's definitely zombie flesh," Dane murmurs Rainman-like a few mornings later. "Definitely. Zombie. Flesh."

Yes, we're back in his stupid room.

Yes, we're studying stupid pictures of stupid Val on his stupid computer.

And no, we're not doing anything else. Not one little thing.

Dude. Is. Obsessed.

"You don't know that," I remind him for the 673rd time.

"Look!" he says, as if he's suddenly remembered I'm in the room with him, as if I haven't already given it 1,000 looks, as if my neck isn't going to snap in half from looking so much. "Look at the way the concealer is smudged on her wrist in this one picture. See, I've blown the image up. Now, I ask you, who else but a zombie would have gray skin underneath?"

We're looking at another random club picture of Stamp with the Val chick hiding playfully behind him. Her small, pale hand is clutching the sleeve of his black-and-white-striped hoodie, and Dane has blown it up as far as he can without all the little pixel thingies showing up.

"Maybe the concealer is gray and her flesh is pale," I counter, mad because if we don't put this Is-Val-a-Sentinel controversy to rest soon, I'm going to start looking into ways to unzombiefy myself—permanently.

"Yeah, that sounds reasonable." He scoffs in that I've-been-a-zombie-longer-than-you way that always irks me for some reason. "What human in her right mind wants her skin to look like ours?"

"Speak for yourself," I huff, standing from the twin bed next to his computer, since he's been hogging the desk chair all week. "While you've been obsessing over Val and her potential zombieness, I've been hitting the tanning booths without you, so I think I look pretty normal."

In fact, though I would never admit this to Dane, I kind of look better than normal. (Zombie normal, that is.) My new zombie skin doesn't hold the tan as long as my human skin once upon a Before Life, but if I go for an hour every other day or so, I at least look less gray and almost, vaguely human.

Enough to take my hoodie down on the way to work the last few days and not tug on my long sleeves till they cover my wrists and fingers all the time. And after one more teeth-whitening session, I might even be able to smile again. You know, not all the time, but at least more than I do now. Lots more.

Wow, imagine that. Smiling versus biting my lip.

I never thought I'd do that again.

"You looked fine before," he grunts, finally turning around in his chair and giving me some attention as I linger at his doorway. "I mean, you look fine now, but there was nothing wrong with you before."

"That's kind of nice of you to say." I grin but not all the way. "I think."

"We are what we are," he says somberly, ruining it. "Tanning beds and teeth whitening and facials and all that stuff—I've been there, tried that, and it's a lot of work. To keep up with, I mean. And expensive. You'll see. Besides, I kind of like the real you."

"Wait," I say, ignoring the kind-of comment. "You mean, the old real me or the new real me?"

"Which do you think?"

"I think you dance around the answer too much."

"The new old you, before you started trying to impress Val for Sunday dinner or whoever you're trying to impress now."

I shake my head and slip from the room, leaving him in rueful silence. This is all getting too funky. With Dane and Stamp under the same roof, I mean. It's too much. I know he wants to keep us all safe, but I need to move out. Seriously.

It's too much like marriage up in here. Family. Nine

to five. Like my mom and dad used to be once upon a time, and look how that turned out. Mom taking off with the yoga instructor. Dad working 70 hours a week to get over it. Me rubbing graves after school.

But this is even worse because we're kids, really. And we're still figuring it all out. Between us, I mean. The moody silences and giddy rushes and slamming doors and dancing in the middle of the night—when we're not exercising, that is. And Stamp coming in at all hours, and Dane resenting it, and me hating it. Ugghh. Just . . . I can do soap opera on my own.

I drift into the living room, which still looks like a living room in case Val ever makes it for dinner, which Stamp keeps promising she will even though Dane and I both know that, no, she won't.

Which is kind of okay with me because, frankly, I don't know if the million-dollar spaghetti I froze from the other night will taste as fresh. Not that I care. I won't be eating any of it. Still, if he cares about her that much—and, of course, if she's not a Sentinel trying to trick us—I'd like her to at least enjoy the food.

Stamp has already come and gone for the morning, despite the hour. He likes to stay away from the apartment as much as possible, coming home late and leaving early to drift through the local mall or go from coffee shop to coffee shop, testing how far and how fast he can blend with the Normals.

I have to admit, even with my latest efforts at playing

it human, Stamp has me beat. Dane, too. Maybe it's because Stamp's newer. He's certainly been a zombie for a much shorter time than Dane has. Whatever the reasons, he's just more Normal-looking.

Dane says that happens sometimes. Just like there are tall zombies and short zombies, boy zombies and girl zombies, there are some real zombie-ass-looking zombies and then there are zombies who look more like, you know, the human people they once were.

Yeah, but I don't know. Maybe I'm just imagining it all or remembering his prezombie self too strongly to ever see him as anything other than alive. But it certainly doesn't hurt him with the ladies. Of all those pictures on his phone, every one was full of adoring human lady flesh.

I walk through the empty living room to grab the morning paper from the front porch, wondering what it would be like to stroll through the world so confidently that you don't just pass as a Normal but you're actually physically attractive to Normals as well.

The locks—all three of them—sound stiff, and I quickly open the door to the chilly dawn. I bend to grab the paper from the cheesy, scratchy welcome mat we bought at the dollar store when we first moved in. It's faded fast and the *O* and *M* are pretty much missing, but we're too cheap or lazy to replace it. I shake the dew off the paper's plastic wrap and carry the news inside, triple-locking the door behind me as I go.

The stationary bike is in my room—has been since the night Val didn't show—and I open the paper and unfold it onto the flimsy black reading tray Dane drilled in place between the handlebars weeks ago.

If you're thinking it's some big romantic gesture he did for me, don't. He just wanted to be able to set his game player on it after the hunk of junk ran out of juice.

Still, it works for the paper as well. I pedal as I read the national front-page headlines. It's about 20 minutes before I finally get to the local section. Then I stop.

Stop pedaling. Stop reading.

And if I could, I'd stop breathing.

"Uh, Dane?" I say sternly to the thin bedroom wall. "Can you come in here for a minute?"

"What'd you do? Break the pedal off again?" I hear the chair creak and his sneakers whisper on the cheap shag rug as he walks into my room.

"Maddy?" he says when he sees my face. "What's up?"

"Does this building look familiar to you?" I point with a trembling finger to the picture of the large gray structure, the one with the faded blue trim, on the front of the local section.

"Wait, hold up. Is that our place?"

I nod.

He leans in behind me, skin luxuriantly cold against the back of my neck.

Actually, it's Building D. We're Building C. But the picture is definitely of The Socialite, our ironically named cheap-ass, skid row apartment complex.

"What happened?" he says.

But I know he's just a few words away from figuring out, so I zip it until he does.

"Oh." He walks away to lean on the chin-up bar in the corner. And again: "Oh."

I stop pedaling. I didn't even realize my legs were still going without my brain attached. I turn toward him. "Oh? One of our neighbors goes missing from one building over, and that's all you have to say? Oh?"

He shrugs, shoulders firm in a V-neck T-shirt from his never-ending supply. I'm convinced he was a main shareholder of the Hanes Corp. in his Before Life. "We're not in Barracuda Bay anymore, Maddy. This is the big city. Stuff like that happens."

I nod, because, yeah, I'm not stupid. But if that's the case, then why is he avoiding my eyeballs so hard?

"Okay, well, so it's okay for you to obsess about Val's fake concealer smudge and stare at it for hours on end, but I can't even discuss an actual neighbor going missing in the last few days without you rolling your eyes at me?"

He shrugs again.

I read the most alarming passage aloud, just to get his attention:

Mrs. Ortega explains that her teenage son, Rudy, went out early Sunday evening to grab some milk and bananas from the bodega across the street and never returned. .

Rusty Fischer

The Ortega family drove around for hours that night, searching in vain, before reporting Rudy missing early the next morning.

"This isn't like him at all," said Mrs. Ortega when asked for a quote. "He has his cell phone on him constantly, even to run a simple errand just across the street. If he could, he would call. I think that means he can't."

Local authorities say that—

"Sounds like Rudy just doesn't want to be found," Dane says.

I toss the paper back onto the wobbly black tray.

"And if I was a human teen living in this dump, I'd run away too." He grunts.

"That's not funny."

He nods, meeting my gaze for a moment before quickly looking away again.

"Think about it. This all went down on Sunday night. This Sunday night. Million-dollar-spaghetti Sunday night? Val-standing-us-up Sunday night? I went to that bodega to pick up some fresh cream probably just a few hours before that kid went missing. That's not making your limbs go tingly or anything?"

I think of how Stamp always calls that bodega the Culturally Confused Convenience Store because of the Latin music and the Asian shrine and the variety of crazy ingredients it sells. I think of how the guy behind the counter knows when I need a phone card or just a bottle of Gargantuan Grape soda. I picture Rudy in there, wandering around, looking for bananas and milk. Maybe we were even there at the same time and I never noticed.

Dane shrugs, starts to say something, must know I'm going to verbally spank him for it, and wisely keeps his mouth shut.

"So hold up. You don't think it's even the least bit fishy? A local teen going missing in the same complex as a trio of zombies? Are you forgetting the Curse of Third Period Home Ec?"

He snorts. "I'm not forgetting it, but one kid going missing is hardly a curse."

I can't tell if he's so obsessed lately with unmasking Val that he's not hearing me or if, more likely, he doesn't want me to worry. And yet, it's all too creepily familiar to ignore.

I can't help but picture my BFF, Hazel, sitting in Home Ec, endlessly twisting one long, red lock of hair around her finger, sounding as alarmed then as I do now. I blew her off. "There's no curse," I said. "You're imagining things," I said. "Grow up," I said.

Who was I trying to protect all those many mortal months ago?

Hazel? Or myself?

And look at what happened to us then! One zombie—sorry, Zerker—infestation later, and here we are. Cursed. Forever. No more Hazel, no more Chloe, and the bodies are still piling up. Or, in this case, being hidden away.

I quickly discovered what few people know: not

just what it's like to be undead but that there are two kinds of undead. Us, the good guys, the zombie zombies who choose to live among the Normals, eat medically donated or ethically acquired brains, and avoid violence. And the bad guys: the Zerkers.

The Zerkers are the ones who can't or won't control themselves, who eat brains, flesh, bones, whatever they can devour, only try to pass when it suits their needs, and do everything they can to make a regular zombie's life hell on earth.

The Zerkers are the reason the Sentinels exist in the first place. They're why zombies need cops: guys in uniform who enforce the laws and keep the world safe, not from zombies but from Zerkers. And if it weren't for Zerkers, Dane and Stamp and I wouldn't be here right now. We'd still be passing for Normals back in Barracuda Bay, wearing lots of makeup and Goth clothes. Maybe sticking out a little but basically fitting in.

Instead, the Zerkers decided to mess with us, break the Zerker-Zombie truce, and back us into a corner. If we hadn't stopped them at that Fall Formal, by now they would have turned half of Barracuda Bay, maybe all of it. But try getting the Sentinels to understand that.

Okay, okay, so maybe Dane's right. Maybe one kid from our apartment complex going missing—skipping town, fleeing to the nearest *American Idol* audition, or whatever—isn't exactly the same thing as the Zerkers picking off my Barracuda Bay High classmates one by one. But still, it's enough to make me pick the paper up, fold it tightly, and save it just in case.

I turn to find Dane studying me from across the room. It's not a big room and more cluttered now than ever with the three exercise machines we moved in. His dark eyes are even more piercing than usual, which is saying something.

"What's going on?" I say quietly.

We've been circling each other so carefully, between Stamp's feelings and work and Val being a Sentinel or not, that I'm hungry to just talk to him.

He opens his mouth but stops. Finally, he says, "I don't know," and he doesn't look away.

"So what should we do? You always said to be packed and ready at a moment's notice."

I look toward my closet, where a single backpack has everything a good zombie could need for a fast getaway: leggings, socks, sneakers, hoodie, shades—all black—switchblade, Swiss Army knife, umbrella, three cans of cat food with brain as the main ingredient . . .

You know, all the essentials.

He follows my gaze, then looks at me.

So I say, "Is this 'in case'?"

He shrugs again, velvety muscles rippling beneath his tight shirt as the sunrise glows through the barely open blinds behind my head. "I don't think I'm ready to pick up stakes and skip town after all we've done to fit in here, but I do think it's time to get more serious about Stamp."

"How do you mean? 'Cause I've been thinking and, well, I know this sounds petty and all, but I totally think we should ground him, straight up. That would do it."

He chuckles lazily at my even lazier attempt at humor. "I'm not sure our boy would stand for that at his age. But what he doesn't know might be good for him."

"Sounds sneaky. Go on . . ."

6

This Isn't as Fun as It Looks

"You think he'll notice us?" I say as we tail Stamp out of the bustling employee parking lot after work later that day.

Stamp guns it straight into early evening traffic.

Dane, a more careful and patient driver, prefers the ease-in approach. He grips the wheel and tries to stay close to Stamp's rugged green Jeep—but not too close. "Maybe I should have borrowed someone else's car, huh?" he says helplessly as Stamp races two car lengths ahead.

"Next time." I force my fingers out of the dashboard and fold them together on my lap instead.

Dane drives a giant, ancient four-door, which he bought used for $600 and spent our first month in Orlando restoring night and day. We're talking 30 straight days of changing the oil, switching out belts and checking the timing, and rotating the tires. Now it runs like a top, even if it looks like something my dad might drive to a crime scene.

"If there is a next time." He grunts, pushing through a yellow light so we don't lose Stamp completely.

Stamp has a real lead foot. I never knew this about him. I mean, maybe it's a recent thing because when we were dating, if anything, he drove real slow. Trying to get to the movies on time with Stamp was like trying to get Dane to listen to anything but smooth jazz, i.e. hard work.

Then I think maybe he's just really eager to see Val. Then I frown because, seriously, why did he never seem that excited to see me?

"This isn't as fun as it looks," Dane says through gritted teeth as we leave Orlando's resort area and head toward the scruffy side of its glittering downtown, dodging insane tourists who don't know where they're going, all the while keeping an eye on Lead Foot Stamp Crosby himself. You know, without Stamp keeping an eye on us.

"Yeah, I've always wanted to follow someone, but it's really stressful—and I'm not even driving."

"Tomorrow you drive." Dane smiles, but I know he means it. Macho as he is, he's definitely not old-fashioned. He's just as happy for me to drive as him, and when it comes to hunting for brains, he's more than happy for me to go meet our creepy contact behind the local morgue rather than do it himself.

Stamp pulls off I-4, the main east-west interstate running through downtown Orlando, on two wheels.

"Hmmm," I murmur as Stamp blows through a stop sign to steer down a mostly deserted industrial center. "I don't remember Stamp ever breaking so many laws to catch up with me after work."

Dane smirks as we inch into weed-covered, giant-warehouses-on-every-block, scary-movie-after-dark territory. "He probably figured you had a little longer to wait around than a human girl."

I slug him, and he pulls on the brakes.

"Dang, I didn't hit you that—"

He shushes me, pointing out the window as he backs into a dark alley on the opposite corner from a giant, brown warehouse. "He's stopped."

I peer out, but he's backed in so far I can't see anything.

"Dane." I slip from the car and only partially close my door so Stamp won't hear me.

"Maddy, don't."

But in two steps he's right there behind me.

Stamp's Jeep is parked in front of a four-story warehouse. There's a fence around it, rusty with barbed wire on top, but it's open. Broken windows line the building's top floor, and there's a rusty fire escape from the roof all the way to the ground.

"Val's?" Dane whispers, pointing to the front door.

It's not dark out yet, though it's getting close. We stick by the wall to the alley, walking so slowly we're starting to get on each other's nerves, all because Stamp has yet to get out of the Jeep.

"What is he *doing* in there?" Dane says.

"Don't get me started. Dude is *so* slow."

"No, I know he's slow, but what can he be doing in the front seat of his car for so long?"

"Well, let me count the ways. First he fixes his hair in the rearview. Then he'll straighten out the coins in his ashtray. He'll drink the last of his Sports Slurp because he doesn't want to waste any. He'll take the knots out of his seat belt, and that's all before he cues up his music for the ride home—"

"Wait, what? Doesn't he just listen to the same music on the way home?"

"Are you kidding me? He has playlists for everything. Working out, not working out, making out, not making out, walking, running, going someplace, coming back, sitting still, standing up."

"But what's the difference? Going someplace, coming back. Isn't it all the same?"

"Not to Stamp. He likes fast music for going someplace and slow music for coming back. Duh."

Dane shakes his head. Then he looks at me funny, as if he's surprised I would pay attention to my boyfriend's music. And in a way, he kind of seems impressed. I think he always thought I was using Stamp to make Dane jealous those first few months after we left Barracuda Bay burning in our rearview.

I think that's why Dane was kind of distant after Stamp and I broke up, like he thought I was just a bit of a user or something. But lately I think he's seen how much I care for Stamp, boyfriend or ex, and he's warmed up to me a little because of it.

Either that or I'm totally losing my mind and making it all up.

Finally Stamp's door creaks and his long legs bleed onto the pavement. He stands tall and looks around, and I wonder if in his carelessness this is the first time he's stopped and checked to see if anyone's following him.

I look at Dane and can tell by the set of his jaw that he's thinking the same thing. We both turn back to Stamp in time to hear his phone ring. Hmmm, I guess we are pretty close to the action after all.

He frowns at the phone, sees the incoming call, and then, as if the caller can see him, smiles.

"Val," Dane and I say at the same time.

"Hey, babe," says Stamp, all goofy smile and eager-to-please voice. "Yeah, just got here. What? You told me to hurry! How can you not be—? Oh, wait."

He waves, clicks off the call. I could swear he's waving at us, but in fact, he's waving to someone walking by on the opposite sidewalk.

Dane and I duck, peeking through dented, empty trash cans the whole while.

It *is* Val, the chick from Stamp's cell phone pictures. But this time she's live and so close we can hear her shoes scrape the concrete, hear the little jewels hanging off her pink purse jingle against her gently shaking rump.

She looks sexier in person. She's more petite than short and thinner than she looked on-screen with Dane blowing her up bigger and bigger each time we looked at her. She's wearing slinky black yoga pants that match the stripes on the sleeves of her hot-pink hoodie. The hood's down to show off her spiky blonde hair. It's black at the roots but purposefully to match her dark eye shadow and grubby black fingernails. Her pink-and-black sneakers give her an extra inch or two, and she walks with the limber jaunt of a human, plus a shake-it-don't-break-it strut.

She's pale, but so many girls are these days. Not so much to avoid skin cancer or tanning beds but just for fashion's sake. Besides, she doesn't show much skin anyway. Her wrists, maybe. A little ankle when she takes a quick step. Her throat. Her face. That's about it.

"Waddya think?" I say, watching Dane watch her firm backside.

"Nice," he grunts.

I don't slap him. I punch him. Hard. Like, Whac-A-Zerker hard.

Even so, it's a little like granite getting punched by granite. Neither one of us budges. Much. Okay, so I budge a little.

"Oh, sorry," he says, avoiding my glare. "I can't—it's

hard to tell. We'll need a better look."

"How did I know you'd say that?"

Val doesn't walk so much as ooze to Stamp, like greasy green amoebas do to one another under a microscope, slipping and sliding all over each other until you can't tell, and don't much care anymore, which is which.

He's so tall and she's so petite, it's easy for her arms to wrap around his waist as her chin hits his chest. He somehow manages to lean down enough to plant a cold, dry kiss on her open and willing lips.

I groan. Out loud, and I don't much care who hears it at this point.

Dane nods, but I notice he's still eyeing the skank's derriere appreciatively.

Stamp opens the door to his Jeep, and she slides up and in, dark eyes still on him as he shuts the door and races around to his side.

"Somebody's whipped," Dane says.

I nudge him. "You know I hate that term."

"Maybe so, but the evidence is all there."

"Don't remind me," I say a little louder as Stamp's engine grinds to life.

His Jeep backs up roughly and speeds past our hiding spot.

"Come on," Dane urges once we can no longer hear the Jeep engine.

"Why? What are we doing?"

"Breaking in."

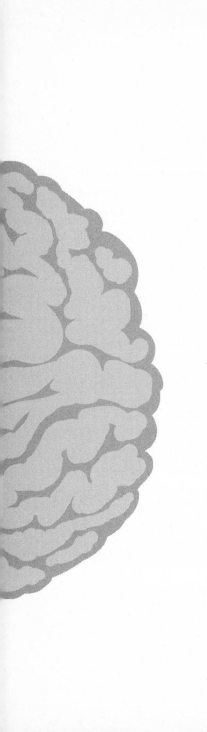

7
Breaking In, Freaking Out

I guess you could call Val's place a loft since most of the warehouse is empty and she apparently uses only about a quarter of a quarter of it to actually live in. Still, that quarter is pretty sweet. (This coming from a chick who shares an apartment with two of the most inconsiderate zombies on the planet.)

"Check out that killer TV," Dane says loudly, as if we're not breaking and entering at that very moment. "It's gotta be 60 inches, if not more."

"I didn't even think they came that big." I've never been a big TV girl, but seriously this is a *big* TV. We're talking never-need-to-go-to-the-movie-theater-again big.

In fact, this TV is so big it's the focal point of Val's whole living space. There is a kind of kitchen area, with one of those small dorm fridges like Dad keeps in his office back home and a microwave and a coffeemaker and a hot plate.

I see a washtub and a clothesline, where teeny-tiny panties and bras and lots of yoga pants and hoodies hang. There is a cot with dirty, twisty sheets and a leather couch and a love seat and that TV and a huge stack of DVDs, mostly chick flicks and monster movies.

And that's about it.

The different areas of the loft are separated by those cool Asian screens so that you can't really see one until you're in it. There are four screens, one red, one black, one brown, and one unvarnished pine. Some have little slats with opaque white paper in them, and some have slats with no paper, and all are amazing.

"See." I admire the dark red one, bringing it to Dane's attention. "This is what I was suggesting for our place."

"Maddy, focus. This isn't Dockside Imports, okay? It's potentially a Sentinel's lair, and we need to be serious about all this."

Then he looks a little more closely. "One of these would be cool. But, no, come on. We'll shop later. For now, find me some zombie evidence, 'kay?"

But I spot him looking back at the screen more than once even as we continue to search.

"I dunno, Dane, she looks pretty human to me."

"So do we." He looks under throw pillows and peeks behind the panty-strewn clothesline. "That's the whole point of passing, remember? If she's a Sentinel, she will have taken a class in all this stuff."

We start in the fridge, where it's standard single-gal-living-alone stuff: yogurt cups and cans of coffee drinks. In the cupboard are gluten-free protein bars. But that's not enough for Dane. He actually looks in the trash to make sure there are empty yogurt cups, cans, and protein bar wrappers. There are.

I smirk but am not really happy about it. Something in me would almost like Val to be a Sentinel. Not because I have a death wish or anything, but it would make me feel better if she were seducing Stamp as part of a mission rather than, you know, actually being in love with him. Selfish though it sounds, I'd rather Stamp get played by a Sentinel than have Val really have the hots for my ex.

But so far she's looking pretty human. The hot plate is coated in dried and burned food, ramen noodle dregs cling to a sticky pot in the sink, and clean overturned glasses rest on a dish towel.

"Come on, come on," I say, convinced Val and Stamp will walk through the door any minute. "I hate doing this stuff. Let's go."

"This is what we're here for. To make sure. We have to take our time and do it right, despite the risks."

"I know and I'm doing it, but . . . don't you ever watch the movies? The good guys always get caught doing this stuff. Let's be smarter than them and get out."

"We are smarter than them. We're zombies, and we've lasted this long without being caught by the Sentinels. Why? Because we do stuff that sucks: never driving to work the same way twice, triple-locking the door every time we leave, avoiding big crowds. Now buckle down and do this, and we'll be gone long before they get home."

Yeah, famous last words.

I follow him around just the same, urging him along.

"I can't find anything," he says, and his tone is downright mournful.

"Good. So she's human, just another one of Stamp's dumb skanks, right? We're good."

We stand there, in the middle of Val's loft, looking at each other.

"I don't think so. I really don't. Who lives like this? Alone, in a warehouse, where she can do whatever she wants any time of day or night, with no Normal neighbors around? That sounds like zombie behavior, not skank behavior."

"Maybe, but if we get caught here and she *is* a Sentinel, isn't our goose pretty much cooked anyway?"

Dane looks at me funny. "Maddy, what do you think we're going to do for the rest of our lives? Put on makeup and entertain guests at theme parks? *This* is our life now. Get used to it. We will always be on the run, and the Sentinels will always be chasing us. We will never know

if one is standing right next to us if we don't start checking out everyone who even tries to get close. Now we
have to find out if this is one of those times—for our
good, for Stamp's good—so chill."

I take a step back and nod twice. Maybe he is right.
And if she is a Sentinel? And she does come back and try
to stomp us? Well, it's two against one. Dane and I have
won with those odds before.

"Okay, look at this place. What's her hobby? Obviously, it's watching TV. Look at that bad boy. I mean,
you don't get a 100-inch TV screen if you're not a major
couch potato. So let's look for a cable bill or something.
See if she's renting movies on demand at all hours of the
night, right?"

Dane nods, his round eyes showing me he's
impressed. He finds a stack of bills in the drawer of one of
those build-it-yourself desks you can get at Family Value
Mart for $19.99. I swear we have the same model—only
in black, natch.

I watch him rifle through the power bill, the water
bill, some credit card bills, until his eyes get *really* big.

"What?"

"Chick spent nearly a grand last month at Wisteria's
Secret Lingerie Corner in the mall."

I smack him.

He drops the bill, pulls up another, then clicks his
tongue. "Jackpot." He unravels her cable bill. It's like

Santa's naughty list or something. It stretches to a full three sheets. "Dang, this chick is in some serious love with all-night cable."

But it's more than that. Every night, from about midnight through 8:00 a.m., Val rents movie after movie, night after night. It's not just once or twice a week, like when a Normal might have insomnia. It's every night.

A horn sounds in the distance, and we both look up.

I'm suddenly aware my hands are trembling.

Dane shoves the papers in the drawer, and we make tracks out the same door we came in, locking it behind us and slipping the spare key under the rock where the dumb skank leaves it.

But it's a false alarm. There's nobody outside when at last we crouch alongside Val's car, creeping our way back toward Dane's. The sky is dark now, and we have no idea where they've gone or when they'll be back.

"So what now?" I ask as we settle into his car. "Are we gonna have a good, old-fashioned stakeout?"

Dane rubs his long fingers across his stubbly scalp—never a good sign for the bad guys. "I have a better idea."

8

Zombies Don't Collate

"What are we gonna do, staple her to death?" I ask Dane as he careens off the street into the 24-hour Office Profits store a few blocks away.

A smile creeps across his face, as if he's seriously considering the notion. "Well," he says, slipping the keys out of the ignition, "it's a little early for that yet, but let's keep it on the back burner."

His smile is gone, and I'm not sure if he's joking. If not, look out.

The store is a lot less deserted than I figured it would be. I mean, who needs office supplies after business hours? Lame music plays overhead while I reach for a cart.

It's habit, I guess, but Dane stills my hand with a gentle touch. "We don't need that."

I nod and follow him through an aisle full of nothing

but—I'm not making this up—paper clips. At the end is a little store within a store called Copy Tronix. Or, at least, that's what the neon sign announces over the bored teenager's head.

She fiddles with a calculator, then perks up when she sees Dane coming.

Most girls do. I try to look at him from her perspective: close-cropped hair, that prowling walk of his, the placid face, the endless pools of his dark eyes, his razor wire muscles and tight-fitting clothes.

She looks a little like the old me right now, the one who used to linger outside Dane's Shop class just for a peep at him. Dazed, confused, intrigued, not under-standing why.

He's not classically handsome. He's too dead for that. But there's definitely something about him that makes your senses sit up and do a double take. And under these harsh retail lights, I ask you, who *does* look human?

"How can I help you?" she asks. Him. She asks him, like I'm not even there.

I wish I knew what we were doing here. I'd answer for him, make her look at me. She's young and cute in that fleshy, alive way, with the tan skin and full lips and lungs that breathe and heart that beats. She has on black jeans and a red golf shirt, the same uniform of Office Profits employees I've seen sauntering around the place, although none of them were bursting out of the seams the way this chick is.

Wait. That's a name tag. Brittni. Of course.

Dane leans on the counter casually. "Actually, Brittni, we were hoping *you* could help *us*."

I smell something funny and look at his face, and he's chewing gum. Where'd he get gum? And why?

"How so?" She giggles.

Dane finally looks at me. "My girlfriend and I here, we're trying to play a prank on a friend."

I stand a little straighter while Brittni's face does a kind of double crumble. What a weirdo Dane is. He chews gum for her but in the same nonbreath calls me his girlfriend for, like, the first time ever. Weird. Sweet, astonishing, brave, kind, and generous but totally, lovably weird.

I slink into him a little more, waiting to hear where this is going.

"We're trying to get some information out of him without coming right out and asking, so we were hoping you could help us think of a survey."

She's gotten over the whole crush-worthy-guy-has-a-girlfriend thing and perked up again. Mood swing much? "Like, what type of survey?"

Her voice is kind of chirpy, and I like it. She reminds me of someone I'd be friends with if I still went to high school. How odd. Only a few months ago I was attending the Fall Formal as a student, and now I'm looking at this chick as if she's from another species: high school student.

Yeah, I feel old, ugly, pale, and thin next to Brittni, but still there's something about her I like.

Now Dane looks at me. I guess *survey* was as far as his mind has gone.

I look back at Brittni and smile awkwardly. "Well, like, let's say we had a company and we were going to send people out onto the streets to ask them questions. That kind of survey."

"Yeah, yeah, a survey taker's survey," Dane says.

Brittni puts on her thinking face: pouty lips, flared nostrils, closed eyes.

Dane and I give each other an arched eyebrow look.

Brittni opens her eyes. "Well, what industry?"

We give her major WTF faces, and she smiles. I knew I kinda liked her.

"I mean, you need to build the survey around some-thing your friend is interested in. So, like, skateboarding, dirt bikes, energy drinks, what?"

See, this is the problem with lying. You tell one, you gotta tell 99 more.

Dane looks at me. I can see where he's going, and watching him look helpless is kind of a joy. It's not a friend we're trying to stump, and the survey is really just an excuse, I'm figuring, to walk up to Val and introduce ourselves without looking like stalkers.

I wish zombies could read minds, 'cause it would be

really nice to bounce ideas off him right now. I think of Val and her loft and blurt, "TV!"

Dane looks relieved. "Yeah, let's pretend we work for some company surveying, what, her viewing interests?"

Brittni gets into it, whipping out a notepad. "That's good. That's good. We can ask what kind of movies she likes. Thrillers or rom coms—you know." She has a pink pen with glitter in it *and* on it and an even pinker fuzzy ball on top, and she whips it around furiously while she makes up fake questions.

We work on it for nearly an hour, Dane, Brittni, and I. She's kinda awesome once she gets going, and I find myself wishing Stamp would go for someone who was at least fun to hang with, unlike the last few chicks he's brought around: rude, anonymous, empty-eyed, bubble-head girls you'd rather strangle than spend 10 minutes talking to.

When we've listed enough questions, Brittni helps us work up a template for the survey, complete with a company name—that takes awhile—and formats the pages on the computer. She's really good, detailed.

"It'll take about 40 minutes to print," she says with pouty lips. "We're kinda backed up."

Dane smiles. "That's cool. Listen, do you know any-where that sells clothes at this hour?"

We follow Brittni's directions to an all-night Clothes Mart a couple of shopping centers over. They're all connected, and since we're just looking for some pants and a couple of shirts, we walk.

"She's nice," Dane says as we wait for the crosswalk light to flash white.

I slug his shoulder. "Is *nice* code for hot or something?"

Dane shakes his head. "It's weird, but live girls are almost another species, you know?"

I do a double take because that's what I was just thinking. Get out of my head, dude.

The streetlight casts more shadows than usual on his pale face.

"So what does that make me?" I say, only half-joking.

He bumps me with his hip and says, without looking at me, "It makes you my species."

Before I can figure out if that's a compliment or a dig, he takes my hand and we cross with the light.

Hey, for Dane, that might as well be flowers and chocolates.

9
Surveying the Sentinel

"Don't you think she'll know we're full of it?" I ask a few hours later as we return from the Office Profits store downtown, printed surveys in hand and scented with sweet Brittni's cheap perfume.

Dane smiles wickedly, walking a little taller, a little meaner, now that he's in charge again and ready to kick a little Sentinel butt. "That's the whole point. This way we get to see if she's a Sentinel. If she's just some random, clueless hot pants who digs pale, cold, heartless guys like Stamp, she'll giggle it off. But if she's the real deal, if she thinks we're onto her, hell, yeah, she'll be ticked."

I dig it when Dane gets all evil mastermind–like.

It's nearly midnight by now, and Stamp and Val have just pulled into the warehouse driveway. She's pouring herself out of the Jeep the same way she oozed herself in, not waiting for him to hold her door anymore. She's laughing at something he's just said.

What? Stamp's a comedian all of a sudden?

Music blasts from the stereo, one of Stamp's clubbing playlists, no doubt. Or, even worse, maybe some list she made for him. Grossness. It cuts out as he yanks the key from the ignition.

The night goes quiet. The only sound is Val's shoes scraping the pavement.

We hang close to the nearest warehouse next door.

Stamp is still in his latest favorite hoodie, the black one with the white stripes and the extra-long sleeves that cover his hands. His hair's still spiky, his cords gray, his sneakers black.

I hold my new clipboard anxiously, clicking and unclicking the top of my new pen.

Dane leans in and gently holds the top of my hand still.

We share a glance so close, so intimate there is nothing to do but kiss softly in the moonlight.

A bark of laughter interrupts us.

Dane looks up, past my head, and smiles. "Showtime." Moments later, he's saying, "Stamp?" and purposefully scuffling forward in his brand-new dress shoes.

We pass the barbed wire fence surrounding Val's warehouse. Come to think of it, what's the frickin' rent on your own personal warehouse anyway? 'Cause, the way she's texting Stamp 24/7, it's not like the chick could possibly have a job.

I pick the seat of my ill-fitting black pants out of my wedge and straighten my thin black tie as we approach. They're still flirting and holding hands by Stamp's Jeep.

Stamp sees us first, eyes getting big. Then he nods, then smiles. God love this kid. He's just a big teddy bear with pecs.

"Dane? Maddy?" he says, sounding genuinely surprised.

But it's not Stamp I'm watching. It's Val.

And she's pissed. Pissed behind a smile but pissed just the same.

And suddenly I'm with Team Dane on this one. If she's just a Normal club chick with a buzz and the munchies after a night out with Stamp, why is she being all passive-aggressive with us?

"Stamp?" she squeaks past the smile glued to her lips.

But Stamp's still kind of marveling at the spectacle of us.

So now she's yanking down on his hoodie sleeve to get his attention. "Stamp, honey? Are these the friends you've been telling me about?"

Her voice is so phony, I can feel the scorn at 15 paces. I mean, she practically barfs the word *friends*.

"Yeah." He chuckles, goofily, like he's still in the club and we've just walked up. "These are my, uh, roomies." He looks at me a little pointedly, as if to say, *Don't go all crazy ex-girlfriend on me now, okay?* Then, still smiling, he adds, "Guys, this is Val, the chick, er, the girl I've been telling you about."

"Has he ever!" Dane extends a hand, and his extra-long cuff rasps against his dead skin.

Time slows down just a smidge as we wait for her to shake it. Because you can fool a Normal if you have the time. You can sit on your hands when you know a Normal's going to touch them. But Val hasn't had the time.

So when or *if* she reaches for Dane's hand, all bets are off. He'll feel it, for sure, and then we'll know. And then we can—

"I can't believe it." She giggles in a burst of nervous energy, raising her hand to cover her mouth like some girls do. "What on earth are you doing here?"

"Yeah," Stamp says, suddenly curious. He looks at his watch with a wide rubber strap. "It's nearly midnight. Shouldn't you guys be at home working out together or something?"

"Actually," Dane says in the ultrafake voice he's suddenly adopted, "we are working." He pops his new white collar to show he's dressed for work.

"Yeah," I blurt too soon, jumping the script ahead a few pages and catching a glare from Dane, who rehearsed it in the car with me about 62 times. "We weren't making enough with the monster show, so we had to take second jobs. We were hoping you'd take a quick survey so we look good on our first day—"

Val approaches, no longer hiding behind Stamp. In her eyes is a kind of predatory glee, like she's the one catching us instead of the other way around. "At midnight?" she says, rolling her eyes. "May I ask what job requires you guys to go walking the streets at midnight?"

"A new one," Dane assures her, stepping just a little closer because, before the night is out, this dude *will* find out if Val is a zombie, one way or the other. "We're just eager to please. New employees and all."

"Yeah, but guys," Stamp says with a rumpled look on his normally unlined face, "this is a pretty rough neighborhood." He looks around, as if we haven't seen it for ourselves.

"It's not rough," Val says, as if this is some kind of pleasant suburb and she's in an apron and we're all standing outside her white picket fence. "But it is deserted. And, how convenient that you just happen to run into Stamp and me on this otherwise completely vacant street."

Dane nods.

The way she's talking—so superior—I have to interject. "What about you, Val?" I say supersweetly. "I'm pretty sure Stamp said you live alone. What are you doing in this place all by yourself?"

She is momentarily stumped, but then a sleazy smile crosses her leathery white face. "Oh, well, Stamp here keeps me company most nights, don't you, lover?" She does that whole oozing amoeba thing again, sliding under his arm.

But even Stamp looks uncomfortable and shoots me a quick apologetic look past Val's blonde spikes. "W-w-well, not every night."

"Yeah," Dane adds a little gruffly, shuffling closer. "I mean, Stamp's home some nights like a good little boy, so you must get pretty scared staying out here alone, huh?"

Val shrugs and loops her arm almost violently through Stamp's. "Not really. I'm pretty tough, right, Stamp?" It sounds almost like a warning. She tugs him toward her and nearly folds him in half with the effort.

He looks a little startled, then embarrassed.

My throat clenches. Sentinel or not, zombie or not, Val is not someone Stamp should be with. And I'm not saying that as his ex. I'm saying it as his friend.

Suddenly I can't help but wonder why sweet Stamp has gone so sour. Has it been just to get away from us, like Dane says? Or did he always have an edge as a Normal that I missed because I was so caught up in being a zombie?

Or maybe I'm just reacting the way most girls do when they see their ex's new girlfriend. I honestly can't fathom how a guy who was ever attracted to me, even in the slightest, could be attracted to a girl like Val.

"So what is this new job of yours?" Val says, stepping in so that Stamp is pushed to the background.

Dane and I share a look because, well, it's the kind of move he taught me in the same scenario: protect your weaker link. So does that mean she has Sentinel training, or is she just an alpha witch? I'm getting alpha-witch vibe, but maybe that's just me.

"You guys must be *really* eager to please if you're

wandering around deserted areas in the middle of the night."

"Reader Response Corp," Dane blurts, reading the name we made up for the top of the form. "They do surveys, customer satisfaction mostly, on all kinds of retail products."

"Really?" Val whips the clipboard out of Dane's hand so fast he barely has time to react.

I watch Val's face as she scans the six stapled pages of questions we worked hard to write. (Well, Brittni did, mostly.) Things like this:

> Would you prefer to watch a thriller or chick flick on a first date?
>
> How often do you go to the movie theater in a month? Please circle the appropriate answer.
>
> Once.
> Twice.
> Three times.
>
> What is your favorite movie snack food? Please select one of the following items.

Val's face is priceless as she reads them. She goes from triumphant, clearly thinking she's going to stump us and reveal some blank page BS that we just threw together, to petulant that we've stumped her, to finally looking downright impressed.

"Wow. This is quite an elaborate survey for big-screen

TVs. How ever did you know I had one?"

"We didn't." I sigh, trying to out-act her. "But most people do these days. Do you? If you did, it would be great if you'd answer some of these. Maybe we could even go inside and—"

But Val's not having any of that. Instead, she has whipped out her cell phone and is reading the number on the survey form, the one right under the completely false Reader Response Corp logo Brittni helped us design.

"Val?" Stamp looks at us uncomfortably, bordering on shooting us major WTF face. "Honey? Who could you be calling at this hour?" In his voice I hear the gentle, almost timid boy I fell in love with back at Barracuda Bay High. In that second of concern for her, for us, I hear the heartbreak that his existence has become since I saved his life—you know, by killing him. Again.

He never wanted any of this. He never deserved any of this. And now he's in danger because he's running away from this.

I shoot Dane a look, and he looks at me as if he's thinking, *Calm down.* After all, the number goes straight to his cell phone voice mail, where helpful Brittni has recorded a greeting in her best bouffant-hairdo, polyester-skirt, headset, fake-receptionist voice:

"Welcome to Reader Response Corporation. Your opinions are greatly valued. Our offices are open from 6:00 a.m. to 9:00 p.m. eastern standard time. Please call back during regular business hours to speak to a live operator. Thanks again for your valued contribution to our continued study of customer buying habits in your region . . ."

I smile to hear Brittni's voice now. We really should have tipped her more considering how much she helped us, though she seemed pretty stoked about the $20.

Val hangs up in not-so-private frustration. "Of course it's a recording." She pockets her phone and hurls the clipboard toward Dane.

Seriously, if he was human he'd be dead already. Witch has some serious arm.

He catches it on the fly, avoiding certain decapitation, and puts another foot forward. "So I take that to mean you won't be helping us with our survey tonight, Val."

No one, not even Stamp, can ignore the outright menace in his voice. Few people can evoke fear the way Dane can with that growl.

But this Val chick? She's hardly fazed.

I'm inching away from him, and I know the dude.

Val steps up. "No, Dane, we won't. It's late, and to be quite honest, I think you're full of it. You and your little friend here and your clipboards and your clip-on ties—all of it."

"Really?" he barks.

"Honey," Stamp says, wedging between them. "Come on now. Why would they lie? And look at their outfits. No self-respecting"—Stamp looks at us, and I know from his saucer eyes that he was about to say zombie—"kid would wear those getups."

"They're spying on us." Val turns on her heel. "They're just jealous. Jealous of us! Now let's go."

"Wait, what?" Stamp stands his ground. Well, sort of. "Aren't we, I mean, can't we even invite them in?"

"No, we can't. Now are you coming or not?"

And that's that. Val is gone.

Stamp lingers, face all crumpled, looking back and forth between us like he's at some tennis match.

"Stamp," I say, edging a little bit closer to help him make the right decision. "Dude, come on. This is all . . . I mean, does this feel right to you?"

"Really," Dane adds, putting a hand on his shoulder. "Come home with us, okay?"

Stamp chews his bottom lip like he used to as a Normal when he wasn't sure what to do. But that was over little things, like whether to choose A or B on a multiple-choice test or what flavor of milk to get in the lunch line. This is life-or-death stuff here.

"Stamp, it's not just about us snooping around. You know that, right?"

He nods at me, looking over his shoulder as Val rattles open the warehouse door in a big, look-at-me kind of way. He winces a little.

"I don't," Dane says, looking at me. "I mean *we*

don't think it's safe here."

And that's when we lose him. Stamp's face changes as he scoffs openly. We had him, and then we lost him. Because we forgot what Stamp hates about being a zombie the most: being protected. He wants to be his own zombie, in his own way, and now it's changed from us being concerned about him to us wanting to protect him, and he can't have that.

Won't have that.

He turns and walks away. "I'm a big boy, Dane," he says, but I know he wants to add my name. "I can take care of myself."

As we drive away, I hope he's right.

But I doubt he is.

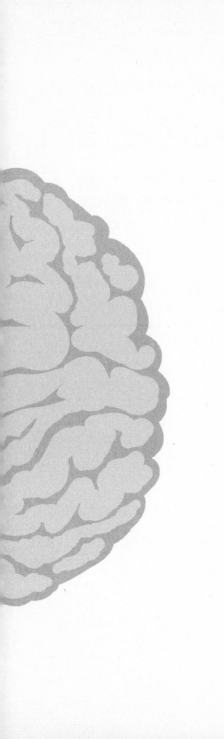

10

Do Those Brains Come with Sprinkles?

"Why do I always have to do it?" I say, slurping on a candy red hot in my mouth.

"He's your friend."

"Friend? That's pushing things, don't you think?"

Dane grunts, sinking deeper into the passenger seat. Yeah, like anyone's going to notice him at the busiest ice cream parlor on the planet.

Literally. It's in the Guinness World Records or something. Look it up. Frozen Planet. Never heard of it? Me neither. At least, that is, until I moved to Orlando, otherwise known as the Neverland of Chain Restaurants.

Frozen Planet is about as big as your average restaurant, only it serves nothing but ice cream 24/7/365. The building itself is painted brown with little black lines crisscrossing it to make it look like a waffle cone. All the windows have sprinkles painted over them: red, green, white, pink, and orange. On top is the world's largest scoop of ice cream. They say you can see it from the top of the Epcot geosphere, though I don't know who would know that except maybe the unluckiest maintenance worker in the world. This ice cream cone is huge, I'll give it that, and it's ringed by neon lights so you can see it at night too, which is helpful if NASA runs out of power and the shuttle needs a little help landing.

We're parked in front with about a dozen other cars, despite it being late as hell. This town never sleeps. I see all kinds of kids in there too. Eating ice cream in the middle of the night? Yeah, that's good parenting. Real good.

My phone is on my lap. I texted Iceman about 10 minutes ago that we were on our way for our weekly pickup. He said he'd text me with the phrase *chocolate chip* when he was ready.

"God, he takes this stuff so seriously," I say to Dane, window down, the evening warm and muggy and soft on my arm. In my mouth, the red hot heats things up by about two degrees a minute. By the time I'm inside, I should be hot enough to pass as human. Kind of. Maybe.

"Probably watches a bunch of spy movies or stuff."

"Or zombie movies." I grunt.

Dane grunts back.

That's how we met, actually. In an online chat room for zombie fans. It was a week or two after we'd moved to Orlando and we weren't having any luck finding a friendly local grocer, coroner, or funeral director to help us out in the brains department. We were getting desperate but feared that if we tried breaking in someplace, the Sentinels might have it under surveillance.

Dane and I hopped online and found this site called *Zombies R Us* and set up my profile. (My screen name is LvingDedGurl, by the way.) We found Iceman in a late-night chat for humans interested in the taste of brains. Yes, such people exist. In this world. In Orlando.

Dane and I perked up, and I asked Iceman what that was all about. He said he'd love to tell me in person, so we set up a date at his second job. At Frozen Planet.

His first job? The local coroner's office.

Trust me, we checked first. Dude was legit.

Dane showed up early for that first meeting, got a seat, ordered a sundae, didn't eat it but tipped well, so the waitress let him stay. I got there an hour later, took the corner booth as directed, and boom, five seconds later this giant of a kid shuffles over in one of those paper hats, peppermint ice cream stains all over his XXL shirt, and introduces himself.

"Living Dead Girl?"

"Iceman?"

He sat; we talked. His breath smelled; I pretended not to notice.

Eventually I showed him a wad of cash and said that

if he could get me three human brains a week, I'd make sure he'd never need to work overtime again.

So here we are, nearly five months later, and I have to go do the trade-off.

The text comes in: Iceman.

I shiver and take the envelope full of cash out of the glove box. Every week Dane, Stamp, and I put $60 from our paychecks toward our brain fund. Every week, I hand it over to Iceman. Brains, meet mouth.

A cowbell over the door rings, and the smells of ice and cream and sugar and peppermint and chocolate nearly knock me over. My zombie senses are on high alert, and this place is like a tidal wave of gross!

I take the last booth on the left corner, as always, and in minutes I see Iceman shuffling over. His real name is Robin Rice. He's 22, lives at home—of course—and he'd be an okay-looking guy if he wasn't so smarmy.

"Hi, sweetheart," he says right off, sliding uncomfortably into the booth so that his massive stomach won't spill over the top. (See what I mean? *Sweetheart*? Really?)

I hold back a retch. "Hi, Iceman. How's work?"

"Which job?" He sighs.

Seriously, he says the same thing every week. I'm in no mood. "Pick one."

He notices. "My, aren't we short tonight?" He pulls the Frozen Planet bag, presumably containing three to-go containers of brains, toward his side of the table.

I smirk and play nice. "Sorry. Just . . . long day."

"What's with the getup?"

I look down, realizing I'm still in my fake survey taker's uniform. "Like I said, long day."

Iceman shrugs. Then he gets down to business. "So how were last week's brains?"

"Scrumptious," I say, like they were his or something. "The best yet." This is the worst part, feeding Iceman's ghoulish ego.

"I guess I should try them myself someday."

"You really should," I say, eyeing the bag still clutched in his grubby fingers.

"Maybe you can cook them for me one day?"

I take great glee in crushing the hopeful look in his sweaty face. "Cook them? Real brain fanatics eat them raw. I thought you knew that."

He frowns. "I guess I'm not a real fanatic, then."

No, I think just a freakish ghoul who sells human brains for cash.

I slide the envelope over, eager to end our transaction, get home, and start the feast. He takes it eagerly, shoving it in his Frozen Planet apron.

Finally, the bag comes my way. I have to force myself to wait and be pleasant, though what I really want is to grab it and run. But where would that leave me next week?

"Thanks, Iceman," I say, inching out of the booth.

"You're welcome, Living Dead Girl."

Then he does this thing, this thing he does every week, where he sits there, a king on his throne, and juts out his right cheek. I lean down, red hot nearly gone by now, and kiss it. His skin tastes like sugar and sweat. If I don't get away soon, he's going to get an earful of red hot upchuck, that's for sure.

"Until next week," he says dreamily.

I can barely hear it with the cowbell ringing overhead on my way out the door.

Where the Cemeteries Have No Name

"Soy sauce or no?" Dane says from the kitchen a little while later as he splits up the fresh brain.

I'm in my room, taking off my makeup and slipping out of my phony survey taker's uniform. I find Dane's keys in my pocket and walk to his room to set them on his desk.

A piece of red string is sticking out of his top drawer. What? Is he knitting now? Making me one of those old-school Raggedy Ann dolls for Christmas? Or a scarf, maybe? Some mittens for my always cold hands?

Hearing the water still running in the kitchen, I slide the drawer open just a smidge. There's no doll, no mittens. But there is a map: a local map, with red string tying several black dots together.

The dots are plastic circles with sticky backing so

they stay glued in place, and I recognize the map as the one that came with our welcome packet when we paid our initial deposit and moved into The Socialite.

"The hell?" I murmur as I sink into the desk chair.

I lay the map out flat, trying to get my geography straight. It never was my favorite subject. I notice our street highlighted with a red dot. X marks the spot.

The red strings all tie around the red dot and make an almost perfect circle as they pull out to all the black dots. It's like a giant wheel, stretching out from our street, each red string like a spoke in the wheel.

Next to each black dot, Dane has written in his blocky handwriting a name, then a date.

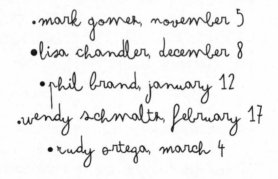

•mark gomez, november 5
•lisa chandler, december 8
•phil brand, january 12
•wendy schmaltz, february 17
•rudy ortega, march 4

Wait, that last one. That name sounds familiar.

I look in the drawer and see why. It's come from our local paper, the one I showed him the other day, about the kid who went out for bananas and milk and never came back.

The sneak! He must have taken it off my stationary bike when I wasn't looking. But what for? I dig a little deeper and find several more clippings beneath it, each with the name on the map highlighted.

I look at Rudy Ortega's picture in the paper. It's from his school yearbook. Turns out he was a junior at the local high school, Cedar Point. He's got a big, round face and weepy eyes but a wide smile. His hair is short, with a little ducktail at the front. I grin, then stop myself.

The clipping beneath Rudy's is for a big-boned red-head. Her name, Wendy Schmaltz, is highlighted. She was a nursing student at some local tech college after dropping out of high school during her senior year. She has laughing eyes, buckteeth, and a spray of freckles across her nose that stand out even in black-and-white.

Every clipping, tied to every string, is about a local kid who's gone missing. One a month, apparently, since we moved to The Socialite. I count the strings, touching them gently. None of them go too far from where Dane and I live. A few miles at the most.

I don't know how freaked out I should be, but I'm pretty. Freaked out, that is.

Yeah, I know every neighborhood has its strange goings-on, its disappearances and violence, but five in five months? It's not like we're in a war zone or something. Sure, we're not living on Rodeo Drive, but we're still in the United States.

I could understand one or two, but even that would be pushing it. Five?

"So now you know," Dane says from the doorway, drying his hands with a dish towel. "Why we went through the whole survey-taker charade. Why we had to start tailing Stamp. Why I pressed Val so hard tonight."

I let the newspaper clippings slide off the map I'm clutching and back into the drawer, where they settle with a rustle, a straggle of red string hanging over the open drawer.

"You think she knows about this?"

He shrugs. "Not knows, exactly, but I think she's involved, yes."

"How?" I drop the map as if it's poisonous. "Why?"

"Look at the pattern," he says patiently, sitting on his bed next to me so close I can still smell the cologne he wore to impress Val. "We're the red dot, and all the missing people are the black dots. See the dates? Every month, a new kid goes missing. And never farther than a few miles from right where we're standing. One month gets her closer to the next month and, with each kid, she's closing in on us. It's like she's working her way in, warning us we're next. Or maybe Stamp's next. I dunno yet."

I shake my head violently. "I get all that. I meant, how could you keep this from me? Why would you?"

He seems taken aback by the question, his eyes pleading. "Isn't it obvious?" Then quietly, "I guess I didn't want to scare you."

I snort. "Oh, 'cause I'm some kind of shrinking violet or something? 'Cause it's your job to protect not just Stamp but me too?"

I stand, clenching my fists, circling him like Val might be circling us. "Who made you the gatekeeper of what I should and shouldn't know? This is my safety we're talking about here too, okay? I mean, you saw me freak out about one person going missing. You don't think it would have helped me to know that four, no, five people have gone missing?"

He sits there passively, watching me fuss, waiting for me to burn myself out. When I finally do, he says, "Not until I found out why."

"And how were you going to do that? No, wait. Here's what I really want to know. When were you going to do that? Tomorrow? Next week? Next month? Next year? When it was too late?"

"I've been trying. It's hard with—well, I can't seem to shake you." He knows he's done it but can't take it back.

I feel my eyes get big but not nearly as big as my mouth. "Oh, so now it's my fault you haven't been able to investigate all these missing people. Well, if you'd just told me about them, I could have helped you instead of you having to shake me!"

I storm from his room, grabbing my kit out of the tiny closet by the front door. The hollow door shakes behind me as it slams, and I feel bad as I triple-lock it. It's barely 2:00 a.m. Outside there is still a little chill in the

March air. As I walk away, I notice a couple of the neighbors have dressed up their doors for St. Patrick's Day.

I stride past Dane's car, the night sky lit up in its usual yellow glow of my zombie vision. I walk through the parking lot, hearing night noises in my wake: a TV blaring some horrible commercial through an open window; house music thumping against a thin wall; a cat scratching at a sliding glass door screen, meowing desperately to be let in.

I straighten the messenger bag over my shoulder. It's new, since I left my old one behind, and I haven't been using it much. It never fit quite right, but what do you expect for three bucks on clearance at the Family Value Mart?

It's light blue with pink trim. Not exactly grave-rubbing appropriate but, again, the price was right. There's some pop star's face on the front that I guess I'm supposed to know because her name isn't printed anywhere on it. I guess all of Dane's smooth jazz has kept me off the pop charts for the last few months. Besides, Hazel was the one who always kept me current on trends, be it lip gloss or sandals or pop stars. Without her, I'm kinda lost. In more ways than one.

Dane thinks these bags were cheap because they ran a few thousand of them off without the chick's name. I just think they were trying to be artsy and failed. Whatever. They should have cared less about the starlet and more about the bag and how it hangs too low and jangles too loud.

I take the sidewalk to the right, walk a few blocks until I'm in the little cemetery behind the big church. It's a Catholic church, the Church of the Resurrection, which is nice. They always have the best guests, as Dad always called them. It was one of the reasons I asked Dane to choose The Socialite as our new home: the cemetery just down the road.

It doesn't have a name, which kind of sucks. I always feel like a cemetery should have a really good name, you know? The Doomsday Acre. Fields of Gloom. Orphanage Alley. I dunno, something Gothic and cool like that. Plus I like to sign each of my grave rubbings and date it and put the name of the cemetery there too. I don't know why.

I had to leave my whole library of rubbings at home when we left Barracuda Bay, so I'm starting over and not real sentimental about such things anymore. Still, some habits are hard to break.

There's a small gate to get in, and it creaks, so I just step over it. Duh. I guess the Catholics are more trusting than most cemetery folks. Then again, most Normals aren't as excited by cemeteries anymore. I used to be, but don't go by me. I was never a normal Normal anyway.

I stroll through the graveyard, letting the heat from Dane's comments roll off me in waves. I know what he meant. We do spend way too much time together. I get that. But even though I'm a tomboy and one of the Living

Dead doesn't mean I don't have feelings.

He says he can't shake me. *Shake* me? You shake someone you want to get rid of, like a cop on your tail or some stalker chick who can't take no for an answer or a piece of gum on your shoe. You don't shake somebody you care about, someone you're supposed to actually love, even if you've seen them 24 hours straight every day for months.

I'm so upset I'm deep in the graveyard before I realize it. I look back and can't see the gate or the road from here. Even so, I don't feel scared. I mean, if there are Sentinels or even Zerkers in the area, they wouldn't want just one of us. It's the whole banquet they're looking for, not just the appetizer.

Besides, Dane will be along soon to apologize. And nowadays I'm scarier than most thugs who'd be out this time of night.

A medium-sized gravestone is calling my name. It's graced with a bulging, moss-covered gargoyle right in the middle. I sit in front of it, sliding off my bag and digging inside for a paintbrush I bought at the dollar store. I gently brush off the moss until the stone is clean and dry. Then I take a smaller brush to weed out the cracks, sending dirt and bugs and little moss boogers flying everywhere.

I pause by the owner's name: Jace Hawkins, b. 1917, d. 1934.

Seventeen. Just like me. Seventeen forever. Just like me. Jace. Boy or girl? That name could go either way. Jace. It sounds so Civil War, so Southern.

I picture Jace in overalls, barefooted, fishing in a stream, a bowl haircut, a freckled nose. Then again, Jace could have been one of those frilly Southern belles. Sheesh, back then, they married you off at 15 or 16. Jace could have had a kid! What did him/her in?

I let these thoughts fill my mind as I gently tape a poster board–sized sheet of onion skin across Jace's gravestone, using strips of gray duct tape to fold the edges around the side and keep them secure.

I grip a piece of fresh charcoal and gently, gently rub the gargoyle from Jace's headstone onto the onion skin. The charcoal rasps against the paper, revealing an ornate forehead, then lonely eyes, a sharp nose, and fanged teeth.

Then I go and ruin it, pressing too hard. The thin paper tears, and I have to start again. It's after I'm through taping the crinkly paper back to the headstone that I hear the footsteps.

Dane.

But no. The footsteps are too heavy, and there's one pair too many. And they sound ugly.

I realize I'm alone in a graveyard in the middle of the night, and I think fleetingly, *Of course there are two pairs of footsteps: Stamp and Dane. Duh.*

I turn, half-smiling, just in time to see a giant boy-man-thing crouching over my bag. He smells not of death but of sweat and smoke and booze and bad intentions. His eyes are alive and glassy and young. Fourteen, maybe fifteen young. He is soft and fleshy, but that flesh? There is lots of it, and you can't be weak to carry that much around. I immediately wonder, *What are they feeding him?* He has on a black T-shirt and a gray ski jacket, the puffy kind that budget rappers wear. He has white sunglasses pushed on top of his shaved head.

The older one, though still young, stands, tall and bony, waving a switchblade in each hand. The blades shine in the moonlight, sharp and threatening but nowhere near as cold as the gleam in his angry eyes.

"Stupid," he says, looking at the crumpled paper beneath my trembling hand. "The other one was fine."

How long have they been watching me? And why didn't I hear or sense them sooner?

I go to stand, but the bigger one puts a hand on my shoulder. "That would be even more stupid."

Their voices are dark and menacing, like they've practiced for this in the mirror a few hundred times. They don't sound as young as they look. Then again, if this was happening, say, at Burger Barn at two in the afternoon, they probably would look as young as they are.

The big guy's eyes are half-lidded, his three greasy white chins covered with blond peach fuzz, but he's not so drunk or stoned or tweaking that it's weakened his grip on my shoulder any.

"Take your hand off me," I growl, shrugging.

His hand stays clamped right where it is.

They both cackle merrily, the taller one closing in. "Off you?" he says, sliding one of his blades against my cheek. "Babe, we're just getting—"

I snap his wrist happily, snatching the blade out of the air before it can dive into the loamy graveyard dirt at his feet. I don't even give him a chance to scream. I shove the crumpled grave rubbing into his mouth and clamp a hand over it. Tight.

The paper goes in so hard I swear I hear a tooth snap, but maybe that's just wishful thinking.

Fat boy lurches, yanking me off balance with a hand on my gray hoodie.

I pivot and drive the blade down, deep down, into his grubby sneaker. The scent of fresh blood fills the night air.

He screams until I slap his lower jaw shut, right onto his bleating tongue. A quarter inch of it tumbles to the earth as I scoot my shoe out of splatter range. I snatch the duct tape from my messenger bag and muzzle them both, then drag them one at a time to the cemetery gate.

Their eyes are fearful and pained as they shake their heads.

It feels too good, this strength I have now. And

there's an anger I didn't have before. It comes in a flash, so it gets hard to control myself. I know they're human boys, young guys, despite their size, and still I dispatched them as if they were 200-year-old Zerkers. That can't be good.

Remorse waves over me, expelling the rage, making me feel stupid and vulnerable all at the same time. As I watch them, they get more and more pitiful with each step. Even so, I yank their arms behind them through the bars and use every last inch of tape to bind them tight.

They wriggle. Maybe they'll get free before the church janitor finds them in a few hours, but I doubt it.

I stand in front of them, watching them squirm, sneakers digging into the dirt as they try to get away from me. The night air smells of their fear, of their sweat . . . and worse.

"Thanks, boys," I hiss to their wide-eyed, frightened faces. "I needed that."

I walk from the graveyard, grabbing my satchel on the way.

I hear more footsteps, and this time it is Dane, whose face is crumpled with concern.

"The hell?" He looks at my torn hoodie and bloody hands.

I do too. I hadn't noticed either before.

"A couple of punks jumped me." I smirk, limbs sore from the effort. "They're fine."

"You sure?"

I shake my head. "Go check." I sigh. I know he

won't be happy until he sees I haven't broken their necks and sucked out their cerebellums, boiled-peanut style.

"Go," I insist, stopping and turning to watch him dodge three gravestones to walk deeper into the cemetery. "I'll wait."

He goes, shoes crunching on dry leaves and rustling in the thick, black dirt. I hear the sound of skin hitting skin, a soft groan, and then his feet crunching again. He is smiling when he returns, and before I can ask, he brags, "I just knocked them out, you know, to stop the bleeding."

"Hmmm." I remember the feel of the big one's hand, hard and insistent on my shoulder, and wonder what might have happened if I wasn't a zombie, if I could feel pain, if I hadn't trained with Dane five days a week since moving to Orlando. "I should have thought of that."

"I'm sure you would have. Minus the shock and all."

He lingers at my side as we weave through the rest of the headstones. I keep waiting for him to take my hand, but he never does. It's not that he doesn't want to, I don't think, just that it's not his style.

I'm not defending him. He doesn't need me for that. He's just never been a chocolate and flowers and sweater-over-his-shoulders, hand-holding guy.

I wipe the guys' blood on the side of my jeans and stoop to rinse off in a puddle of standing water in the church parking lot.

"What happened?" Dane says.

115

I shrug. "Nothing much. Just common late-night thuggery. This neighborhood seems like it gets worse every day."

"Then it's good you're here to keep Normal grave rubbers safe, right?"

I figure he's joking, but when I look up, I know he's not. He has his thoughtful face on: lids half-shut, cheeks sucked in, lips tight. Stamp always called it Dane's grim face.

The thought of Stamp makes me smile.

We walk back to the apartment, then past it. Dane pauses at the entrance, standing in the silhouette of a dozen broken Christmas lights wrapped around The Socialite sign, still waiting for someone to take them down before it's time to put them back up again.

"I need to think," I tell him when he follows reluctantly.

"Okay, yeah, good idea. Listen, Maddy, about the map. I'm sorry. I just—"

"You know what I was thinking of?" I interrupt, ignoring him. "When those guys jumped me back there? I was remembering the first time Bones and Dahlia did the same thing back in Barracuda Bay."

"And?" he says when I don't immediately deliver the punch line.

"And it got me thinking," I huff, waiting for him to catch up. "I don't think Val's a Sentinel, Dane. I think . . . I think she's a Zerker."

12
Val's His Gal

"This is awkward." Stamp smiles as we sit in the same booth at his favorite café. It's midway between work and home, but that's not why he likes it. They serve carbonated espresso shots, and he's as addicted as a zombie can be to something other than brains.

The place is one of those funky, poser, retro coffee shops with floor-to-ceiling windows and stark, uncomfortable black chairs and matching tables, black-and-white framed art of random couples kissing in France, and baristas who haven't bathed in days and are damn proud of it.

They all know Stamp by name and have his order practically waiting for him when he walks through the door, while they look at me and my Mountain Dew Voltage as if I've just ordered fried chicken at a vegetarian buffet.

It's not just that I'm undead. It's that I'm unhip. Stamp, in his endless effort to pass among the Normals, has managed to expertly navigate a world I'm still trying to understand. Even months after being reanimated, I'm still experimenting with the right layering of my makeup, trying not to look too pale or too gray or too orange or too fleshy. I'm still working on finding long-sleeved shirts that don't look dorky and leggings that don't make me look 12 years old.

But Stamp? He's mastered this world. Not just the living world but the teenage world. I keep forgetting I was never hip when I was alive, and Dane could never be anything other than a bad boy—good for making your dad mad, bad for dinner parties and cafés and poser clubs.

But Stamp was already heading toward permanent cool before he died. Now he's just made it his life's mission to belong. And here, in a place like this, with funky so-retro-its-hot-again remixes of old '80s songs on the overhead speakers and hipster baristas with stringy beards and carbonated espresso, it's like his home turf and I'm the sore thumb.

It's after work and he's dressed for another long night out, in snug black leather pants and a shiny gray shirt that manages to make his skin only vaguely pale. His favorite black-and-white hoodie is tossed across one corner of the table, his shiny cell phone resting atop it.

He looks good, but I know that's mostly because he wants nothing to do with me.

"Awkward how?" I say, pushing my soda away. "Because I didn't order some froufrou coffee drink to impress all your friends?"

He smiles charmingly, complete with dimples. How can he still have dimples with, like, 0.002 percent body fat? Whatever. It's just another of life's little mysteries, like why he can still pull female digits at Mach 10 while guys literally (no lie) cross the street to avoid me.

"Uh, because we haven't been alone since Dane went in to pay for gas on our way out of Barracuda Bay."

I blurt on autopilot, "That's not true." But it mostly is.

He starts to say something, obviously sees there's no fight left in my eyes, and stops. "It was always him, wasn't it?"

I cluck my tongue.

He fiddles with his spiky black hair. "I know, I know. We've done this to death, but—"

"It wasn't always him. It was you, first and always. And then, well, things changed."

"No, they didn't," he says, turning his dark eyes toward me. Oh, how I used to love looking into those baby blues. But for all of us, whatever eye color we had has long since bled out. Now we have the same dark eyes, with Stamp's just a little lighter than most because they were so darn blue before. "Things never changed between us because they never really got started, Maddy. It wasn't your fault. It wasn't my fault. It just happened. But quit trying to pretend it didn't."

"I'm not pretending. I don't have all the answers either, okay? About what we are or who we love."

"Maybe not, but you and Dane sure act like you've got all the answers now."

"Why? Because we're careful? Because we're trying to stay off the radar and you're doing everything to get noticed?"

"Like what?" he barks.

"Like going out every night, exposing yourself to all those humans—"

"Hey, just because you and Stamp want to hide away and pretend you're not one of the Living Dead, don't try to—"

I shush him, leaning in. "Why don't you say it a little louder? I don't think the barista's cousin in Wyoming heard you."

"Why shouldn't I?" He kind of stiffens, contorting his fine features into something feral. "I'm tired of hiding. Or what do you and Dane call it? Passing?"

"Yeah, Stamp, we know."

"I am careful." He says it like he's trying to convince me.

I shake my head. "You can't be. Not with all these new friends, all these new girlfriends. Not with Val."

"You don't know anything about her."

"Do you?" I snap, 'cause now he's just pissing me off.

"Sure. Lots."

Liar.

"What, then, Stamp? Besides her address."

He shrugs. "I know that she likes monster movies and frozen lemonade and thongs and—"

"Give me something real," I say, trying hard to erase the mental image of Val in a thong. "Like, oh, where does she come from? How does she afford an entire warehouse? What does she do for money? Where is her family? Who is her family? Who are her other friends?"

He shrugs. "She doesn't know that stuff about me either."

"Don't be so sure."

"What's that supposed to mean?"

"It's supposed to mean that you have to be more careful. That we have to be on guard for Sentinels posing as hot young club chicks."

"Are you kidding me? You really think Val is a Sentinel?"

"Or worse," I say, but he's so self-righteous he doesn't stop to hear.

"Please. That's the dumbest thing you've said all night, and you've been tossing off some doozies, lemme tell ya."

"Have I? They only sound like doozies if you're living in dreamland and refuse to come back down to earth."

He shakes his head, avoiding my eyes because, deep down, he's got to know I'm right.

"What do I need to be careful for anyway? I've got you and Dane to show up to interrogate her for me, right? Isn't that what you clowns were doing last night? And don't think she didn't know it. She was really upset."

"Who cares if she knows it? That's what friends do. They look out for you, even when you don't, or won't, look out for yourself."

"Whatever," he says, waving a hand.

I grab it fiercely. But not because I'm pissed, exactly. "What are all these rings?" There's one on every finger. Silver, mostly, or fake silver. Skulls, one spider, a claw, the usual Goth crap. I only ask because he wasn't wearing them at work, and I've never seen him wear a ring at home.

"When in Rome," he says casually, yanking back.

I still hold on tight, making him really work to get that hand back.

"You should see some of these clubs and what the guys wear. This is tame by comparison."

I bite my tongue. Yeah, well, I'm about to find out. Without him knowing it.

Just then his phone rings, belting out some rancid heavy metal ringtone that elicits frowns from the other customers.

As he slips it from atop his folded hoodie, Stamp still looks miffed—until he sees who it is. "It's Val," he whispers excitedly. "Hey, babe, guess who I'm sitting here with? No. What? I barely know that guy. No, it's Maddy! You know, from last night? Right, the census taker—"

"Survey taker," I correct. Hey, it may be a pretend

job, but I worked really hard to make it look real. The least he can do is—

He looks appalled that I'd dare interrupt and, with big gray eyes, whispers so Val can't hear, "Maddy, please!"

I groan and stare out the window at midevening foot traffic passing by the Poser Café. (No, it's not its real name, but it works, so I'm keeping it.) God, is there anything worse than listening to your ex flirt with his current, at the same table, hearing his stupid skull rings hit the black Formica every time he waves exaggeratedly 'cause he's such an epic, cheesy, love-dumb spazz?

"Seriously?" Stamp's voice changes from puppy-dog lovefest to seriously confused. "Sure, I mean, she's right here, so okay . . ." He hands me the phone with a frown and mouths, "Val wants to talk to you."

I squinch my nose and have to stop myself from blurting, "What? Gross! Why? No, thank you, but just—no, gawd!"

Instead I take the phone, paint on a smile, and say in my best motherly voice, "Val? Is that really you? How great to hear your voice again . . ."

I know it's lame, but what else was I going to say? "My sometimes boyfriend thinks you're a Sentinel, and if I catch you betraying my sometimes ex-boyfriend I'm going to personally remove your limbs with my newly whitened teeth"?

"It was so . . . nice . . . meeting you last night," Val says.

I can't hide my distaste at the gruff sound of her voice and her passive-aggressive, stop-start style of speaking really fast then really slow.

"Stamp had told me so . . . much . . . about you. It was . . . great . . . to finally meet you in person. And Dan seems really sweet too."

"Dane," I kind of growl because you know and I know after nearly clocking him last night, the witch remembers his name.

Stamp hears my tone and gets all big-eyed again.

I shoo him down with a reassuring hand, but he's still leaning way too close to me over the table.

Ooh, and was that a dig? The way she paused there around the word *much* when she said she'd heard so much about me?

Why, yes. Yes, it was.

That. Bitch.

"Oh," I weasel right back, really oozing it on as Stamp sits there, smiling cluelessly. "Stamp has just had *so* much to say about you. It's a shame you couldn't invite us in last night. That would have been a real treat."

Finally Stamp frowns and mouths, "Hey!"

There is a slight pause before Val croaks, "Oh, well, you know how it is with new lovers. Stamp and I just wanted some . . . alone . . . time. But maybe next time. We can do it at your place, right? I heard I missed out on your fancy thousand-dollar spaghetti."

Oh, it's on! Bitch knows it's called million-dollar spaghetti! Who the hell calls something thousand-dollar anything? Unless, you know, it actually costs a thousand dollars.

"Oh, well, it's waiting on you. Hey, listen, what are you doing tonight? I'm sure I can defrost it in time for dinner, if you're not too busy."

"I'd love to," Val croaks, sounding like a cross between Dane and some poor schmo who's had his jaw wired shut, "but Stamp and I are heading out to that new club downtown. Spartans? It's too bad you can't dance. I know Stamp would love to see you—"

"Who said I can't dance?" I say perfectly sweetly, so it's surprising that Stamp's eyes get huge. Again.

"Why, Stamp did, sweetie. He tells me everything."

Sweetie? Really?

"Oh, did he now?"

With more than mortal speed, Stamp whips his phone from my hand and babbles into it, "Well, Val, he-he-he, I've got to make sure Maddy gets home safe, and then I'll come pick you up so we can head to the club, okay? What's that? No, you hang up first. No, you! Oh geez, you're so funny. Okay, I'll—"

"Done," I groan, snatching the phone and pressing the End button so I won't hurl my last three servings of brains all over his carbonated espresso. "That's seriously annoying."

"Yeah, well, what's more annoying is that since I hung up first, she's going to call just so she can hang up first. See. There."

The phone rings, and with speed and skill I both silence the ring and power the phone down. "Done and done."

Stamp makes a big show of trying to get the phone back, but I can tell he's secretly relieved. At least a little.

"She'll be mad." He sips his fizzy drink.

"What? Are you scared of a little girl?"

He shrugs, and I figure he'll deny, deny, deny.

But then, after a pause, as if maybe he's thought his answer over a little, he blurts, "She's tougher than you think."

I shiver, recalling the way she tried to back Stamp down on the sidewalk last night. "I bet." I drink my soda. "Sounds like you guys are getting all serious and stuff."

"Kinda."

"What's your strategy there?"

"Strategy?"

"Yeah, exit strategy. You know, before things get too serious."

Stamp frowns, then sneers. "That's the difference between you and me. I'm not constantly thinking about getting out of a relationship while I'm still in it."

He stands abruptly, and I linger until it's clear he's ready to leave and not just get another fizzy drink refill. I pocket the phone as I rise, thinking maybe he'll forget it. That would give Dane and me another chance to mine it for clues.

But the minute we're outside and standing on the curb, Stamp winks. "Hand it over."

I smile. A wink was always our little code that things were okay after harsh words were spoken. "Fine." I sigh dramatically, sliding the phone out of my hip pocket. "But before I do, answer an honest question."

He rolls his eyes but stays put, another good sign. "What?"

"Do you love her?"

"Who?" He squinches his face. "Val? Love? Maddy, we just met."

"Yeah, I know, but you're already doing the you-hang-up-first bit, and that's usually a sign of true love. Or dementia. Whatever."

He snorts.

I hand him the phone even though he really hasn't answered the question.

"In this case," Stamp says, almost looking around as if she might hear, "it's more like a sign of true scared."

"Really?" I say. "Stamp, you don't have to go tonight. Let's get Dane, and we'll go pretend to eat somewhere, like old times. Val will understand."

"Not really," he says, not nervously but close enough. "Besides, you don't stand Val up. Ever."

"Why? She stood us up without much worry."

"Yeah, well, it doesn't work in reverse. Just trust me. But it's cool. We're cool." He puffs up his chest before slipping on some sunglasses to shield the last of the afternoon sun.

"You sure?"

He sniffs and changes the subject. "Look, I'm serious about driving you home. It's on the way to the club. And look, it's still early. That place doesn't really get hopping until well after midnight."

I picture Dane in the borrowed car still idling around the corner in the Burger Barn parking lot. "It's cool. I don't want to get you in trouble with Val."

He winks again and turns, sunglasses blinking in the sun.

I watch him go, never suspecting it could be the last time I see him re-alive . . .

13
Nightclub of the Living Dead

"Bitch is a zombie," I grunt, flopping into the passenger seat a few minutes later. "Straight-up undead witch from hell, no doubt."

Dane doesn't smile often, but when he does, look out. The last of the day's sun colors his gray skin orange and lights up his teeth. I'm so relieved to see him, so freaked out that Val's among the Living Dead, that I impulsively plant a kiss on his thin, pale lips.

I can feel him smile even as we kiss. I pull away just to see it some more.

"What finally convinced you?" He puts the car in reverse and exits the parking lot.

We idle in traffic until Stamp's Jeep appears in the left lane a few cars up.

"Stamp handed me the phone and made me talk to her." I groan.

"Ugh." He makes a face. "I hate when he does that."

We share a wince like girlfriends.

Dane eases in to follow Stamp. "So," he says a few streets later as traffic begins to thin. "Are you feeling better about this now? I mean, I'm not sure how her behavior last night didn't convince you, but—"

"Yeah, lots better." I'm jazzed to get started and get this night over with. "Where'd you get the car?"

"You know Chuck from work? The wardrobe dude?"

"The fat white guy with the dreadlocks?"

He gives me a funny face. "No, that's Ralph. You know? Chuck? The one with all the Star Wars shirts?"

"Oh yeah, gotcha. So . . ."

I'm watching Stamp's Jeep, now a few lanes over.

Dane is really drawing this out. "Anyway," he finally says, "Chuck was helping his girlfriend move tonight, so I told him he could borrow the sedan. She collects a lot of comic books, and his backseat wasn't big enough for them all. This way Stamp won't recognize the car, *and* it looks like I did a favor for Chuck instead of, you know, the other way around."

"Nice thinking," I murmur, watching Stamp turn left. Before I point it out, I hear the blinker switch on.

"So what did she say one-on-one?"

"Nothing but grossness on toast. Playing all nicey with Stamp right in earshot."

"Sexy," he cracks as he slows down. "Did she tell you why she couldn't invite us in last night?"

I make an ick face, but he's paying more attention to the road than to me. Story of my life. "She said she and Stamp were young lovers and needed their alone time."

Stamp has turned in to Val's neighborhood, which looks even sketchier now that we know our way around and I can pay more attention to details. The other warehouses here are completely deserted, and for a moment my mind flashes to Val building her own Zerker army, chaining them up in all the other warehouses and just waiting for the right time to release them on us.

Dane pulls in to the parking lot next door but close enough that we'll see Stamp's Jeep when he leaves.

"I really hate this neighborhood," Dane says, squinting against the dreadful orange light from the street lamp we've parked under.

"Yeah," I say, manually locking my door. "I'm glad I'm already dead."

Stamp's long legs launch him out of the driver's seat. He's wearing his skinny jeans again and that ridiculous black-and-white-striped hoodie, plus the shades still, even though it's close to midnight by now.

"You know," Dane says as Stamp disappears into the warehouse, "I never thought I'd say this, but I think I preferred it when Stamp dressed like a jock."

I snort. "He just seems so lost. Like he's trying so hard. He seems vulnerable, don't you think?"

Dane nods but then shakes his head. "Stamp's tougher than you think. He can handle himself."

Rusty Fischer

"Oh, really?" I nudge him. "So what's with all this, then?"

"Don't you want to know if she's a Sentinel or not?"

"Or Zerker."

He nods and says absently, "Or Zerker."

"So what's the plan? I mean, other than follow them to some stupid club?"

He chews his lower lip. "I'm still working on that. But we need to isolate her. It may take force. You up for that?"

"I am." I grin, thinking of those thugs in the cemetery the other night. "But what if she's not what we're pretty much sure she is? What if Stamp's right and she is just some crackpot Normal who digs living dangerously and watching scary movies on TV all night?"

He looks at me, nods.

"We apologize? Here they come." I subconsciously inch down in my seat.

Stamp is reaching for his door as the thin, blonde menace saunters to hers. Val stands patiently even as the car shifts from Stamp's weight in his seat.

"Ouch," Dane says, clearly enjoying this.

"Yeah, he never was too good with the gentlemanly stuff."

"Me either." Dane's still watching Val, who's tapping her toe impatiently.

I know Dane's kind of fishing for a compliment, so I ignore him. "*What* is she wearing?"

132

She's got on white-and-black tights to match Stamp's jacket. Lame. Her foofy gray skirt looks really expensive. But then she's in a cheap, ripped tank top and . . . a red boa?

"Kids these days." Dane shakes his head.

At last Stamp gets the message and springs from the car, shimmies over, and opens Val's door. Even from down the block, we can see her mouth flapping and his shoulders shrinking.

"Told you he was whipped."

I roll my eyes. "More like scared."

"Really?" The cheap leather of the borrowed car seat cracks as Dane turns to look at me.

I nod.

Dane grabs my head and shoves it nearly to the floorboard. Seriously, my head's scraping the gas pedal, but he's gazing out the window. What's wrong with this picture?

He turns his lights off and follows Stamp's Jeep, lucky to catch him as he roars from the industrial side of town and back onto the interstate, heading for downtown.

We follow them from afar, Dane paranoid that Stamp or Val might spot us and head for the hills.

Halfway to the city lights, I say, "Dane, this is ridiculous. So what if they spot us? It's America, right? Can't two zombies go to the same club as one known zombie and another suspected zombie?"

"I guess so, but I still like the element of surprise.

I think we shook Val up pretty bad showing up out of nowhere last night, and Stamp saw it. It wasn't quite enough, but I still prefer surprising her to the other way around."

"Great. Fine. I get that, but enough with the cat and mouse, okay?"

"Okay, yes, you're right." But still he drives all hunched and sketchy.

Finally Stamp pulls off the second downtown exit and we follow, merging with the nightlife as old and young alike fight for parking spaces in the lively downtown district that blends both upscale bistros and cafés with trendy nightclubs and hookah bars.

We spot the club Stamp was squawking about over coffee: Spartans, which I guess has a kind of gladiator theme or something judging from the giant gold doors that look like shields, with swords for door handles, of course. Stamp parks, and we circle the block.

We park behind a bustling Cuban restaurant, which looks a ton more fun than stupid Spartans, let me tell you. I pump a ton of quarters in the hungry meter before we cling to the last of the line waiting to get into the club.

It's pretty obvious the rest of the kids are all mouth-breathing, pulse-pounding Normals: healthy skin, flushed cheeks, beads of sweat on their foreheads, bodies so warm and amped up on energy drinks I can feel the heat coming off them at three or four paces.

Stamp seems to know them all as he hustles and jives

with all kinds of freaks of nature, from the kid with the glittery green Mohawk to the chick with the shiny gold chain strung from her nose ring to her nether regions. (Not that I'm a prude, but attention-grab much?)

"This is worse than I thought," Dane says, nodding toward Stamp, who's doing some elbow-cracking hand jive with another ghoul of the night. "Lucky they're all freaks, or he'd stick out like a sore thumb."

"So maybe he hasn't been as careless as we thought."

Dane doesn't look over when he says, "Maybe not, but it's not the crowd scenes I'm worried about so much as the after party, if you know what I mean."

"Yes, Dane, I know what you mean. You don't have to keep rubbing it in every night, okay?"

He senses my tone, as do a few of the Normals, and they all look my way. I peg the chick with the nose ring and say, "Yeah? What?"

She rolls her fake contacts and turns around, puffing heavily on a nasty clove cigarette that I'm tempted to shove down one of her lung holes.

Dane puts a hand on my shoulder. "Hey, hey, are you here to make a scene or what?"

"No," I grumble. "But you've spent the last two nights reminding me Stamp has a ton of extracurricular activities and, well, it's not so easy to hear."

He smirks. "Yeah, well, how do you think I felt while you two were going out?"

I groan. "It's not the same. You knew my heart was

with you. I don't know what Stamp's doing anymore. You and I never felt like strangers. With Stamp, that's all I—"

"There. Look. They're going in."

I watch Val flirt with a giant bouncer in a toga as Stamp gives him one of those bro shoulder hugs before they quietly slip inside. The open door releases music so loud I can hear it from 10 couples back.

We wait, more anxious now than ever, as the huge bouncer in the tent-sized toga buddy-shakes and bro-hugs every man, woman, and child in line in front of us.

"Come on, come on," Dane whispers tensely as we finally get close enough to make out the foil leaves woven into the big dude's fake crown. "Why does this guy have to write every couple a love letter?"

I watch as the freak with the nose chain leans in and whispers something to the bouncer, eyeing me with a look so chilly I'm tempted to check for frostbite. Then she smirks at him, and he nods knowingly before she sails right in.

Two couples later the bouncer looks at us. "Sorry, guys, club's full."

The door is ajar, bass pumping out.

"I see plenty of room," I say.

He slams the giant, shield-shaped door with one leather-sandaled foot. "I said the club's full."

A dozen or more couples wait behind us, enjoying

the show. It's clear we're outsiders here, Dane and I, with our black jeans and leather jackets and nonspiky hair and no nose rings attached to our hoo-has.

Dane and I look at each other and smile. All the obstacles we thought were confronting us—losing Stamp and Val in traffic, expecting a recon team of Sentinels at every turn—and the biggest one turns out to be some bouncer in a toga?

Dane whispers, "Can you lend me a diversion for a few seconds?"

"Gladly."

I turn to the emo Goth behind me, a mousy guy with a dyed black mop covering his left eye. "What are you looking at?"

"A couple of losers who can't get into the club." He giggles.

His tall emo girlfriend with the skunk tail hanging out the back of her fishnet stockings whispers something in his ear.

I growl at her but turn just in time to see Dane leaning in to the bouncer, two fingers pinching the big guy's wrist.

The bouncer's face reddens, and his glistening forehead drips sweat. "Okay, okay."

Dane releases him and grabs the giant gold door, swinging it open as if it were made of balsa wood and not 380 pounds of hammered brass.

"Thanks for your understanding." I beam at the big

guy, who favors one wrist and uses his toga shoulder fabric to wipe his brow.

Inside it's clear the club is pretty sparsely populated. Either that or it's so damn big you could fit a million more kids inside and still not make a dent. White curtains billowing from the roof are tied to each wall with giant gold sashes. Cocktail waitresses in *much* tinier togas than the bouncer's dash from cluster of kids to cluster of kids, handing out earthen mugs foaming with dry ice inside. The dance floor is throbbing with colored lights and twisting bodies, and the DJ in the booth above wears a gladiator costume with sunglasses.

I don't see Stamp or Val anywhere, but it's hard to concentrate with so much stimuli from every corner of the club.

We can't hear much because the awful music is 15 times as loud as it should be, especially with our super-zombie hearing powers.

"Ugh," Dane says, bellying up to the neon-blue bar. "I'm so glad I died before clubs like this became popular."

While he orders two sodas, I ignore him and watch for Stamp. It's hard to find him because he looks just like every other megadouche in the joint, down to the black-and-white stripes, spiky hair, skull rings, ridiculous white shades, and—

"There he is." I nudge Dane.

He hands me my soda, and I sip it absently.

Dane's dressed simply in black jeans, black T-shirt, and a snug black leather jacket, the kind with white stripes down the arms. I like the way the rotating strobe glistens off his closely cut hair.

We slip on our sunglasses to fit in but mostly to add to the disguise.

Val and Stamp are talking to a bunch of identical-looking clowns, and she's whipping that sparkly red boa something fierce.

Stamp looks nervous, jumpy, and I can't tell if it's because he suspects we're onto him or if, like he implied at the café, he really is afraid of Val.

She certainly has him under her spell. That much is clear. He gets the drinks, pays, and brings them to her. He nods patiently, smiling appropriately while she talks. And talks and talks and talks.

"Is he even having any fun?" Dane says, leaning in close so that I can smell the fizzy soda on his cold tongue. "I mean, they all look like her friends."

"They don't even look like her friends." I walk toward them, Dane tagging along. "They look just like Stamp. They look like her servants."

And that's when it hits me. They're not her friends. They're not even friends with each other. "Do they look familiar?" I say, flashing back to the map in his room.

I'm looking at one in particular, a vaguely Latin-looking dude in blue jeans and a long black coat that's too big.

He looks out of place, jumpy but eager to please, and young. So young.

And familiar. "Is that . . . Rudy Ortega?"

"Who?" he says, leaning in as I point toward the Latin kid.

"The missing kid from our apartment complex. You know, the one from the newspaper the other morning? He went out to get some bananas from that bodega across the street and never came back."

He shakes his head but doesn't stop looking.

"And that girl next to him. The redhead with the sad eyes? She was one of your dots as well."

"No, it can't be. You mean the nursing student from over by Sea World? Wendy . . . Wendy Schmaltz. That's it. Been missing for a month. But she looks so different now."

"Yeah, well, compare Stamp's yearbook picture with how he looks tonight."

He looks at me, and we look back to the small semi-circle of club punks surrounding Val. There are five. Besides Rudy Ortega and Wendy Schmaltz, we can't name them. We'd need Dane's map for that. But this much is clear: all are young, all look out of place, and all are kissing Val's butt big-time. Just. Like. Stamp.

"I don't get it," Dane says. "Why would the Sentinels be recruiting Normals? It doesn't make sense."

"It makes perfect sense if Val's a Zerker."

Dane slides his empty soda glass toward the bartender,

who's wearing a plastic Roman breastplate. "So you think Val met Stamp on the nightclub scene, figured out what he was, and started picking off kids who lived around him?"

"Well, if she was a lone Zerker without any backup and found that Stamp had two zombies for roommates, she might have wanted her own personal army to make sure she could take us all."

"So you think that's why she hasn't made her move yet? She wants enough fellow Zerkers to make sure she's never outnumbered?"

I nod. Makes sense to me.

For a petite girl, Val has a pretty imposing, Zerker-like presence. In a way, she reminds me of the only other female Zerker I know—or knew. Dahlia.

Dahlia might have been compact, but she was fierce. Fierce in a way that went beyond her size or her status as one of the Living Dead. I'll never forget the last time we tussled or the look of murderous venom in her black, endless eyes.

And now I'm having some kind of déjà vu of the Living Dead. We're talking, this chick could be Dahlia's spirit sister.

Val's arms are firm, if a little on the slim side. And if you don't count that booty in her skirt, there's not an ounce of fat on her. The veins in her neck stand out when she laughs, and her eyes are fiercely alert. Too alert.

"Look out," Dane says, but it's too late.

She's spotted me.

Or has she? I can't tell if she's looking at me or through me or if she'd even remember me in the first place. She brays laughter, looking away.

Stamp nods uncomfortably.

A few of Val's lackeys look our way, then past us, then back at us.

"False alarm?" I say.

Dane shrugs. "How should I know? Whatever she is, she's better at all this than— Shoot. Now Stamp's looking."

"And whispering," I add. "That creep—"

Dane's eyes are wide. "Yeah, that didn't look too obvious. Ooh, wait, they're coming over. Maddy, Maddy, look normal. Seriously."

I turn to see Val leading her stiff lackeys plus Stamp, who trails along in the background reluctantly, looking all kinds of awkward.

"Maddy?" Val says in that throaty voice that always sends chills up my spine. "Dane? What are you guys doing here?" She turns to Stamp. "Did you . . . did you tell them we'd be here tonight?"

"You did," Stamp says.

Val turns on him so quickly, so fiercely, that I flinch. Even Dane flinches.

"I mean, r-r-remember? At the café tonight, I heard

you ask Maddy if she—"

Val doesn't let him finish. Instead, she turns to us. "Last night you show up on my doorstep, and tonight you're here at the same club? If I didn't know any better, guys, I'd say you were following us."

Dane and I share a glance, only to find Val's friends ambling toward us.

No, not just toward us. Around us.

Dane sees it too late.

By the time we're both alert, we're surrounded.

The Rudy kid from our complex is bulky in his big leather coat. There's glitter in his spiky hair but fear in his eyes.

Wendy, the would-be nursing student, looks thin but strong in a red leather jacket to match her flowing red hair.

The others cluster around, hulking and ready.

Val saunters through the center of the circle while lights throb and music pulses. I see her eyes are blue, then green, depending on the light. The lights move away. Under her obviously fake contacts, her eyes are flat, ugly, and . . . yellow.

We were right. Val's not a Sentinel. She's a Zerker.

"Back off!" Dane grunts, also sensing it. "Give us Stamp, take these others with you and get lost, and nobody gets hurt."

"Silly boy. We're all zombies here in this circle.

Nobody gets hurt anyway."

The music pounds, and the bar disappears into the background. Bodies flit by, half-naked, sweaty, glittery Normals oblivious to the Zombie-Zerker showdown among them. Somebody drops a drink, and none of it matters.

"Who are they?" Dane juts his chin toward Rudy, then Wendy.

They look back at him uncomfortably.

"What?" Val cackles, yanking Rudy so harshly the sunglasses fly off his head. "Don't you even remember your own neighbor?"

Rudy grunts, flashing yellow teeth that I swear contain bits of fresh brain.

She releases him, and he blends into the crowd of Zerkers at her back. "Took you long enough to come check me out," Val says, nodding at Dane.

"Who says it's our first try?" he says.

"They do." Val smiles triumphantly. "My little friends here have been watching you. What? You think I turned them just because I was hungry for a little human flesh? Trust me, I have way more discipline than that."

"What do you want with Stamp?" I say, nodding in his direction.

Wait. He was just there, in the back slightly and to the left.

Or wait. Was he over there to the right?

"Where's Stamp?" Dane barks so loudly that the

dancing Normals outside the Zerker circle actually stop to check us out.

Wendy, the doomed nursing student, hisses at Val's entourage. They promptly scatter, and she turns to me with a self-assured smile.

And I promise myself that, before the night is over, I will wipe it off for her, innocent victim or no.

"Stamp who?" Val presses in as the circle of her Zerker friends tightens around us. "I don't see anybody there, do you?"

I see Dane's fist tighten, his eyes narrow to slits, but I know what he's thinking: Too many witnesses.

"Give us Stamp back!" I'm standing toe to toe with Val now. I poke her stupid boa with every syllable: "Give. Him. Back."

She stands, intractable, and pokes me back. Hard. "Come. And. Get. Him."

Just then rough hands pull us apart, and I'm tossed into the bar. I hear a scream—a loud, girly, civilian scream—as the strobe lights flicker and the music blares. I turn to find Val gone but her friends shoving me every which way.

But not all of them. Wendy is here. And the Rudy dude from one building over.

So where are the rest?

A couple of others surround Dane.

He tackles one, twirling to avoid the hands of another.

I turn and hear a whack, feeling Wendy's palm on my face right before I'm sitting, stunned, on the floor. Vaguely, in the background, I hear the stomping.

Normals running.

Rudy stumbles forward.

I feel bad, but it's him or me. And really, all that matters now is Stamp. I lash out, the bottom of my shoe connecting with his knee.

He comes down hard on the other foot.

We're face-to-face.

My palm slams his nose upward. Something snaps, and Zerker goo oozes from Rudy's shattered nostrils. I'm yanked away before I can see him fall.

Wendy hoists me up under the bar.

My head cracks the electric neon. Bulbs burst, and fuzzy white powder fills the air. I scramble to still her hands.

She shoves a finger into my ear, probably hoping it's my eye.

I grab her thumb and wrench her down to the floor with me.

Chaos is all around us. Normals run and shout, "Security! Security!"

Wendy snarls as she struggles to rise.

I plant my sneaker on her throat and press down. "Where. Is. Stamp?" I treat her throat like a gas pedal with each word.

She shakes her head, trembling violently, one gray eye and one yellow eye pleading now that a fake contact has obviously been knocked out. When I lift my foot, she spins around, shoving me against the bottom of the bar with both hands. She spits through black goo between her teeth, "Wouldn't you like to know?"

She is rank, her one eye glowing yellow now that we're face-to-face, and I know . . . I know she's gone. Zerker gone. Like Bones and Dahlia were when I first met them back in Barracuda Bay. Like my favorite teacher, Ms. Haskins, after they got to her. Like half the football team and the entire cheer squad.

Nobody home but rage now. Hard, cold, Zerker rage.

I lift my feet against her chest and kick out, shoving her halfway across the floor. It's nearly empty now. Most of the Normals are gone. Spilled drinks and wet cocktail trays are the only things littering the floor.

I turn to find Dane wrestling with Rudy, the bigger Zerker seconds away from gnawing on Dane's beautiful, glistening skull.

I'm too far away to stop him. I find a bottle that's fallen off the bar and launch it their way.

It lands with a thud against Rudy's temple, but he doesn't even flinch. Dane does, though, grabbing it with a free hand, breaking it against the bar like something out of *Road House*, and shoving the pointy end right under Rudy's exposed throat. Most Zerkers are so strong and old and leathery and tough, it's like trying to jab your way through a rhinoceros' hide. But Rudy is a young Zerker, meaning fresh. The broken bottle slides into his throat so far that half of Dane's hand goes missing, then pops out the other side of Rudy's skull, bits of brain and gore sticking to the jagged edge as goo gushes like an oil well from the back of Rudy's head. The guy keels over, pawing at the bottle top sticking out of his throat as Dane inches away. Rudy dies—again—with a confused look in his yellow eyes, hands reaching out to us as what's left of his brain short-circuits from the inside out.

"Poor Rudy." I frown, looking around the deserted club.

"Poor Rudy? Dude almost turned me Zerker!"

I shrug, looking for any signs of Stamp. "You would have pulled out of it."

"Not without that flying bottle trick." His eyes are all gooey and grateful. I think I like it better when they're hard and black. "Here!" He finds a service exit under a blinking red sign and steps over several damp wooden crates as we find ourselves in some back alley. There is no one left: none of the Zerkers Val turned, no Val, certainly no Stamp.

There are voices around the corner, hundreds of club kids squawking and texting and complaining to the Spartans' bouncers at the same time. Then sirens in the distance.

Dane says, "Come on," even though I'm two steps ahead of him.

In the club's lot we see the empty space where just a few minutes earlier Stamp's Jeep was parked.

We skirt the crowd, taking another back alley to reach the car in the back of the Cuban restaurant.

"Witch!" Dane opens the driver's door so roughly the hinges crack. It's not even his own car!

"So what was that?" I say.

He tears out of the parking lot, over the curb, and into the street.

Cops pour in from the other direction.

"A setup," he seethes, speeding through stop signs and past shocked pedestrians. "I should have known better than to follow just Stamp. I should have been following Val."

"Well, how? We didn't even know where she lived until recently."

"Exactly my point." He slams his large palms against the shiny steering wheel and stops short of running over a big blue mailbox on the next corner. "I've gotten lazy, letting Stamp run around town at all hours, not even knowing who he's hanging out with. I should have been following him weeks ago."

"You said you wanted to trust him."

Dane turns on two wheels at a nearby corner and roars onto the interstate, passing cars at an unsafe rate of speed and trajectory.

"Yeah, well, look where trust got us," he says. "Stamp's missing and I don't even know who took him."

"Val took him."

"I mean, I don't even know who Val is. That's my point."

"She's a Zerker. And she outsmarted us. All those

kids missing for months now. And we were totally stumped."

"I was stumped," he says, focusing on not killing us in downtown traffic. "I should have told you about those kids, about Rudy and Wendy. I should have made you come with me to check them out. I was stupid. I thought after what we'd been through, it would be the Sentinels coming after us, not the Zerkers."

I grit my teeth and hold on as he flies from the highway, dipping into the same industrial neighborhood we've been staking out.

"There's his Jeep," I blurt as Dane screeches to a halt in front of Val's warehouse loft, nearly sending me flying through the windshield.

The neighborhood is deserted at this hour.

We get out of the car, the engine still running, and carefully approach the silent warehouse.

"Looks dark," I say.

"See what I mean? We've been set up."

"But why? What's her game? She could have taken Stamp anytime over the last few weeks. Why tonight? Why now?"

He tries the warehouse door, yanking it six ways to Sunday and ringing the bell half a dozen times.

No one's in there. We both know it. We're just trying to do what we can to avoid getting back in our car and driving away.

Away without Stamp.

Dane turns to me, his jaw flexing and dark eyes flashing in the beam of a random street lamp. "I don't think it's Stamp she wants."

"Then who?"

He shakes his head, walking toward Stamp's Jeep. "I don't know. That's my— Shit!"

"What's your shit? I thought you said we couldn't— Oh, shit!"

We see the note on Stamp's windshield at about the same time. It's written in some trampy red lipstick and takes up most of the glass. It says:

If you ever want to see Stamp alive again, be at Splash Zone by 3 a.m.

Val

P.S. Bring your swim trunks!

"Splash Zone?" Dane strips the gears in poor Chuck's car as he backs away from the warehouse and throttles toward the interstate.

"It's that cheap-ass water park on International Drive by the outlet mall," I say.

"You mean . . . the one with the sharks?"

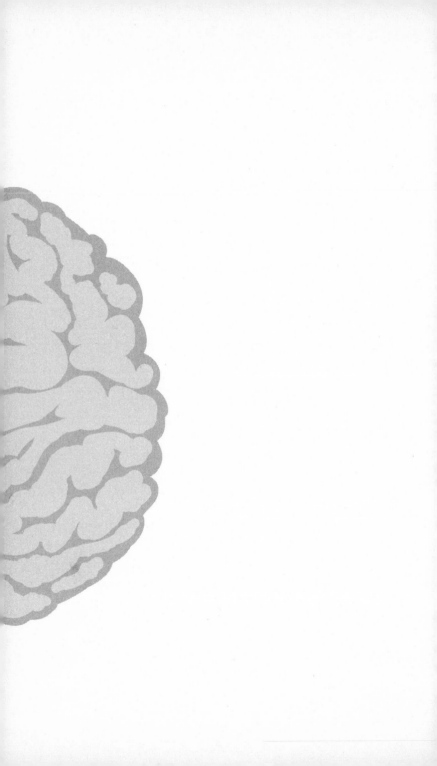

14
Splash Zone

Splash Zone is deserted at this hour, but the stadium lights surrounding the two-acre water park are all on. It's on the butt end of International Drive, one of the tackiest and most popular tourist strips on the planet, and at three in the morning the only things open are a few random truck stops with an attached diner or two. All are a few blocks away, and nobody eating there is exactly Splash Zone material, if you know what I mean.

It costs eight bucks to park, but the four guard stations are closed.

Dane picks one and blasts right past, cracking the black-and-yellow gate arm into splinters. We jostle over speed bumps, our teeth rattling.

"Where the hell is she?" He rounds the thin strip from the guard stations and enters the ginormous parking area. It looks empty all the way ahead to the huge wave sign announcing Splash Zone Family Water Park. A blinking neon-blue sign beneath it says, Home of the Hourly Shark Feeding!

There are no other cars in the parking lot, but that doesn't mean anything. She could've parked around the back.

"How the hell do we even get in?" Dane says, gunning it across the middle of the lot.

"There." I point to the entrance gate.

Dane stomps on the gas, forcing me back in my seat, but only for about five seconds. We slide to a stop next to a darkened ticket booth and nearly smash into it. Apparently Dane's worried the brakes too hard this night.

"Why do I feel like I should be wearing a tuxedo and bringing you a corsage?" Dane says as we leap from the car.

We test the first gate and find a linked chain threaded through the rusty metal bars.

"It does feel strangely familiar," I gush, helping him yank the chain apart. He's always been more limber than me and never more so than in an emergency.

We push the massive, creaking gate open just enough to squeeze through.

I follow Dane inside the park, trying to block out the mental image of Barracuda Bay's Fall Formal and what happened last time someone kidnapped Stamp and focus on what's in front of me.

Splash Zone is a water park–slash–aquarium featuring

the usual slides and gushers and slushers and arcades and penguin-shaped, chocolate-covered ice cream bars. Dane and I kept saying we'd go, we'd surprise Stamp and make a day of it, just the three of us, but we never did.

Now here we are, about three in the morning, and I don't think it's to eat ice cream and ride the water gushers. But Splash Zone isn't just fun and games. It's got live animals, hence the penguin ice cream bars, and flamingos in a pond. But there is also a chance to swim with the dolphins. And, in a special steel tank, there are sharks. Real, live sharks that, as the entrance sign announced, you can feed by hand every hour on the hour.

And maybe it's just the pessimist in me, but I can't imagine this night ending without sharks involved.

The park is built around a giant lake, where fireworks explode at night and ski shows entertain during the day. You know the kind, with girls in bikinis making pyramids out of each other.

Dane and I race around the empty park, but we don't know where to go or what to do or, frankly, who to do it to. There are pink slides where daytime customers can pop out of flamingo mouths. There's a kiddy pool with the water still running. The arcade sign is still blinking, though all the machines are dark.

And no Stamp anywhere. Not even Val tripping us as we pass.

We pause by a concession stand, and I'm glad we don't have heaving lungs drowning out clues of where

Stamp could be. But the silence in the deserted park is deafening.

Until we hear the urgent shuffling.

Dane looks behind him, but there's nothing.

Same with me. I creep away from the pink molded plastic of the concession stand and peer around a corner. Nothing. No one.

The footsteps are closer, closer until finally from behind a dolphin merry-go-round a security guard clomps forth.

I can tell right away—from his askew hat and bloody tie—he's no longer living but freshly reanimated.

"Zerker," Dane says through gritted teeth as we instinctively crouch together.

The groaning guard sees us—or more than likely smells us—and quickens his shuffling. The thing about Zerkers is they're mean. Especially at first.

Older Zerkers like Bones and Dahlia from back home, or Val now, or even Rudy Ortega and Wendy Schmaltz have had a while to settle into their Zerker tendencies. The frenzy in their brains has calmed, and once they've eaten human flesh, they'll eventually repose into the bad guys they're destined to be.

But for awhile there, say the first 24 hours after they've been bitten, or turned, Zerkers are badass hombres.

Like us, they feel no pain. They don't need to breathe, so they can't run out of steam, and they'll run on bone stumps if their feet fall off. They're the zombies authors write about and moviemakers portray: hungry, soulless, angry, confused. But mostly hungry. The worst part is, if it wasn't for Zerkers, zombies would have a much easier time. But no, every few months or so, some random Zerker loses it, chomps on the neighbor, starts an infection, and boom—zombies everywhere get a bad rap.

And that makes a 175-pound, six-dollars-an-hour security guard who's just been turned into a Zerker your worst. Frickin'. Nightmare.

I look around for something to defend myself with—a fire alarm axe, the bar off a kiddy swing set, a discarded Popsicle stick—but there's nothing.

Dane drags me to the nearest gift shop. With one thwack of his boot, he sends the front door's glass cobwebbing and smashing to the ground.

We stand back as the white, frosty shards rain to the concrete.

The guard hears it and turns.

We're inside, tossing shelves and stuffed orcas.

Dane finds something he obviously thinks will snuff out a newly reanimated zombie with the least effort. He's smiling, hands behind his back so I can't see his big discovery.

I'm thinking a medieval sword or a spear studded with shark's teeth or one of those tridents that Poseidon dude uses—now that is some Zerker-killing mojo right there. Then he tosses me whatever he's been hiding.

I catch it and immediately roll my eyes. A brass dolphin statue?

"Hold it like this," he says, palming a granite base and wrapping his fingers around the dolphin's thin tail.

I have to admit, it does look pretty lethal the way he's holding it.

"And jab it like . . . this!" He uses a stuffed manatee to make his point, spearing its defenseless nose with the tip of the dolphin's snout (beak?) until the poor manatee's stuffing lies all over the floor at our feet.

Glass crunches behind us.

I turn, instinctively doing as Dane says and shoving the dolphin's beak into the guard's face.

Teeth crunch and tongue tears until the statue is wedged in the guard's jaw so tightly it won't budge. His mouth is wide open, the underside of the base poking out as his fingers claw at the statue. His yellow eyes widen, and thick goo gurgles out around the statue.

The guard backpedals through the broken glass. His anxious attempts to rip the brass statuette from his mouth only shove it in deeper.

It should've been a kill shot. And it would've been, except for the tiny little fact that, like zombies, Zerkers are already dead. He could live like that for days. Weeks.

It's knock out the brain or keep fighting the Zerker.

"Throw me another one." I sigh.

Dane does but shakes his head. "Okay, fine, but don't do that anymore. We can't lug brass dolphins all over the park all night!"

The guard tosses his head to and fro, desperate to dislodge the dolphin from his cracked and crumbling dentures.

Dane sneaks up behind him, knocking over a stack of postcards in the process, and shoves his own dolphin's beak into the Zerker's right temple, unleashing a geyser of black goo.

It does the job. Down goes the guard, never to rise again.

Dane wipes gore on his black jeans and looks up at me, hands on his knees. "She must have turned the security guards," he says, overstating the obvious.

I cluck my tongue. "It must be nice to have no conscience. You can just turn random, innocent people like Rudy and Wendy and security guard guy here into your own mobile army. Forget Rudy's parents or Wendy's boyfriend or this poor dude's family."

"She's a Zerker, Maddy. What'd you expect?"

I ignore him and keep walking, feeling ridiculous but much safer with my pointy dolphin beak held high.

We go deeper into the park, expecting Zerker guards to pop out from every water fountain, picnic bench, or restroom. Splash Zone is huge, by the way, and full of the dripping of hoses and tanks and drying slides.

There are no footprints to guide us, no spiky Stamp

hair to follow, just this endless, giant water park and the smiling faces of stuffed dolphins and penguins and sharks staring out from every snack bar and gift shop window.

We walk purposefully to clear each area in turn. First the kiddy slides, then the food court, then the arcade, and then the seal show. We expect to find Stamp at every one.

We don't. Not yet. We're walking toward the starfish pond when I hear slapping behind me, like flippers or wet socks.

I look back.

Behind us waddles a dolphin trainer, still stuffed in her neon-blue wet suit and black flippers. Her skin is cement gray, and her eyes are yellow. Blood's mixed into her seaweed-green ponytail, which rasps across her rubber shoulders with every step.

"Maddy," Dane shouts, but he's too far away to help.

Dolphin trainer flounders toward me.

I crouch behind the nearest turtle shell–shaped trash can and take aim at her knee. The minute she pops into view, I kick out until my shoe connects in a bone-crunching snap.

Dolphin trainer goes down. She's still too fresh to be able to speak but well past feeling anything like pain. Her expressionless eyes look past me, a fiery yellow but blank and dead inside. Dry blood cakes her teeth as she looks around, openmouthed.

I know I can't feel, that I'm not supposed to feel, but still my heart seems hollow when I think about what's about to come.

What they never show you in the monster movies is how hard it is to kill someone—something—that still looks human.

A vampire has fangs. No problem: stake through the heart.

A werewolf has fur. No worries: pop a silver cap in that ass.

Frankenstein has bolts on his neck.

A mummy has miles of TP.

But a zombie?

How do you kill a humble security guard? Some missing kid from your own hood? A cheerleaderrific dolphin trainer who probably grew up running a petting zoo in her backyard every summer just for fun?

"Maddy!"

The dolphin trainer spots Dane and growls, her shattered kneecap tearing through the blue rubber of her suit as she struggles to stand.

"I know. All right," I shout, madder at him than I am at this poor stranded Zerker. "Just—I got this!"

Images of undead footballers and reanimated cheerleaders and Zerker Home Ec teachers back in the Barracuda Bay High gym flood my mind as I yank the dolphin trainer's ponytail back and shove the dolphin beak through her left eye, digging deep until I'm sure her brains are permanently scrambled.

I yank the statue out and watch her writhe on the concrete, right flipper kicking in a chlorinated puddle until it stops. Forever.

"What'd Val do? Turn everybody left in the park?" Dane huffs, standing next to me with an arm over my shoulders.

"That's what you get for working overtime," I say humorlessly, taking no joy in wiping an innocent woman's gray matter off on my own black jeans.

We walk on now, gore under our fingernails, smelly water beneath our feet.

Overhead a speaker squawks, and Val's voice bellows, "Warmer, kids. You're getting warmer."

Dane looks up immediately, as if perhaps Val is a fairy-zombie-mother floating above and he can knock off one of her wings with his brass statuette. Of course that witch is safe, probably in some invisible DJ booth, noshing on some innocent security guard's cerebellum while we stumble around looking for Stamp.

"We should split up," I say. "You go find her. I'll go find—"

"No damn way." Dane speeds up a little. "You don't know what's waiting for you at the end of this ride, and I'm not letting you go it alone anymore. That's what got

Stamp into this mess in the first place. We abandoned him."

I nod and follow him. I wonder if he's right. If we'd be here now if we had tailed Stamp 24/7 since we got to Orlando. But how? How do you protect someone who doesn't want to be protected?

And what kind of Afterlife is it when all you do every day is look over your shoulder for the next Sentinel, the next Zerker, the next random thug to hunt you down?

Another squawk, and this time I'm near enough to a light pole to see a speaker clamped to it high overhead. It's white and boxy, but there's no doubt. That's where Val's voice is coming from.

"Warmer," Val croaks. And then, as if we're some kind of dense or something, she starts humming the theme song from *Jaws*: "Duh-duh, duh-duh, duh-duh-duh-duh . . ."

And just as I'm about to toss my brass dolphin statuette at the damn speaker, I turn the corner and see a sign that says Teeth Time. The letters are red with blood drips down the sides, and the sign is shaped like a giant shark's jaw. You know, the kind they always have in pictures.

I hear the splashing, see the fresh puddles, and know Stamp is in the shark tank even before Val says, "Very good, kids. Hurry up now. He only has a minute or two left."

But she's lying.

Stamp is already half gone by the time we get to him.

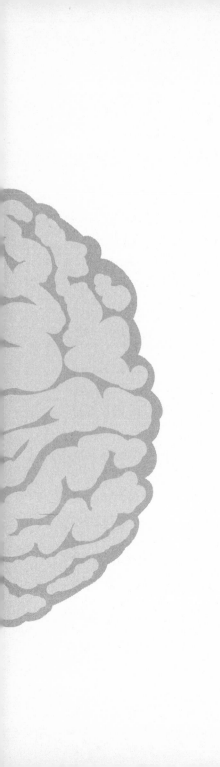

15
Teeth Time

Teeth Time is like a giant pool. Metal stands surround it, and one of those movie theater ropes zigs and zags to keep the guests' lines from getting too chaotic. A small booth has an empty cash register and a sign: Shark Chow: $25. It sounds steep, but that includes 15 minutes in a shark cage where, next to a certified dive instructor, kiddies and grownups alike can feed real, live sharks.

The cage is empty. I'd hoped Stamp might be there, safe, even if submerged and surrounded by sharks. Sharks who couldn't get to him.

The pool itself is alive with activity, gray water rippling and bits of fabric and worse clinging to the white-capped waves.

Fins puncture the surface of the saltwater tank, making it hard to see Stamp through the ripples and the black goop that is zombie blood. But there he is, finally, secured to the bottom of the shark tank with what look like cinder blocks and bike chains.

It's not being underwater that's threatening him. We don't need to breathe, so big whoop. It's the damn sharks circling him, some close, some not so close, all interested. They are sleek and slippery and brown or gray. They're not big, like movie sharks, but their teeth are.

I can see the black-and-white stripes of Stamp's hoodie and the saucers of his eyes as his mouth moves and nothing, not even bubbles, comes out.

I crumple beside the tank, looking for an opening, letting my dolphin statuette clatter to the wet concrete. It's no use now. You can't stab a shark with that and watch it die. They're like the Living Dead but not actually.

Six sharks circle Stamp, their fins slippery, their jaws chomping. And then I notice why. There are parts of Stamp inside.

"Dane," I shout helplessly even though he's kneeling right next to me. Suddenly I'm kicking off my shoes. I don't know why I do that except it's what you do when you go swimming, right? I'm hysterical, shouting as I leap toward the water.

Rough hands snatch me back before I can even get wet, then toss me 10 feet onto the concrete.

I rush back, full steam.

Dane literally pile drives me into the ground. "Stop! Maddy. Back. Off."

"We can't let him die like that." I shove with all my might and manage, with two knees and one well-placed elbow, to get Dane off me.

"We have to," he says from behind.

Something clatters to the ground.

I look closely to see Dane grabbing a copper stake from the rubber handle end, where it's safe for him to touch.

"W-w-where did that come from?" I stumble toward the shark tank.

"I always keep one handy, Maddy." He hoists it high.

Now it's serious. One touch from the copper business end, and that's it. It's lights out, Maddy. And I can't have that. I need to get in that water and tear those sharks in half. He has to understand that.

"Dane, just, it's *my* choice. You couldn't control Stamp. You can't control me!"

"No," he says as he inches toward the edge of the tank. "I can't control you, but I can save you."

"Just, okay, just let me see him, okay?"

He holds the copper stake close. It's about the size of a fireplace poker, and I wonder whether he hid it up his sleeve or down his pants. I see the protective leather cover lying on the ground next to his feet and wonder why I never noticed it before.

Water splashes me as I reach the edge of the tank. A shark's tail flaps at the surface, and his jaw clamps down, tearing something off Stamp's body.

I yelp and turn away, then turn back. I peer into the

water, feeling Dane's hand on my collar, and try to find Stamp's eyes. But there is too much tissue in the water, making it cloudy, too much swirling around.

I'm not doing it. I'm not sitting here while Stamp gets pulled to pieces. I yelp and leap.

Dane yanks me back again, tossing me to the floor and sticking the business end of the copper stake deep in my throat.

I gurgle and grind and hear a molar crack in my mouth, and then the lights go out.

16
Deader Than Usual

I wake dripping wet but not because I've made it into the tank.

My head pounds like someone is beating a drum inside, a side effect of the copper short-circuiting my electrical system and shutting me down cold so that, in effect, my zombie brain's had to reboot for me to wake up.

Dane and I call it a copper hangover, usually laughing because we're not on the hangover end.

Right now I feel dead. Deader, I guess, than usual.

I blink, the blurry frame gradually coming into focus but slowly. So slowly.

My clothes are soaked. That's the first thing I notice. But also the dripping of water from, well, everywhere. There is a flapping sound everywhere I turn, like someone's just dumped a bucket of fresh fish onto a dock.

I blink to see the sky, yellow with my zombie vision. My joints are sore from the copper hangover.

A shark is next to me in the open air, tail flipping, eyes gone white. It's clearly dead, impaled by a brass dolphin statuette shoved to the hilt inside its dull brain. Red blood pours from the wound and mixes with the green saltwater puddles all over the deck.

I sit up to find five more sharks, each one deader than the last, each with a dolphin statue–sized hole in its skull. My eyes stay open as I take in the scene. It's like one of those end-of-the-world movies where the camera pans to show dolphins washed up on otherwise empty shores.

Although these sharks didn't die from the elements or global warming or some tidal wave. Someone killed them.

"What happened?" I blather, tongue still partially paralyzed as I struggle to stand. It's too hard, and I crash on my rump, resting my arm on a dead shark tail to steady myself.

Dane turns, dripping and seeming dead inside too. "I tried, Maddy. I tried to save him—"

"What? *Tried*?" I scream.

I rush to his side and see the tank empty. The cinder blocks and chains are there. The water still laps against the side of the blue pool. Little bits of black-and-white cloth swirl in the water. But no Stamp.

"Where is he?" I shout, tongue gradually regaining its composure.

Dane struggles to speak, his face dripping and

crumpling as if he might cry, but we both know that's impossible.

"Dane, where did he go?" My voice sounds desperate and dangerous, even to myself.

"He's gone." Dane averts my gaze, pointing to the sharks bleeding on the deck. "He's gone."

I limp toward him and, with each step, say, "Where. Did. He. Go?"

Dane points to a shark. "H-h-he's in this one and this one here and—" His voice breaks, and he turns his face away.

I reach for the nearest shark. Its belly is fat and firm and tears easily beneath my rock-hard fingers. It's like ripping open a wet suit, rubbery beneath my skin. It splits with a gushing sound as water and blood and body parts rush out.

I see Stamp's wrist, leathery and gnawed, and his ankle chewed off at the bone and still clad in half a sock, teeth marks puncturing his cold, gray skin.

"All?" I whimper, thudding to the ground and reaching toward, but not touching, Stamp's battered extremities. "They're all like this?"

Dane nods, kneeling next to me.

"At least he didn't feel it, Maddy." Dane looks at me now. Finally, I look back.

"But he's gone," I say quietly. "He's . . . gone."

"I know."

"No," I say more urgently now. "I mean, he's gone.

Last time I could bite him and bring him back. Now I wouldn't even know where to start."

He waits a beat, as if wondering if I'll overreact to what he's about to say, then says it anyway. "Maddy, this isn't where it starts. It's where it ends."

"But it can't end here. Not here. Not like this."

He nods and says no more.

I sit there, dripping and hopeless, staring at Dane's dark eyes.

He gently draws me close to him. I shiver but can't cry. My eyes are open and staring into the wet, black cotton covering his bony shoulder. I flash on an image: Dane leaping into the tank, fighting off the sharks, tossing them onto the deck, snatching pieces of Stamp flesh from their cold, dead jaws.

But I don't feel proud of him, exactly, or even grateful to him for trying. I only feel emptiness and the sickening knowledge that nothing will ever be the same. That nothing will ever be worth it again if a kid like Stamp can be torn to pieces just for some crazy Zerker's enjoyment.

I push Dane away too hard.

He falls over the nearest shark and down onto his butt on the wet concrete. He sits there looking startled and surprisingly helpless, and my heart breaks all over again.

"Sorry." I sniff, helping him up and ignoring the bit of black leather belt stuck in the shark's teeth as I glance in its direction.

Then I look at Dane's hand and notice something missing.

"Where the hell is your pinky?"

Dane looks down and shrugs. "Maddy, they were sharks in there, not kittens."

I barely push him, and he nearly stumbles again.

Now I see why. There's a chunk missing from his right calf, glaring and bloodless through his torn jeans.

"Dane!"

I turn him around and see nicks all over his back, his arms, but nothing else is missing.

Suddenly it washes over me: Dane jumped into a shark tank to save Stamp.

And here he is, limping and missing a whole entire finger.

I kneel and slip from my leather jacket, tearing off a sleeve and yanking it into strips.

"Let me look at this. Jesus," I murmur, turning him around as I gasp at the sight of his calf muscle just out there for the whole world to see.

There is a four-inch gash where the skin has been sliced open and raw beef pokes out from inside: withered, gray zombie muscle and white, petrified tendons. I avert my gaze and tie two strips of leather around it to keep it covered.

"Will it heal?" I say, already suspecting the answer.

He shrugs as I wipe the last two strips of leather around his left hand, covering his jagged pinky stump.

"It'll get hard and useless but, no, I don't think it will heal. Guess my days of wearing short shorts are all over."

Neither of us chuckles.

With my nursing duties over, Stamp in pieces, and sharks lying at my feet, all I want is to get going.

"Where is she?" I stomp away.

When I don't hear Dane's footsteps splashing through the shark guts, I turn to find him standing there in the same place, a worried look on his face.

"Don't you, I mean, shouldn't we—?" He kneels, reaching toward a piece of Stamp.

It's part of an arm, ragged at both ends.

Before he can touch it, I blurt, "Shouldn't we what?"

"Well," he says, stopping short of touching it, "shouldn't we try to bury him?"

"No. We should try to avenge him. Now where did she go?"

He stands, looking almost relieved that I've shot down his burial theory. Yeah, I know it seems cold, but what are we supposed to do? Cut each shark open? Grab every body part? *Every* one? Bury the sharks with Stamp to make sure? And where? When? For how long?

I already buried Stamp once, back in Sable Palms Cemetery. It was wrong to dig him up then, to take him from his natural death and give him an unnatural life. It would be just as wrong to toss his pieces, what's left of them, into some shallow grave now.

"Well," Dane says, dragging me toward a metal

stairway between the shark and dolphin tanks, "she stopped laughing about 10 minutes ago, but I think I know where she is."

We tromp up the stairs, my fists clenched so hard my nails will leave scars on my palms. That's the least of my worries.

At the top is a booth cleverly hidden behind a banner: Win One for the Flipper!

The booth is about the size of my old counselor's office at Barracuda Bay High, with tinted windows overlooking both the shark tank and the dolphin swim areas. It must be a control booth of some kind, where technicians can make announcements or swivel spotlights or play music to start the show.

There's a red sign on the white door: Keep Out! Employees Only!

With his good leg, Dane kicks in the door only to find an empty chair and another note taped on it, this one scrawled on the back of a food court menu featuring fried shrimp and hush puppies.

So sorry about Stamp. See you in Barracuda Bay. If the Sentinels let you go, that is.

XOXO,

Val

We look at each other, eyes big and mouths open, like two characters out of an old-timey silent movie reel.

"Barracuda Bay?" I gasp.

"Sentinels?" Dane says. But I can tell it's not really a question. It's a statement. He's pointing out the tinted window of the control booth to the pavement below.

A team of Sentinels pours into the park. I watch two, three at a time shoulder each other out of the way as their black berets bob and weave while they race their stiff zombie legs.

We can see them from afar with our vantage point, and we both know there's not enough time to run. Not anymore.

They are striding with purpose, passing all the landmarks we did on our long, meandering loop around the park, only in half the time: the snack bars, the arcade, the food court, the trash cans, the Otter Climbing Wall, the Barracuda Bungee Jump . . .

Each has a Taser in one hand, the other hand free to pump like a piston as they march gracelessly in their black cargo pants with plenty of pockets up and down each side.

I count 10 of them, all twice our size, before they reach the shark tank and I give up completely. And I'm not just talking about the counting.

Their thick, black boots splash through the puddles left by Dane's shark attack. Their berets duck floating balloons and pennants while the Sentinels scour the deck for us.

A few break rank to kneel next to the sharks, nudging them with their Tasers and watching as the rubbery bodies bounce back.

A couple of them chuckle as they open the shark's jaws, rubbing dead, gray skin against the sharp teeth and making faces. One picks up a piece of Stamp's body and tosses it to a friend.

Stupid, heartless Sentinels.

I retch, even though I can't throw up because there's nothing to throw up and my long-dead stomach muscles wouldn't let me even if there were. It's a reaction, I guess, some holdover in my human DNA to express the shock and disgust I feel.

Maybe Zerkers aren't the only bad zombies after all.

I think of Stamp and that night so many months ago. How badly I wanted to see him. How I snuck out of my house in the rain to go to his stupid party. How excited I was, how dangerous it felt to be slinking through back alleys in the downpour, how much I wanted to kiss him and him to kiss me. How much I wanted him to want me and suspected he did.

The fact that I died that night, on the way to his house, has been a part of me ever since. And Stamp has been a part of me ever since. Love him, hate him, date him, break up with him, but an Afterlife without him—an eternity to grieve—will be no life at all.

I look away and slump in a seat in the control booth.

Dane does the same. He swivels his chair toward me and holds my hand. After a long minute, he says, "She tricked us. From day one, this was all about setting us up."

"Doesn't matter."

"But, Maddy, the Sentinels. They'll find us. We're cooked."

"Doesn't matter."

"Yeah, it does. Once the Sentinels get you, that's it. Might as well try breaking out of federal prison."

I look back at him and say, as if on autopilot, "Dane, it doesn't matter."

He tightens his grip but says no more.

The first of the Sentinels trudge up the stairs, making the booth tremble.

I say, "Don't you want to know why it doesn't matter?"

"Sure," he says, but I can tell his heart isn't in it.

"Because, Dane, if it's the last thing I do, I'm going to rip Val's head off with my bare hands."

17
Her Brother's Keeper

We ride in silence, for the most part, in the speeding SUV. My right arm is fastened to the armrest with those zip-tie handcuffs TV cops always use. They're stronger than they look for being so thin and see-through, though at this point I'm not really dreaming of getting away, merely surviving.

They're Sentinels, see? And we've been on the run for, what, nearly five months now? They've probably spent thousands of man-hours and tens of thousands of dollars looking for us, and we've pretty much made fools of them from day one. So I'm figuring if they don't rekill us right away, it will just be to tear off our limbs one by one.

Either way, our future's not exactly bright at the moment.

I don't try jiggling the restraint, not even once. I

just sit there numb in a seat next to a giant Sentinel who stares bleakly ahead as the miles spin beneath our tires.

Dane is in the seat behind me, strapped in as well, with his own personal Sentinel sitting beside him, also huge, also silent.

Two more Sentinels fill the driver's seat and passenger seat in front of me. They're so tall their trademark black berets scrape the ceiling every time they move their heads, which is infrequently.

The rising sun barely penetrates the thick-tinted glass as the driver takes an exit. I can't see which exit it is, but I don't care where we're going or how to get back. We zip off the highway on two wheels.

As I lean to compensate, I watch the tie dig into my wrist and feel my shoulder rub across the Sentinel next to me. He nudges back, like I did it on purpose. I huff, he huffs, until we're back on four wheels and speeding forward, ever forward, all over again.

Two more identical SUVs follow us as we merge from a modern highway to a backwater, two-lane strip of pothole-ridden asphalt near the Florida-Georgia border. I jostle, lips sealed lest I scream Stamp's name over and over and over again.

I have to keep my eyes open and stare at the back of the Sentinel in front of me. If I don't, I'll keep flashing onto things best never seen again: Stamp's black-and-white hoodie, arms waving at the bottom of the tank, chains wrapped around his legs, dead sharks and body parts, bloody water on the deck, Dane's eyes, the look on his face as I came to.

He's gone. He's gone . . . Dane's quivering voice echoes in my mind. Why don't these damn Sentinels talk to each other, just once, to drown it out?

Things happen quickly after our four silent hours on the road. The SUV approaches a sign: The Crestview Rehabilitation Center. The pine trees and setting sun on the wooden sign seem to say, "Come here and stay . . . forever." I wonder if Dane is right: if once the Sentinels grab you, they never let you go. And again, it doesn't matter.

I'll get out. I have to get out.

Either that or die trying.

The sign looks weathered as we pass, as does the rehabilitation center itself: a barren three-story brick building.

The Sentinels pull around to the back to a kind of garage area, where more Sentinels wait. Lots more. They stand in formation, five rows of three Sentinels each, all dressed in black. Their thin lips are stitched together. Not literally but they might as well be.

This is the point at which Dane or I would normally crack wise, say, "Glad you could bring out the welcome wagon," or something totally lame like that, but I just watch, lips zipped as tight as the Sentinels'.

Maybe I'll become one after all. I feel double dead

inside, which is what most of them appear to be. Maybe that's the kind of rehabilitation Crestview is offering: taking civilian zombies and turning them into fighting, ugly, angry killing machines who apparently need a dozen pockets up and down each leg. But, hey, if that's the only way I'll ever get out of here, well, sign me up. I look good in black.

The engine shuts off, filling the grim morning with even more silence since the Sentinels rarely have anything to say. The drivers get out as the Sentinel next to me reaches into one of his many pants pockets. He pulls out a switchblade, the thuggish kind, and flips it open with a click.

He looks at me carefully, eyes dead and dark, with the hint of a smile quivering at one corner of his gray lips.

I look back at him, chin up, eyes just as dead. The smile, if there ever was one, disappears.

With one slice, he frees my bonds.

The door next to me slides open, and two Sentinels grab my arms.

Behind me, as we walk through the garage and into a back entrance, the sounds of boots on asphalt and whispering black pants mingle with Dane's voice. Little snippets reach me as I'm marched into the building.

Dane's voice increases in volume as I'm led ahead: "Where are you taking her? . . . But she didn't do anything! . . . Why can't we be together?"

I flinch hearing his desperate tone but don't look around, not even to wink or mouth the words, "It's okay. I'm fine. Don't worry about me."

The sooner Dane is rid of me, the better. For him, anyway.

Inside the hospital-smelling building, the floors are squeaky clean. I stare straight ahead, watching white wall after white wall, door after door, corner after corner, until I spot a door marked Intake and know that's where we're headed.

And then . . . we walk right on by.

And keep walking, passing through doors and corners and corridors until it seems we've been walking for days. I feel like I did with Dane at Splash Zone, running around in circles looking for something, for someone, not there.

And yet I've been around Sentinels before. They never do anything or go anywhere without a reason. Maybe they're running us around in circles because they want us to feel confused and disoriented. Or maybe this place just has a really crappy layout. I dunno.

Finally we come to a wide, clunky service elevator in the back. It has tan doors and no music inside. We ride to the top floor. The door dings and opens onto green walls instead of white.

We walk the long corridors. It's not so much a maze as a track, one that never really seems to go anywhere.

The hallways are wide, like in a nursing home or Dad's morgue, and now once in awhile Dane and I can see each other if we glance to the left or right. Whenever I do, Dane is watching me carefully, as if I might crumble at any moment. I remain expressionless, even though I know a smile would ease his mind.

Still, it feels wrong to smile this day. My clothes are still damp from the place where Stamp was slaughtered. His killer is still somewhere out there, footloose and fancy free, heading to my hometown—where my dad lives, where he's vulnerable.

Gradually, though, Dane and his Sentinel guards slow down. They're still with us—us being me and a Sentinel on either side of me—but no longer beside us. I haven't seen Dane's face in many minutes.

He calls my name but is quickly muzzled by the thump of what sounds like an elbow to the stomach, or maybe the head, and then . . . no more. I still hear his footsteps, softer, quieter than the Sentinel's, but even they begin to fade out.

Finally we get to a large room with one table and two chairs. It looks like one of those interrogation rooms you see on cop shows. The Sentinels bring me inside and sit me down. I don't resist.

They stand there for a minute, and I'm waiting for one or both of them to chain me to the table somehow, but they don't. They are as silent and grim as ever. Then they simply walk out of the room and stop.

I turn to face them a little, just to see what they're doing, and it's basically . . . nothing. I see the backs of their heads through the Plexiglas windows on either side of the door. I shrug and turn back to face the wall.

It's cinder block, like the rest of the place, and painted a generic off-white. Not quite tan, not quite white. After awhile I no longer even see it. Maybe that's the point.

I look down at my lap, which is covered in the goop of the heads of the security guard and dolphin trainer. And I wonder how many Splash Zone employees Val turned just to slow us down on our way to the shark tank.

The goo has dried and stained my jeans, even though they were black to start with. That's how black Zerker blood is—blacker than black. After I stare for several minutes, the stain looks like one of those inkblot tests they give you in the counselor's office when you act out after your mom runs out on you in sixth grade. If I stare at it long enough, it changes like a cloud: first a pirate ship, then a proper lady's face, then a grizzly bear.

I'm glad, in a way, that I never got Stamp's blood on me. I couldn't handle that, having it on me, staring at it, watching it grow and shift and merge into odd shapes.

I look away, back to the white-not-white gloss of the opposite wall.

Dane said Stamp didn't feel anything, and logically I know that's right. Dead nerve endings mean no pain. I've been punched, kicked, knocked in the head with a bat, shoved around, and none of it ever actually hurt, not one second. But I knew what was going on. I might not have felt the pain in my skin or muscles or bones, but I felt it in my soul.

I've felt scared and anxious and apprehensive and hurt and betrayed and hopeless pretty much every day since I got this way, and no one's ever going to tell me that I wouldn't feel all that to the 900th degree if, say, a shark or four or five were tearing me apart and I couldn't do a damn thing about it.

I shake it off, quit blinking so I can stop seeing Stamp's hand lying there, bitten in half, on the wet deck of the shark tank. I keep my eyes open and listen to the squeaking from down the hall.

It's purposeful but slow, almost cautious.

It sounds like someone wearing Sentinel boots, but the footsteps are softer, lighter than a Sentinel's. I wonder if maybe since Dane was wetter than me they've given him a change of clothes, including boots, and now he's coming to sit with me while we wait for something else to happen.

But I know when the door shuts behind me and only one pair of footsteps approaches the table that I'm wrong. I won't be seeing Dane again today.

This is what they wanted: divide and conquer. It was too much, too good, to think they'd let us stay together. Maybe later, after they've done what they're going to do.

But now? Now they've got us right where they want us, and there's nothing we can do about it.

"Madison Emily Swift?" says a stern voice.

I turn to find a tall woman standing next to the table. She's so regal, so prim and proper, that I almost feel like standing up. Almost.

"My name's Vera. I'll be your intake counselor."

Vera's dressed in Sentinel garb—thick boots, pocket pants, long-sleeved shirt with lapels on the shoulders, even a beret—but it's all light blue. The color of suits that little boys will sometimes wear on Easter Sunday. Powder blue, my mom would have called it if she were still around.

"How do you know my name?"

She sits, in all her blueness, and slides a thick green file folder on the table. In her free hand is a shiny silver pen. She clicks the top nervously, as if maybe she doesn't want to be in the room with a chick who's just watched her ex get swallowed by some hungry sharks.

"Why wouldn't I know your name?" She cocks her head, still clicking her pen.

Vera's black hair is close cropped, her skin a kind of coppery gray, her eyes a silken black.

"Well, I mean, the Sentinels probably gave you my purse, but the ID inside is fake, so . . ."

The woman stares at me without a readable expression. With those black eyes and not a wrinkle on her face, I can't tell if she's mad, glad, about to shove a copper stake in my eye socket, or what.

Finally she taps the folder and says, "Maddy, this is all yours. Every last page of it." For proof, she flips open the top of the folder and slides out several news stories from the *Barracuda Bay Bugle*, featuring my latest yearbook photo. And then an actual page from my yearbook, copied, with my photo coated in yellow highlighter. There's a copy of my old driver's license, family photos from one of Dad's albums, a picture of Mom.

Mom? Dang, how far back does this file go anyway?

But then Vera keeps flipping through the pile. Buried underneath are more photos. More recent ones. Surveillance photos of Dane and me at our apartment in Orlando, in the parking lot at work, on the stage. A copy of my employee ID badge and fake driver's license.

I sit up a little straighter. "Wh-wh-where did you get those?"

Vera offers her version of a smile. "You think the Sentinels were going to let you run away from Barracuda Bay without a chase? You think we didn't find you or follow your dad or listen to your calls every month?"

"But we were so careful. We never saw a Sentinel the whole time we were in Orlando. Not once."

Vera flips one of her blue lapels with a long finger. "You think we can't change out of these and put on a Mickey Mouse T-shirt and a ball cap and a camera strap around our necks and blend in enough to snap some pictures of you in some monster makeup show? Or at the midnight movies or the mall? Please give us a little more credit than that."

"Well, then why didn't you pull us in sooner?" I say, confusion turning to concern. "I mean, if you knew where we were, where we worked, where we lived, why didn't you just snatch us right away?"

Vera avoids my gaze for the first time and says coldly, "Early in our investigation of the events in Barracuda Bay, we determined that allowing you to remain free would facilitate the apprehension of several Zerkers who were, shall we say, following you."

I nod, the temperature in my body dropping even more. It's not bad enough the Zerkers want us dead. The Sentinels were willing to let them get close just so they could catch them.

"So we were bait?"

"Not precisely." Vera rushes to defend herself, clicking her pen closed and slipping it in one of her powder-blue top pockets. "Like I said, we had you under surveillance 24/7 and could have easily pulled you in if Val hadn't led you on that wild goose chase tonight."

"You were there?" I sit up. "At the warehouse? At the club? At Splash Zone? The whole time?"

Vera nods without expression. "We couldn't show our hand too soon. We had to wait for an extraction team, had to be sure Val was alone, that it wasn't a trap we couldn't get out—"

"How soon was too soon?" I snap, sitting up just a smidge. "Before Val lowered Stamp into the shark tank? Before Val released the sharks? Was one shark too soon? Two sharks? Three? Four? How many limbs did Stamp have to lose before you had enough Sentinels to snatch one tiny Zerker?"

Vera looks back, undeterred. "You don't understand. We have procedures in place. Rules, protocols. You might have known that if you'd waited for us back in Barracuda Bay rather than running away before you could explain yourselves."

"So this is our fault? We were protecting ourselves! The Zerkers were killing kids in Barracuda Bay. Not zombies. Kids. Live kids. One here, one there. Should we have just stepped aside and let that—"

"Dane and Chloe knew the rules, Maddy, even if you didn't. They knew what to do, and they ignored us. We could have stopped the Zerkers in Barracuda Bay before things got out of hand. Before you lost your football team, your cheerleading squad, and half the faculty. Then you ran away from us. Did you not think there would be consequences for your actions?"

"Yeah." I snort, crossing my arms and breaking my no-emotion rule, because this witch right here has gotten under my zombie skin. "Consequences like, I dunno, a medal? A ticker tape parade, maybe? Free teeth whitening for life? Vera, we destroyed the Zerkers in Barracuda Bay. We saved countless lives, and what did we get for it? A life on the lam."

Vera starts to speak, then closes her mouth and her eyes. She shakes her head. "Now is not the time or place. Nor, frankly, are you in a position to argue. You are here now, and that is all that matters. I will be your intake counselor, and I alone will determine when you are to be released. *If* you are to be released. We'll start with a brief interview and—"

"If?"

Vera's eyes are big again. "Yes, if. You are out of options. Like it or not, we are the law, and the laws can't be broken. If it is determined that you played a larger role in Barracuda Bay than my records indicate, then your Afterlife sentence will be, shall we say, extreme."

"Afterlife sentence?"

"How long you remain here at the center, incarcerated, before we feel it's safe to let you walk among Normals again. I have to warn you, some Afterlife sentences are extremely—"

"Whatever, Vera. Sentinels, Zerkers, intake, outtake, release, Afterlife sentence—whatever. Doesn't matter. I'll do what you want from now on. I couldn't care less about freedom anymore. All I want to know is this: Who the hell is Val, and what the hell did she want with Stamp?"

"Why, I thought a girl as smart as you would have figured it out by now."

"What's that supposed to mean?"

Vera shakes her head as if she's disappointed in me, in Dane, in us. "Val wasn't after Stamp, honey. She wasn't even after Dane. She was after you."

"Me? Why? What the hell did I ever do to her?"

"Not to her. To her brother."

"Her brother? How the hell could I know her—?"

Vera finally nods, cracking a vaguely sinister, almost pleased, smile.

"Bones?" I sit at the edge of my seat. "You mean Bones was Val's brother?"

18
Zerker Runs in the Family

"Why do you think we took so many risks before trying to apprehend her?" Vera says, suddenly seeming to take an interest in my damp clothes and mascara-streaked face.

"Trying?" I blurt, beyond myself with disbelief. "You mean the witch got away?" I shake my head. God, Sentinels suck. Seriously.

"Unfortunately, yes, she was able to escape before the extraction team was fully prepared to apprehend her and—"

I slam the table, if only to stop her excuses.

The folder pops closed, and some of the pictures shift.

"She's five feet nothing. Weighs 90 pounds soaking wet, and I just rode here with about 2,000 tons of Sentinel fun. Couldn't anyone stop her? Hell, the way she was teasing us from that DJ booth, she was practically begging to be caught. What's the use of tailing us, using us as bait, if you're not even going to catch the Zerker who's been stalking us?"

Vera shakes her head, absently sliding the old photos back into the thick file. "As I said, we have procedures—"

"Then your procedures got Stamp killed. All those Sentinels waiting outside Splash Zone, and the whole time Val was letting the sharks loose. Dozens of men with their Tasers and big muscles, and they just stood by while those sharks tore him to pieces."

I stop, not because I don't have more to say but because I can see the wheels going round in her head, waiting for my mouth to stop moving.

"Maddy, I know you're upset. I don't blame you. But you don't know the full story. We didn't have dozens of Sentinels in place while Stamp was, was—"

"Save it." I spare her the trouble of making excuses I'm not going to believe anyway. "What's done is done. My question is what are you doing *now* to catch her?"

"We have teams on the ground combing through her abandoned warehouse, checking her cell phones. We'll find her."

"Before she gets to Barracuda Bay? Before she finds my father? Before she tears him apart?"

"I said we'll find her."

"Not if I find her first," I say grimly, avoiding her gaze.

Vera slips her shiny pen out from her breast pocket and studies it. "First you'll have to get through me, dear."

I can't tell if she's challenging or threatening me.

Does she mean literally get through her, like knock her down and run over her back? Or metaphorically, like she's going to have to approve my discharge or something? I guess I don't much care, since both seem pretty far out of reach at the moment anyway.

"Then tell me what I have to do, Vera. What do you want? I'll do it."

Vera stands. "All in good time."

I picture my dad sitting in our cozy breakfast nook, drinking instant coffee out of his cracked Christmas mug, thinking he's safe when all the while Bones' sister is heading straight his way, hell-bent on revenge.

Vera grabs the folder from the table and waits, looking down at me while tapping one booted toe as she stands there, looking triumphant and regal in her uniform.

"I don't have time." I hate the helpless sound in my voice, but I'm just as helpless to stop it. "Val said . . . she said . . . she said she's going to—"

"Your father is safe. Whether he knows it or not, we have him surrounded. Even more so than usual. Now get up or—"

"Or what?" I grip the table, ready for a fight. Why not? She said we were safe, and look what happened to Stamp. She said they were using us as bait but then couldn't even catch Val when she was sitting there, seducing Stamp for two whole weeks. Why shouldn't we fight after all that?

I can take this chick. She's old and thin and wearing

that powder-blue Sentinel uniform. How tough can she be?

She smiles placidly, holding the thick file in one hand and her silver pen in the other. She flicks the pen's top up and down, up and down, almost . . . menacingly.

"You don't want to make me move you, Maddy. Trust me."

"Please." I chuckle. "I've fought bigger and badder and—"

Vera clicks her pen one last time, then jabs it in my neck as I'm bragging. I have just enough time to think, *The hell?* before a whiff of ozone, a sizzle of electricity, the smell of burnt meat, and *whoosh*! I fly like a Mack truck from the chair, across the room and into the wall, sliding down cinder block to the linoleum floor.

Heaped in a corner, every joint tense and brain fried, I try to speak but my tongue just kind of vibrates.

"Give yourself a minute, dear," Vera says as if she's just served me iced lemonade and sugar cookies. "The juice from my electric pen is still flowing through you. Now you were saying something about, what was it? Oh yeah, bigger and badder?"

She smiles down at me, eyes not entirely unkind despite the use of her magic, ass-kicking pen, as the juice runs its course through my body.

Stupid. I was stupid not to know that pen was some kind of weapon with all the clicking and clacking right in front of my face the entire time.

She helps me stand on wobbly legs, then waits as I steady myself with one trembling hand pressed flat against the nearest wall.

"I'm sorry, Maddy," she whispers before she opens the door. "But you left me no choice. I can help you, you know, if you let me."

I can't tell if she's being serious or luring me in with some good Sentinel/bad Sentinel crap, but I keep my distance until she pockets the pen. I try to unclench my jaw. It takes awhile.

Electricity is to zombies what silver is to werewolves, what garlic and holy water are to vampires. All we have left, the only juice still running through our veins, is electric current. It's why brains, which are full of electricity even after they're dead, are all we need, all we want, to survive. So when something conducts electricity, like the copper at the end of Dane's stake or a Sentinel's Taser or Vera's James Bond electric pen, well, it doesn't play fair with our zombie insides.

So forgive me if I'm still a little clumsy on my two left feet as I stumble to the door. Vera walks through and says to the guards, "I'll escort Ms. Swift to her cell, gentleman. That is all."

Her voice is crisp and not at all how she talked to me inside the room. It almost sounds, though I know it can't be true, like Vera's their boss. But if there's one thing Sentinels hate more than Zerkers, it's women. I've never seen a female Sentinel and, according to Dane, there's never been one.

So how can Vera be their boss?

They grumble and make a move to follow, but apparently that powder-blue suit isn't as lame as it appears, because one cluck of Vera's tongue and the Sentinels scatter as if she's just stuck her pen in both of their necks at the same time. I watch them go, wishing I could see the looks on their faces.

I can see Vera's, though. She smiles and leads me down another hall.

At the end of it is a hulking Sentinel sitting at a cheap, metal desk like you'd see in any high school counselor's office. There is nothing on it except his hands, which he raises in a *stop, do not proceed* motion.

Vera says, "I'm here with the detainee."

Hmm, that sounds kind of . . . innocent. Not prisoner, not customer, not client, not inmate. Detainee. Kind of like detention but with a zombie guard keeping watch over the door instead of, you know, some pudgy assistant principal.

But then I wonder, is detainee better than prisoner? Or worse?

The Sentinel grumbles and starts to rise, but Vera says, "I have a key."

He sits heavily, as if relieved.

From a hip pocket Vera slides out a key and quickly

slips it into a round metal lock. There's a resounding click, and the tan-colored door hisses open.

Inside is a long hall. It's brightly lit with flickering bulbs but narrow. A yellow line—I can't tell if it's painted on or just really good tape—stretches in front of a row of cells, maybe eight in all.

Like, real cells.

Jail.

Cells.

Detainee or no, it's clear I'm a prisoner of some sort.

Vera and I stop in front of one.

"I thought you were joking."

"Why would I be joking, Maddy?"

"Isn't this"—I rack my brain for the name on the sign we saw while pulling in earlier—"the Crestview Rehabilitation Center?"

"That? That's just so Normals keep on driving by and don't get in our hair. This is one of a dozen containment facilities the Sentinels operate around the country. It houses detainees from the southeast region mostly: Florida, Georgia, the Carolinas, a few from Tennessee."

"Detainees?" I say—anything to stall going inside that cell.

She nods, reaching in one of her pockets for the same key she used to open the door at the end of the hall. "Sentinels that have gone rogue, zombies who refuse to meet with the Council of Elders, zombies who have been caught eating human flesh—that kind of thing. And Zerkers, of course. If we rehabilitate anything here, it's them."

"You can do that?" I say, and not just to stall. "Rehabilitate Zerkers?"

Vera bites her lower lip, the way Dane will when he's not sure whether to tell me the truth. "Not all. But we're working on some interesting techniques that may hold out hope for the future."

I try to picture a future where someone like Bones or Dahlia or even Val could be rehabilitated. "Is that something we even want?"

Vera looks at me with something like respect or at least interest. "I'm not sure. But . . . don't you think we should at least try?"

I start to answer, but the thought of Stamp's black-and-white hoodie floating among the circling sharks closes my mouth. How do you rehabilitate someone who could do something like that?

She takes my nonanswer as an answer and reaches into a pocket.

I flinch, expecting to get a jolt from the pen again.

Instead she flashes the key to make sure it's the right one.

To buy myself another minute or two, I say, "W-w-well, for such a big place, it sure seems empty."

"It is empty." She slides the key in the last lock and eases the cell door open on smooth, oiled hinges. "Except for you."

She steps aside, and I walk in. What's the point of delaying the inevitable any longer, right?

The cell is wide, if not long. There is no cot, like in the movies, or toilet or even sink. Because, well, what do I need with any of those things? One table and two chairs stand in the corner. That's it. They're steel and bolted into the cinder block wall, so I can't even pick one up and clobber a guard over the head with it.

I turn from exploring the room to find Vera closing the door gently, then pocketing the key. She stands there, file in hand, key and pen in pocket.

I say what's been on my mind since we parted: "What about Dane?"

"Don't worry about Dane right now. There is you, there is me, and that's all you need to worry about right now."

I shake my head. "So what now? I'm supposed to rot in some cell while a crazy-ass Zerker makes tracks for Barracuda Bay, and you think I'm going to stand for that?"

"What choice do you have?"

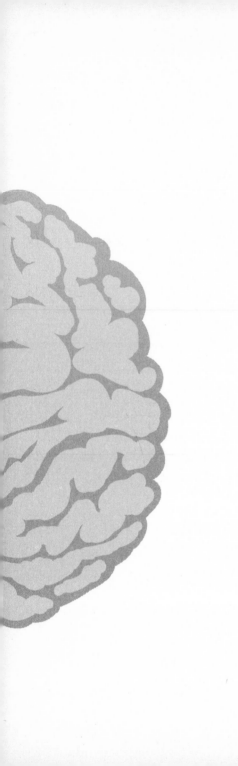

19
A Black Belt in Bitchery

There are no windows in the cell, naturally, but none in the hall either. I've been pacing for, I dunno, hours or days since Vera walked away.

I keep waiting for her to come back, to bring Dane along with her, to drag me to the Council of Elders, to experiment on me, to question me, to execute me—something. Anything would be better than this.

This not knowing, this not doing? Florida is a big state but not that big. Anyone with a lead foot and a dead bladder could make it from one end to the other in a day, easy. Someone like Val, a motivated, deadly, cunning, and gleeful killer? She's probably already there.

And after the Sentinels dropped the ball with Stamp, how am I supposed to believe Dad's safe, as Vera said? Fact is, I don't. The thought of Val in the same town, in the same state, as my dad makes my dead skin crawl.

But for all my zombie strength, the bars are too thick to bend and walk through. So I'm stuck for now. Perhaps even for awhile.

The cell is exactly 14 paces wide, and I walk them over and over again as I fume. I picture Dane, black T-shirt still damp from trying to save Stamp, and how he knocked me out in order to save me.

I think of his missing pinky and the gaping gash in his calf and the dreadful look on his face as he waited for me to come to. How long had he sat there, dripping wet, black goo oozing from his missing digit, surrounded by dead sharks and pieces of Stamp? One minute? Ten minutes? Twenty?

I drift back to Barracuda Bay and remember the first two Zerkers I ever encountered. I can clearly picture Bones, so tall in his shiny white tracksuit, so crafty and clever. His partner in crime, Dahlia, so petite and full of fury. They were a good match, the two of them combining their strengths to be double the trouble for the good zombies who lived in my hometown.

In Val, it's like both were reincarnated on crack with a PhD in mean and a black belt in bitchery.

I shake my head, clench my fists, and pace, but it doesn't change the fact that I'm in here and she's out there. It was a mistake to run. I know that now. I wonder if Dane does. I wonder if Stamp did all along. We should have stayed and taken the heat. For better or worse.

We were stronger together back then. Dane and

Chloe were a force to be reckoned with, like Bones and Dahlia. Two heads were better than one. Dane with his hard angles and rough edges and complete lack of empathy for anything Zerker. Chloe with her utter badassery. Nothing and nobody could get by her. Until, of course, someone—or something—did.

And me? I was so eager to please Dane, so diehard in wanting to protect Stamp, I'd have done anything to keep us all safe and re-alive.

If Val had shown up then, with all three of us on our game, she wouldn't have been able to touch us. Not a chance. Back then Stamp still trusted me and Dane still respected my opinion, and together we managed to stop an undead army complete with footballer zombies, Living Dead cheerleaders, and even a legion of undead teachers.

A punk Zerker like Val? She would have been worm food in 10 seconds flat.

Then we ran, and everything changed.

It was like, as the school burned down in our rearview mirror, we left part of ourselves behind. The best part of ourselves.

By the time we got to Orlando, almost as soon as we crossed the city line, everything shifted and none for the better. I chose Stamp, and Dane melded into the background. He became more father than boyfriend, and the more time I spent with Stamp, the more he knew my heart belonged to Dane.

And the more Stamp knew, the more he changed. Withdrew. He became hurt, and once we broke up for good he was distant. He became less like a friend or even an ex and more like a roommate.

Him staying out all those nights, with some new crowd we didn't know, made him worse than hurt. It made him vulnerable. Bait for a chick like Val and her charms, whatever those might have been.

And now Stamp was gone forever, and Val won. The thought of her, that blonde spiky hair, that stupid red boa, her voice over the loudspeaker at Splash Zone, teasing us. I close my eyes to drive it all away, but it only makes it worse.

I know my heart is dead, but my chest hasn't forgotten the flutter of anxiety that happens when I'm so mad I could burst. I swear I can feel it beating in there, or maybe it's just the electricity left over from Vera's mighty pen.

Vera. She'll be back. She'll want to talk, to discuss more of what's in my file. She'll bring her pen and her key. They will be in her pockets. The pockets of her powder-blue Sentinel uniform. If I can just remember which pockets they're in, if I can just grab them, then I can get out.

And Val can be mine.

20
Human No More

"You're going to have to talk to me sometime, Maddy."
Her tone is halfway between demand and request, equal
parts mother and prison maiden.

"I've talked. I'm talking. What more do you want to
know, Vera?"

We're back in the little room where she first ques-
tioned me. I can't tell if it's been one day, two days, two
weeks, or only two hours. There are no windows here or
in my cell or in the long hallway leading to my cell.

It feels like daytime, or maybe that's just because the
room is so bright. There are no Sentinels waiting gigan-
tically outside the door this time. Either Vera thinks she
doesn't need them anymore or they were just for window
dressing the first time.

I eye the electric pen in her hand just the same. I
think she wants me to.

She doesn't answer right away, just sits there staring at me. I can't tell if she's supposed to be the good zombie, the bad zombie, or both, but I'm not worried much either way. Talk is cheap. Only revenge matters anymore.

Her left hand, the one without the lethal pen, rests gently on my file.

I nod toward it. "Have I been that bad?"

Vera arches an eyebrow but doesn't reply.

"It looks like my file's gotten so big you've had to add a second one to fill with all my misdeeds."

She smiles softly before apparently remembering this is supposed to be some kind of interrogation. "Actually, this is someone else's file. I thought . . ." Her voice, usually so confident, drifts off midsentence as she looks above my head at the window behind me. I turn, expecting to see someone—a team of Sentinels, maybe, or even Dane—but there's nothing but more off-white cinder blocks and bright, white lighting.

Then she fixes her eyes on mine and continues more confidently: "I thought if you saw it, it might help you understand a little of what makes her tick."

"Her?" I snap, sitting up immediately. "What her? That's Val's folder?"

I reach for it, and she clicks the pen once over my hand.

I yank my hand right back. Yeah, I'm not proud of it, but it beats getting knocked clear across the room again.

"I'm not stupid," Vera insists, removing the pen but watching my hand carefully. "I know what you're thinking. I know that nothing I say matters, that you're only thinking of the day you can get out of here and find the person who killed Stamp. But I'm warning you: Sentinels don't take kindly to escapees, and if you think you're in trouble now, just—"

"Can I see the damn folder or not?" My voice, like my jaw, like my fingers on the side of my chair, is tight.

She hears the tone, her eyes get a little bigger, and then she slides it across.

Now that it's in front of me, I'm hesitant to read it.

I've been staring at the mental picture of Val's face so long I'm almost afraid to look at a real picture of it. That probably doesn't make much sense, but it stops me from opening the folder right away just the same.

"Aren't you going to open it?"

"Yeah, yeah, I just . . . I really hate her, you know?"

Vera pauses as we both stare at the unopened file sitting on the table just so in front of me.

"Maybe you won't after reading the file."

"The hell does that mean?"

Vera doesn't even flinch. If anything, she leans in. "It means that once you get to know Val as a person, you might not be so quick to—"

"She's not a person. She's a Zerker, remember?"

Vera ignores my tone and softens hers: "Not always.

Like you, she started out as—"

"Val was never like me. Never."

She nods curtly, says, "You didn't kill all those Zerkers out of revenge?"

"We didn't kill anybody. We defended ourselves. We defended our town and our friends and our parents. There's a big difference."

Vera shrugs. "Maybe that's what Val thought she was doing."

"What? By waiting a few months and then luring Stamp into some shark tank? That's self-defense?"

She opens her mouth and, so help me God, I shove the table in her direction just to shut her up. Its legs skid a millimeter or two on the floor.

Vera kind of gasps, we share a look, and then she shakes her head. "Look at the file. Then we'll talk." She stands, pen in hand—clicking, clicking, clicking—pacing the small interrogation room.

I finally open the file with a trembling hand. The first thing I see are the same kind of surveillance photos that the Sentinels—or the Keepers or the FBI of the Living Dead or whoever the hell—took of Dane and Stamp and me in Orlando.

They're of big-booted, spiky-haired Val doing mundane un-Zerker-like things: getting gas, shopping for mascara, going into a nightclub, coming out of a nightclub.

I'm flipping them over and over and over, sneering at Val's smug face, that pug nose and stupid, *stupid* hair, when the first picture of Stamp pops up. I gasp out loud and don't care that it stops Vera in her tracks.

The room slips away, and I slide the picture out of the folder, holding it close so I can study every detail. Stamp is in a black T-shirt, loose but soft and clingy across his broad chest. It has long sleeves to cover up his zombie skin, and he stands awkwardly, a full foot taller than Val. They lean against some grody brick wall downtown.

I can tell it's from a few weeks back, when they first met, because he's not wearing the stupid black-and-white hoodie he must have bought—or maybe she bought for him—while they were dating.

He looks so young, so handsome, even in his Living Death. I've known him so long, I don't see the death pallor, the drawn cheeks, the hooded eyes, the crooked smile anymore. I just see the boy who ran into me that first day at Barracuda Bay High, the Superman curl he can't get back, and the boy I doomed forever by bringing him back from the dead.

And now he's dead again.

"You're lucky," I croak, not looking up, voice deader than usual, "that zombies don't cry. Or your stupid folder would be ruined."

I hear a cluck or a chuckle and then the shuffling of her feet to the other end of the room.

Reluctantly, I slip Stamp's picture into the file and move on.

There are more of them together: Val and Stamp in

211

a nightclub, Val and Stamp chugging double frozen coffee shots, Val and Stamp at the warehouse. I flip through them quickly. It hurts too much to linger.

There is a yearbook photo of Val, circa 1970-what-the-hell. She's in braces and bell-bottoms and a big, fat, floral collared shirt and feathery blonde hair. I always forget zombies are immortal, that *we're* immortal.

"How old *is* she?" I say, as if this is the biggest sin she's committed: not being an actual teenager.

Vera finally chuckles. "Does it matter?"

I shrug, flip the page, and freeze. There is a second yearbook photo, same '70s-era feathery hair and big, floppy collars and—it's Bones!

"Bones had hair?"

"Lots of it," she says, even though she's staring at her shoes. "Apparently."

Brown, curly, frizzy hair. Big buckteeth. Eyes that were not yellow but green. Val's eyes, too, I find, looking back.

I slip the photos out of the file and line them up next to each other. Only when they're side by side can I see the resemblance of brother and sister. It's in the eyes, the bridge of the nose, the jut of the jaw.

"They look so goofy."

"It was the '70s. We all looked goofy."

"You . . . you were in the '70s?"

Vera rolls her eyes. "You don't wanna know."

There are only a few more pictures in the file.

Younger ones. Bones and Val as little kids on tricycles. Looking awkward in fuzzy red jumpers in front of a Christmas tree.

I put those images back and stare at the yearbook photos.

"Why do they stop here?" I say, already suspecting the answer.

"That's when they were turned." She returns to the seat across from me.

While I stare at the yearbook photos, memorizing each freckle, each eyelash, each pimple, Vera rustles through the few remaining pages of the file to slide out a yellowed newspaper article. I can't see the front as she holds it up, but I see a cigarette ad on the back: 75 cents for a pack of cigarettes. Not too shabby.

"Mysterious illness infects local church," she reads from the article, holding it by the edges gingerly. "Thirty-four members of the Zionist Pioneer Church on 47th and Sycamore were buried in a mass grave yesterday, in accordance with local health codes. The only two survivors of what local residents are calling the yellow flu, named for its resulting flu-like symptoms and yellow eyes, were not in attendance. Valerie Simmons and her younger brother, Randolph, watched the funeral on TV from the local orphanage. Their parents, Bill and Carol Simmons, were two of the earliest victims of the yellow flu and—" She pauses.

I've slid the pictures into the file and closed it. "So they were human. I get that. They had parents, friends. Their whole life changed. So why us? Why did Bones, or this Randolph Simmons dude, get to the point that he hung out in high schools baiting regular zombies and chomping on Normals' brains?"

"Why do any of us wind up anywhere?" Her voice is sad.

I wonder if, like me, she is thinking of her own parents and how she became a zombie and when and why and what she left behind.

"All we know is that Valerie and her brother, Randolph, aka Bones, survived a Zerker outbreak by becoming ones themselves. We could only trace them as far back as the orphanage they stayed at after the funeral. That is, until they broke out. After that, they came up as only blips on the Sentinels' radar from time to time over the years."

I shake my head and slide the file across the table. "So if they were so close, where was Val when Bones was terrorizing me and my friends?"

Vera shrugs. "Another high school, perhaps? Divide and conquer? All we know is that Val showed up in Barracuda Bay a few days after the first team of Sentinels got there to try and find you. A surveillance team tracked her all the way to Orlando, where she apparently located you guys. That's where these photos were taken. After that, well, you could probably tell us more than we already know. If you'd talk, that is . . ."

I nod but don't. Talk, that is.

She sits there patiently.

Suddenly, I remember: "You said this would change my mind about Val. Why?"

Vera shrugs. "She was human once, just like you."

I stand and linger by the door, my back to her. "You forget," I say, my tone so cold it almost frosts over the window in the door. "I'm not human anymore."

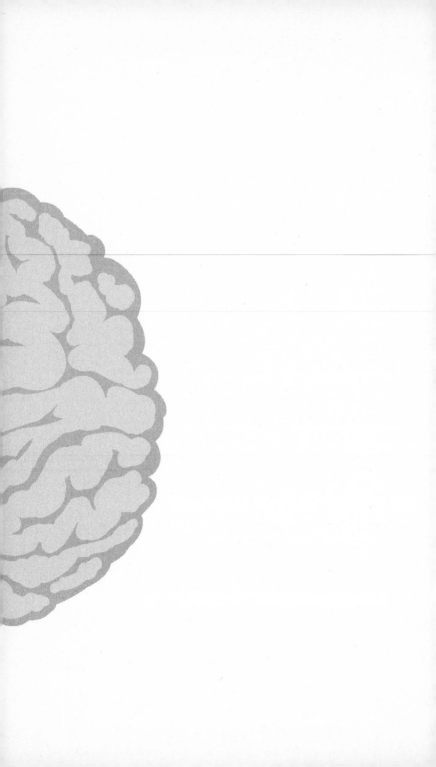

21
She's a Keeper

I'm pacing when I hear the door at the end of the hall open and boots squeak in the hall. Then something starts scraping ominously in time with the boot steps.

Clomp, clomp, scrape. Clomp, clomp, scrape. I stop my pacing long enough to inch away from the bars of my cell, just in case it's some cyborg with a machine gun arm or laser beam eyeball or something.

I know, I know, too much Syfy, but I can't help it! What else am I supposed to watch at 4:00 a.m.?

The clomping and scraping get closer and closer—did I mention, it's a really long hall—until at last I'm nearly pushed against the far wall of my cell and a flash of faded blue enters my peripheral.

Vera comes into focus and sets down the four-legged chair she's been scraping down the hall. She sits in it outside my cell. There's a self-satisfied smile on her face, like maybe she did all that on purpose, just to scare me or tease me or just plain bug the holy crap out of me.

Either way, I go back to pacing.

Each pass I notice something new about how Vera's sitting but more importantly where she's sitting. Just on the other side of the yellow line outside my cell, to be specific. Too far for my arms to reach, and don't think I haven't spent the last few hours trying.

And the way she sits there, smiling, legs crossed, my file on her knee, one foot dangling in the air and every so often kicking a little the way people do. It's like she's read my mind and already knows about me wanting to pickpocket her or something!

"So," she says brightly, as if I'm not in a cell and she's not on a molded plastic chair outside of my cell holding a file that contains every vital piece of information about my life. "How are you feeling today?"

"Today? What day? Isn't it the same day?"

She nods. "Technically, but it's after midnight now, so how are you feeling today?"

I pause by the door of my cell and rest my hands on the bars over the lock, the way you'll see prisoners do in old movies. It feels good to take a break from the constant pacing. Not because I'm tired, but staring at a wall hour after hour gets real old real fast. Besides, like her or not, Vera's at least something new to look at for a change.

"Well, let's see. I'm sad and scared and pissed off and lonely, but mostly I'm pissed off. Why? What are you writing?"

She has an open legal pad on top of my file and is writing what I'm saying. Okay, maybe not every word, because I was really flying through the syllables there at one point, but—

"You're here for intake, remember, Maddy? I can't release you if I don't—"

"Release me? When are you releasing me? Let's do this thing already!"

Vera cracks a rare smile, then shakes her head at the same time. "Maddy, you know I can't tell you that yet."

I groan and turn on my heel and catch a slight whiff of mold from my sneakers. "Well, can I at least get some new clothes, then?" It's not the mold I care about so much as the opportunity to reach out and grab and steal a key from whoever's handing some new clothes over.

She nods absently, then scrawls some more notes. "Someone will be bringing those along for you. Now, before we do, a few updates."

I perk up, sitting in one of the steel chairs bolted to the wall of my cell.

"We've now sent a total of four Sentinel First Responder teams to Barracuda Bay and moved your dad to a safe house."

"A safe house. What's that?"

"A house that's safe, Maddy." Her tone isn't even

sarcastic. "I can't tell you where, for obvious reasons."

"How safe?" I ask urgently, lurching to the edge of my seat.

"Safe, Maddy, as long as he goes straight from work to the safe house and back again."

"And work? I mean, a safe house is one thing, but how do you hide four teams of Sentinels in the county morgue?"

Vera offers another little smile. "You'd be surprised how subtle we can be. After all, we stalked you for months without you knowing, didn't we?"

Yeah. And look how well that turned out.

"Well, I mean, how is he? Did he say anything?"

"About what?"

"About me? Damn, didn't he even ask you why he was being moved?"

She looks at some notes in her pad and shakes her head. "I don't see any of that here, no."

She leaves it out there, just like that. So do I. I mean, what am I going to say? It doesn't sound like Dad to not ask about me, but . . . he does hate change. Maybe he was ticked off when the Sentinels showed up and dragged him out of his warm, comfy home.

"Secondly," she goes on, pausing a little so I can snap out of it and focus on her again, "we've been interviewing Dane and his story conflicts with yours."

"How so?"

"Well, he claims that you were unconscious for most of what happened at Barracuda Bay High School and, accordingly—"

"Wait, what? The Fall Formal? Seriously? Why are we still beating that dead horse? I thought . . . I thought this was about Val and what happened to Stamp. She's the bad guy. She should be in some damn cell, not me and certainly not Dane! I mean, who the hell still cares about Barracuda Bay High?"

Vera cocks her head and runs a large hand over her bristly scalp. "The Sentinels do, Maddy. In addition to the laws you broke by leaving the scene of an active Zerker infestation and not reporting to the Sentinel authorities the minute you three arrived in Orlando, you broke a series of laws back in Barracuda Bay."

"Wait. Hold up. *The Sentinels* still care? I thought you were a Sentinel."

She shakes her head. "I'm a Keeper, Maddy. We're kind of between the Sentinels and the Elders."

I nod. "So you're above the Sentinels?"

That would explain why she can click a tongue and 400-pound zombies in black berets come running.

"We don't think that way about ourselves," she scolds, but there's still a gleam of self-satisfaction in her eyes.

"So, I don't get it. If you're not a Sentinel and you're not an Elder, then what does a Keeper do?"

She shrugs. "What do you think a Keeper does?"

"Keep kids in some stupid jail cell when they should be out protecting their dads."

She nods. "Not quite but, yes, we are the Keepers of many things: of information, for one. Of rules and laws, for another. And when those rules and laws are broken, we keep zombies like you locked up until we can get to the truth. That's how we keep order. That's how we keep ourselves above the Zerkers. I thought you, of all people, would appreciate that."

She waits a beat, as if to see if her explanation makes sense, but really I'm just trying to gather as much information as I can so that when and if I ever get out of here I can know who to avoid the fastest.

Sentinels: avoid.

Keepers: avoid at all costs.

"Back to Dane." She leans in just a smidge.

I watch her closely. It's as if she's finally started talking about what she came here to talk about. "You understand that if he is charged with all the zombie laws he broke back in Barracuda Bay, he could be kept here for up to 10 years. And that if you were to allow him to take all the blame, your stay would be much shorter."

"How much shorter?" I say, not even trying to hide the base desperation and, yes, greed in my tone.

Another head cock, as if she's surprised by not just the question but the tone. "I-I'm not sure." She stumbles for the first time since we've met. "I guess I didn't think you'd let him take the blame for what I doubt he could have managed to do all by himself."

"Who says? Ever seen the dude with his shirt off? He's all muscle, lady. All over. And he's been doing this a really long time. And he really, really hates Zerkers. Does it say that in your file? Because, really? Those Zerkers didn't stand a chance."

"Okay, but you understand that these are serious charges Dane faces?"

"Well, then, he shouldn't have killed so many Zerkers, I guess, huh?" I try to sound flip, but the words feel like acid on my tongue. I wonder if she can see the distaste on my face.

She nods and stops writing. "I see. Are you saying you're willing to let Dane take the rap just so you can flee to Barracuda Bay and—?"

"Of course not!" I gasp, really laying it on thick now. "I would never let Dane be punished for something I did, but if I didn't do it, would the Keepers want me to confess to it? Is that how you guys roll because, from what I've seen, Vera, you guys are better than that."

She shakes her head warily, suddenly distracted by a noise at the end of the hall.

I look at her closely and lean in. If she were only sitting two stupid inches closer to the cell, I could reach out and snatch her bony-ass arm, yank it inside, and get the key.

And the pen. *Don't forget the pen, Maddy!*

"Your clothes are here," she says abruptly, standing and sliding the chair back another few inches.

Damn, can this witch really read minds?

I hear boot steps, lots of them, and wonder how many Sentinels it takes to carry a change of underwear and some stupid flip-flops.

Then I hear the distinct clinking and clunking of chains.

"Dane!"

And I catch Vera's eyes, so alert and so knowing, and I can almost hear her thinking: *Wow, for someone so eager to let her man take the rap for her crimes, she sure is happy to see him.*

22
Dane with Cane

He looks bad: beat down, bruised up, and bandaged everywhere.

Plus, he's limping. And there's this: a cane!

"Hey," I snap at the Sentinels and, by association, Vera. "That wasn't all from the sharks!"

"Maddy," Dane says, hobbling on his cane and getting pulled back mercilessly by one of his giant Sentinel guards when he's too close to the forbidden yellow line of doom. "Don't worry. It's fine. I'm fine."

"You don't look fine," I grumble.

He cracks that crooked smile. "Really, Maddy, I am."

He's holding clothes, lots of them, and goes to hand them over. Before he does, a Sentinel grabs them and shoves them clumsily through the bars, where they naturally sprinkle like grated cheese all over the floor.

225

"Nice," I hiss, picking up socks and a flannel shirt and tossing them onto my shiny, stainless steel table just as carelessly. "Real nice. Can we have some privacy please?"

The Sentinel guards chuckle, but Vera gives them a look and they take four steps back immediately. Dang, maybe these Keepers are badass after all.

"Five minutes," Vera whispers, eyeing Dane carefully before stepping back to keep a safe distance from the stocky Sentinels. She touches Dane's shoulder gently. "And stay behind the yellow line."

Dane looks down and stops his cane right where the yellow line ends. He waits, watching until Vera has joined the Sentinels midway down the hall. She walks past them a smidge, then stops. She's not going any farther.

"Maddy," he says, undeterred, "what is this place?"

"I don't know. Some detention wing or something."

He's in gray sweatpants a size too big and a snug pajama top buttoned up halfway. Part of his chest and his left hand, the one with the pinky missing, are bandaged. One leg of his pants is rolled up to accommodate one of those black plastic casts you can walk around in.

He sees me looking and lifts the cane. "You like?"

It's an old person's cane, with a black rubber tip on the bottom and an aluminum frame and a black rubber grip at the top, for comfort, I suppose.

I smirk. "High tech," I say, wishing everyone could just leave us alone—really alone—for a few seconds.

That's all I'd need to make Dane realize that what I'm doing—what I'm about to do—isn't meant to hurt him.

Instead, I have to speak in code. Or try, at least. "What are they doing to you?" I say quietly.

He shrugs. "Asking me a ton of questions, but who cares? You?"

"Same. I thought we'd be in trouble over the Splash Zone, you know? But all they seem to care about is Barracuda Bay. It's like, no matter how far we run, or how hard we try, we'll never escape our past."

He smiles weakly, and for a second I see the old Dane. My Dane.

"Did you know about this place?" I say. "About places like this?"

He shakes his head. "I've heard rumors, but I've only ever dealt with the Sentinels when the Elders were around. I'm not sure even the Elders know about places like this."

"Why? I thought they knew everything."

He shrugs. "It just seems beneath them somehow."

"So what are we going to do?"

"What can we do? You've been up here the whole time, but I'm still downstairs in the medical wing, and let me tell you, this place is locked up tight. So whatever you're thinking, stop thinking it."

There's a glimmer in his eye, unfamiliar and overzealous. It's like he's onstage.

"I'm not thinking about anything," I snap, the thought of those dead sharks lying wet and broken on the concrete, pieces of Stamp digesting in their still-warm bellies. "I'm doing it and soon. You know about Val, right?"

He leans in a bit but not far enough to catch the wrath of Vera. He lowers his voice. "Do you?"

I nod. "Didn't you know Bones had a sister? I mean, that would have been nice to know. Before we tore him to bits and pieces and set his ass on fire."

"Shut up," he says but not unkindly. "The odds of two siblings being Zerkers is, like, astronomical."

"Says you," I taunt, but only because I enjoy seeing him smile, even if just for a second or two.

I see one of his teeth is chipped.

"What happened there?" I point to it.

He shrugs again, the ill-fitting pajama top lifting up from his sweatpants. "I must have chipped it when I was fighting one of those . . ."

I don't need him to finish his sentence. I nod.

Hurriedly, as if to air the stench of our shared memory from the hallway, he blurts, "They're working on some new stuff down in the medical wing, though, where they say they might be able to grow back some of the flesh."

"How? I thought zombie flesh didn't grow back."

"It doesn't, but they're trying electrical therapy to

revitalize some of the dead tissue clusters. Don't ask me. Just, we'll know if my frickin' finger ever grows back."

He's using that false voice again, and I look at the Sentinels standing downwind. I wonder, idly, if he's been coached.

I look at Vera over Dane's shoulder, but she quickly avoids my gaze. I turn back to Dane, who's still smiling.

Why? Why is he smiling so much?

I look into his eyes, those deep dark eyes, and wait for something to shoot across the air, something magical and true and sincere that only I could see. It never does. He looks down, then up, then down, and I say, just as falsely, "Good for you, Dane. I hope they can grow your finger back."

He stops smiling abruptly and can't start again for a little bit.

When he does again, it's not quite so bright. "I miss you, Maddy."

"Me too," I say. I think, I hope, it's the first honest thing he's said so far.

Behind him and off to the side, we hear a grunt and look at the tallest Sentinel. "One minute," he says.

We turn to each other at the same time.

Dane smiles again, less bright this time. "What now?"

"I don't know," I blurt, voice cracking.

He notices, and his eyes get a little bigger.

I hate that being a zombie still lets me show my most shameful emotions. I can't blush anymore, which is nice.

229

I can't sweat buckets when a cute guy rolls in the room. But my voice can still crack, and that's just not cool.

Still, we're beyond cool now. We're beyond Dane and me.

I look at Dane with his cane, his missing pinky, his chipped tooth, and his bruised and bloodied body, and I know he's not going where I'm going. Not this time. As much as I'd like his help when I finally get to Barracuda Bay, as much as I know he'd enjoy taking Val down so hard she never gets back up, just one look at him tells me for once he's not up for it.

"I guess we lay low," I bluff. "For now."

"But you said"—he shuffles forward with his cane until the Sentinel clears his throat once more—"Val and Barracuda Bay."

"I know, but look at us. You've got a cane. I'm stuck behind bars. Vera says they've got my dad on lockdown with Sentinels all over the place, so let's just hope she's right."

Dane turns when I shift my focus to the tall woman in the light blue beret, just as the two Sentinels move forward.

Dane leans even closer and hisses, "Something tells me you're shining me on, Maddy."

"Right back at you," I say fiercely, even though he's not the one I'm mad at.

Or is he?

He turns before the Sentinels reach him and doesn't look back.

No final words. No harsh comeback over his shoulder. He just hobbles down the hall, leaning heavily on his nursing home cane as the excess of his baggy sweatpants pools around his ankles.

I watch him go, his shoulders seeming not just wiry but frail, and wonder if I'll ever see him again.

"Well, that went well." Vera sighs, sliding the chair over just shy of the yellow line.

"Didn't it, though?" I say ruefully, sitting in one of the metal chairs welded to my cell wall.

She has my file on her lap and taps it occasionally with her pen, probably just to remind me not to step out of line.

"Has seeing Dane changed your mind about implicating him so fully in the Barracuda Bay incident?"

I pause, even though my mind is already made up. For effect, you see. "Yeah, actually, it has. But before I do, I want to ask: What will happen to him if I do?"

Vera shrugs stiffly. "Depending on the severity of his actions, he'll remain here for up to 10 years."

I nod as if I'm still mulling all this over. "And if what he did wasn't that severe?"

"As little as, say, two years."

Two years. Not bad for a guy who has another few hundred years left in him. And maybe it won't be so bad. They've given him a cane, so the Sentinels can't be all terrible. And sweatpants and a pajama top and shuffly slippers.

Besides, at least he'll be safe. Uncomfortable, maybe even unpopular, and probably not at the top of the fresh brains list come feeding time every week or so, but safe. Alive.

Where I'm headed, there's no such luck.

I nod, suddenly remembering she's waiting for answers. "What do you want to know?"

23
Prison Break

Vera returns with several more Keepers the next day, as scheduled. They're there to record my testimony. "For the record," as Vera puts it quite formally, obviously putting on a show for her colleagues, if not exactly her superiors.

All the Keepers wear their powder-blue Sentinel uniforms, down to the cute beret. All are women. The tall one takes notes in a yellow legal pad, just like Vera's. The shorter one holds out a sleek, white digital voice recorder. The shortest points a video camera at me.

It feels funny being filmed. A little nervously, I crack, "Lucky I'm not a vampire or you couldn't get me on tape, right?"

Predictably, only Vera smiles and merely halfway at that.

Vera faces the short Keeper looking into the video camera, who gives a thumbs-up. So does the one with the audio recorder. I'm not sure why they need to do both, since even the camera on my cell phone records audio as well, but I'm thinking it has to do with expediency: Don't have time to watch the video? Here. Listen to the audio.

Then again, what do I know?

When all the technology is aligned and the new Keepers are patiently waiting, Vera looks at me and says, "Maddy, are you ready?"

I nod. "How should I start?"

"Let's start with your name."

"Madison Emily Swift."

The other Keepers nod at Vera.

"Go on," she instructs.

"My name is Madison Emily Swift, and I am innocent of all charges . . ."

Despite Vera's eye roll, I do my dog and pony show for them. I sell Dane down the river.

Big deal. I blame most of it on Bones, that creep, and the rest on Dahlia. But still, that's not enough for them.

"Did Dane willingly engage in open warfare with the Zerkers?" asks one of the Keepers, the one with the blonde hair poking out under her blue beret. She holds out the sleek, digital recorder to get all the juicy bits.

"Yes, but . . . they started it."

"Just answer the questions," Vera coaches from the sidelines.

"They did," I protest because even though I'm a total turncoat, it needs to be said. "Bones and Dahlia were getting out of control, turning kids willy-nilly. They even turned my best friend, Hazel! What were we supposed to do?"

"Yes or no." Vera's tone leaves no room for interpretation.

"Yes," I say dutifully, eyeing the pen as Vera clicks it nervously in her right hand, which probably means she'll be sticking it in her left pocket, out of habit, when she goes to shake the other Keepers' hands before they leave.

"Did Dane try to avoid the conflict with the Zerkers?"

"Yes."

"Was Dane successful?"

"No, but have you ever tried to reason with a Zerker? Sorry. I mean . . . no."

It goes on like that, back and forth, me blaming Dane for just the bare minimum to make the Keepers' trip to the Crestview Rehabilitation Center worthwhile but not enough to send him downriver.

"And Chloe?" says the blonde with the voice recorder, checking some notes in her free hand. "What was her role in all this?"

I shrug, biting my lower lip. No one said anything about dragging Chloe into this. I picture her tall and sturdy frame, her severe face, her pancake makeup, her pierced nose, and her lips that rarely cracked a smile.

"Chloe?" I say, gaze flitting to Vera for guidance.

She offers none.

"Chloe was probably the real reason Dane got involved," I lie.

Hey, what's she gonna do? Come back to life again and glare at me?

"Explain yourself," demands the blonde with the tape recorder.

"Well, I mean, Chloe was pretty adamant about us handling that business ourselves. Dane was all for coming to the Sentinels, even the Elders, about our problems, but it seemed like every time he tried to bring it up, Chloe shot him down."

Vera eyes me warily as the other Keepers look among themselves, then back to me.

"Does Dane not have free will?" the blonde says. "Could he not make his own choices?"

"Sure, but you'd have to meet Chloe to understand. He trusted her, relied on her opinion. I think he honestly believed when she said that by the time the Sentinels got to town, the Zerkers would have won." Then, during the awkward silence that follows, I just have to add, "Having just lived through my second Zerker attack, I'd have to agree with her."

Vera crosses her arms and raises her head, but no one else makes a peep. At least if nothing else, it's on the record. I said it.

Eventually, after a couple of painful (for me, anyway) hours, they nod to Vera and turn off the video camera and voice recorder and start packing up. They don't shake Vera's hand (dammit!), but she pockets the pen just the same to walk them down the hall, pointing at several of the empty cells along the way.

None of the powder-blue berets turn back to thank or even acknowledge me, except Vera. Once. She wears a hard-to-read expression.

I shrug and turn away from the bars. What's done is done. Now I just have to let the chips fall where they may.

For Dane, that is.

I stretch while nobody's looking, stretch, stretch, and listen to the footfalls down the hall.

Four pairs of Keeper boots march away. Only one pair returns.

Vera looks a little ticked off when she walks into view.

"What's that look for?" I say, feeling loose, maybe even cocky, from all the stretching.

"I'm not sure how convincing your testimony was." She stands literally on the yellow line. "I think the Keepers feel like my call in to them was a bit premature."

"I told them everything I told you."

"Maybe it was how you said it. You seemed a little wishy-washy on the facts."

I nod, turn away, then turn back, like there is some huge emotional turmoil going on inside. "Well, what would make them come back?" I say, edging closer to the bars. "What if I told you . . . I haven't told you everything?"

Vera shifts my heavy file. "I'd say you were endangering your own freedom." Her voice is stern and no longer the least bit playful. "The punishment for withholding testimony is often as severe as the crime itself."

"So I won't withhold it anymore." I back away from the bars coyly. "But I'm not telling it to those other Keepers. I'll only tell it to you."

Then I step back and drop my voice an octave. "You're . . . you're the only one I trust to tell my whole story to. Maybe that's why I sounded wishy-washy to those other Keepers. I don't trust them. But I trust you."

"What's that?" she says, fumbling for a voice recorder of her own. "I couldn't hear that last part."

Yeah, dumbass, that's because I was practically whispering so you'd have to come closer.

"Oh, sorry," I say, only slightly louder this time. "I was saying, I'll only tell you the testimony I couldn't share with the others." More whispers.

Now she's moving across the yellow line just a tad. "You'll have to speak up. I can't hear you, and if we don't get all this on the record, then I'm afraid your testimony won't count for—"

"Forgive me if I don't want to shout it to the rafters that I'm betraying my boyfriend, okay?" I shout, still clinging to the back cell wall. "I just . . . you never know who's listening, you know?"

"I'm listening," she says, voice recorder extended just slightly toward the bars. "Right now, Maddy. I'm listening." Her voice is slightly desperate, her eyes alive with ambition as she moves forward just another smidge. I can tell there must be some reward for getting my testimony or imprisoning Dane, something that's making this normally rational woman lose her frickin' mind. "Just . . . tell me what I need to know. I'll make sure Dane stays locked up for a long, long time."

"You better." I creep close to the bars, where she lingers just over the yellow line. "Or none of this is going to be worth it."

"This what?" Fear glimmers across her face as she stands there, too close, but too frozen to step back just yet.

But it's too late. "This!" I leap forward and grab her thumb. I twist it awkwardly so that her hand slips through the bar. Then I yank the rest of her arm all the way in, up to the shoulder.

I break it with a sickening snap and mouth, "Sorry."

She winces and struggles to reach for her pocket with her one good hand.

Quickly I snatch the pen away before she can. With one click of the top, I stick it in her neck, shocking her into unconsciousness before I can look into her betrayed eyes anymore.

Yeah, bummer. But her arm will recover, like Dane's pinky or leg. And Dad? Dad's still human, and Val won't show him the same mercy I'm showing Vera. Not by a long shot.

I help Vera slump to her knees and frisk her until I find the key, then let her fall to the floor. Gently, gently!

The minute I unlock the door, I ease Vera into the cell and undress her. I put the clothes the Sentinels picked for me on her and slip into her powder-blue uniform and matching beret, tying the big boots tight. I lean her on the ground with her back to the cell doors, as if she's—or as if I'm—contemplating the opposite wall. Hey, it won't mean much when she wakes up and starts hollering, but until then nobody should come sniffing.

I slip from the cell door and lock it behind me. There are about eight other empty cells to pass before I reach the door at the end of the hallway. I know this plan has about zero chance in hell of working, but if I don't get out of here now, right now, I don't care what Vera says: My dad isn't safe. In Barracuda Bay. Anywhere.

Right now, that's all I care about.

Hazel. Ms. Haskins. Stamp. And Stamp again. I've lost too many innocents to sit around waiting for some Keeper to decide my fate.

I'm going to save my dad. Period. What happens to me after that, I'll deal with it then.

That is, if I don't die again trying first. And I probably will.

I pass each cell, aware that I have a few dozen giant Sentinels to disable on the way out of Dodge. I swallow air out of habit and slide the key into the door at the end of the hall.

A single Sentinel sits at his single desk and doesn't even look up as I pass. Here I am, loaded for bear, about three milliseconds from shoving the key in his ear hole, and . . . nothing. Not even a, "Hey, how you doing?"

I nod my beret-covered head at him anyway, but he merely grunts without looking up. There are stairs and an elevator in the corner of the little alcove we're in. I want desperately to run for the stairs, to flee and not look back, but I remember Vera rode the elevator and, since I'm playing the part of Vera today, I press the down arrow button and wait. And wait. And wait.

I hear stirring at my back but don't turn around. I mean, if I really were Vera, would I go jumping every time a fly farts? No, I'd stand right here minding my own business, waiting for the world's slowest elevator to—

"Any progress today, Keeper?" asks the Sentinel at my back.

The way he says Keeper, with such disdain, even if I were Vera, I wouldn't turn around to give this slug the time of day.

"Time will tell," I say, trying to mimic Vera's slow and low register.

He grunts. "Waste of time, you ask me. I say lock 'em both up, throw away the key. Serves 'em right, running from us for so long."

I wait until the elevator dings and the doors open to

walk in and turn, making sure the panel with the lighted numbers next to the door is hiding my face. "Guess that's why you're a Sentinel," I say as the doors begin to shut, "and I'm a Keeper."

His grunt is louder than the first, but the doors now shut him out. I cling to my pen, clicking it on and off twice just to make sure it still works. I get to the ground floor quickly and turn left, though I have no idea where I'm going. I just remember turning right when we walked in and hope to retrace my steps.

There is a lot of activity on the first floor. A *lot*. Like, frickin' the-last-day-of-school-out-on-the-quad a lot. All I see are bobbing black berets. All I hear is the squeak of boots as they pivot left and right to go in and out of so many doors.

There's a Sentinel every two damn feet. Since I'm impersonating a Keeper, of all things, they each nod at me. (Who knew Keepers had such pull?) I avoid eye contact, grateful that Vera's jumpsuit doesn't bag too much on me. I keep the beret down so low I'm getting distracted by the field of blue fuzz overhead.

I am lost in a maze of hallways now, desperate to get out and certain that upstairs Vera is coming to in her cell and clanging a metal cup against the bars to get the guard's attention.

How long before the Crestview Rehabilitation Center goes on full damn lockdown mode and they toss me under the building and throw away the key?

I turn around at a dead end and follow the flow of traffic, finally noticing the sounds of engines in the near distance. Engines and slamming doors and boots crunching on gravel. Gravel, not flooring. Car doors, not hallway doors. That must be out front, right?

But is out front where I really want to go?

I finally enter the main hallway, which is wider than the rest and better lit. It's also better trafficked, and I'm starting to pass some of the same Sentinels for the second time. Most don't notice or care. One does a double take, shrugs, and moves on. But how long before one does a triple take and follows me? Because, if I really am a Keeper, shouldn't I know more than a Sentinel? As in, how to get around the center?

I hear a horn honk, a gear grind, and an ignition falter. I head that way. I remember the garage where they shuttled me out of that SUV and into the center. A garage with big wide doors and lots and lots of vehicles.

And I'm heading that way, right away, when I pause. Something in my peripheral vision catches my attention. Just before a bend in the hallway, I see several burly Sentinels clustered with a mortal-sized zombie between.

It's Dane! He's wearing the same getup as he was yesterday and relying heavily on his cane to keep up with the ginormous strides of his monster Sentinel handlers. I'm the only powder blue in a sea of black at the moment, and he spots me right away.

Our eyes lock, and time slows down. His face reacts

strongly at first, then softens as the hall full of giant Sentinels grows claustrophobic and dangerous around him. I can see the glint in his eye, the confusion about what I've done, the hard edge of blame as the Sentinels haul him off to wherever they're taking him, but also a gleam of understanding.

Or maybe it's just wishful thinking on my part.

Then I see his eyes get big, and I look ahead to find myself nearly running into a wall of Sentinels walking the opposite direction. I narrowly avoid striking any of them, though it's too obviously a non-Keeper move to avoid a few grunts and near chuckles as I pass.

I turn immediately, hoping for a smile from Dane, but all I see are the colossal backs of the Sentinels shuffling him away for who knows how long.

How like him not to rat me out, even after all I did to him.

Does he know what I'm up to? Is that why he didn't nark? Or is he just that much of a stand-up guy?

I think I know the answer already, but now is not the time to get all mushy and run back to him with open arms and spouting poetry. Now is the time to get away, as quickly and quietly as possible, and do what needs to be done. If I make it, I can always apologize to Dane later. If not, and he doesn't know the real deal, the real me, then he never knew me at all.

I turn around and buck up, moving forward, ever

forward. *Forget it,* I tell myself. *Forget it. You're doing the right thing. Dane will understand. He has to.*

If this is a suicide mission, like Vera said, then I'm not going to turn it into a murder-suicide by dragging Dane along with me. And that's what would have happened, if he'd known what I was doing.

Well, he probably knows now, but what's he going to do?

Oh, crap! Shoot! Is that macho man going to tell the Sentinels, if only to save me from myself? He did it with Stamp and the sharks, sending me into a copper coma and sacrificing his own pinky and half his calf in the process. What's to make me think now will be any different?

But he smiled, right? Didn't I see him smile there, just before being swallowed up by the mammoth backs of his Sentinel guards? I can't afford to wait around and find out.

I hustle and finally hear the truck engines loud and close. There is a motor pool beyond a half-raised garage door at the end of a side hall. It's kind of the same setup as Family Value Mart, where you're going along, looking at basketballs and jar candles and paperbacks and DVDs and, boom: auto shop aisle—what the hell?

I pause, turn around slowly so as not to look too spazzy, see no one looking, and duck under the half-open garage door. The scent of motor oil and spark plugs on the other side of the garage door hits me right away, an almost welcome smell after the linoleum and floor polish odor of the center.

There are four Sentinels in the motor bay, all working under a hood or two. Their sleeves are rolled up, their berets askew, their cement-gray cheeks splattered with motor oil—and they definitely don't want a Keeper in their midst.

"Did you miss your ride?" one asks, wiping his hands on a greasy red rag. "We just sent three of you packing not 20 minutes ago."

"You did?" I say innocently, trying not to look over my shoulder too often. "I had some follow-up questions for the detainee." I look around, as if the other Keepers might still be there. *Please, God, don't let them be there!* "I asked them to wait."

I'm tapping a foot, pen in my hand, hand behind my back. These guys are big. Maybe not as big as Dane's captors, but big. And I've been lucky so far. Out the door, down the elevator, through the halls without so much as a stubbed toe. No way am I getting out of here without some kind of tussle.

Another one pokes his head out from under the open hood of the car he's working on. More dirty hands, another greasy red rag, black eyes sizing me up and down. "Well, we've only got one civilian vehicle left, little lady."

He juts his chin toward a small black car, an import, that looks like a mouse compared to the sleek black SUVs lined up next to it.

"Fine, great, whatever," I say, so eager am I to bolt out of here before Vera can come to and sound the alarm. "Just hand me the keys, and I'll be out of your hair."

The first one with clean hands looks at the others and says, "Well, you know that's not protocol. We need a work order, a point of destination, and of course you'll need an escort." He inches forward.

Of course there would be protocol. These are Sentinels we're talking about. Why didn't I know that? How am I going to get around all this?

He keeps coming, Mr. Bad News Sentinel. I have the pen behind my back and am about to click it right up his big, fat nostril when another Sentinel steps from a nearby car to my left and says, "Hey, what's that behind—?"

I turn, duck, and bury the pen in the soft flesh of his waist, just above his webbed weapon belt and below his rib cage. He pauses, giant arms a centimeter above me and ready to slam me to the floor when I click the pen once and he shivers once, twice, three times before circuiting out and tumbling to the garage floor.

He falls on me and I struggle, panicking, to hoist him off me. I don't have much time, and I have even less room for error. If just one grease monkey Sentinel walks through that half-opened door and alerts the rest, I'm done. That's it. And all that separates me from that grim reality is the garage door at my back. I slide out from under him, elbow banging against something harder as I do: his Taser.

I grab it, stand, and find the other three Sentinels circling me warily. I can't tell if they've alerted anybody else yet, but I don't have the time to find out. As they see me flickering the Taser in my hand, they fumble for their own.

Before the nearest one can aim his, I jam the flickering volt of white-hot blue lighting into the meat of his calf, just above his tightly laced military boot. He gargles and goes down, a chunk of dead, gray tongue bouncing on the floor at his feet.

God, I hate when that happens!

The other two rush in for the kill, but they're so big and slow I duck under their swinging arms. Their Tasers send blue-white arcs tickling past my hair without a trace. They get wise fast enough, though. Just like that, my size advantage becomes a disadvantage as the two giants circle, eager to go in for the kill.

I juke toward the one in front.

He flinches.

I turn and slam the Taser into the thigh of the one behind me.

He jerks into a frozen position and literally launches

into the air before crashing on the nearest hood, denting it so badly I figure it's probably trashed for good.

Unfortunately, he takes my Taser with him, and now they're both out of range. I'm stuck, defenseless against one looming Sentinel who's smiling like he's already won.

We circle each other. He's flickering the Taser; I'm clenching my fists. He jabs; I back up. I back up; he jabs. The Taser gets closer and closer, and I'm running out of room to back up to. I panic, looking around for a spare lug nut bar or crescent wrench or some horror movie tool-like device, but there's nothing. This must be the cleanest Sentinel garage in all of zombiedom.

Then I remember. The key. Vera's key.

I reach for it in my pocket as he jabs one last time, the stinger of his Taser piercing a fold in these too-generous sleeves and singeing the baby-blue material of my—of Vera's—Keeper uniform.

The Sentinel grunts and I kick the side of his knee with all my might. He goes down to the other knee, like Stamp used to when I'd watch him and the rest of the team huddle around the coach after football practice. I kick the Sentinel again, in the chest this time, and he grabs my leg before I can pull it back. But to do so, he has to use both hands. In the confusion, his Taser clatters to the ground.

I kick some more, three times, four, until he lets me

go. Before he can get up, I grab the large cell door key and jab it straight, and deep, into his ear. There is the slight crush of eardrum and cartilage and then the vague pop of his brain being punctured.

He lashes out, wildly punching me with his giant fists, but the damage has been done: the key sticks tight. I roll away, favoring what I hope isn't a cracked rib, and scramble for his Taser, where it's landed next to a spare tire.

As his eyelids flutter, as his upper body wavers, I shove the twin fangs deep in his chest and pull the trigger. His jaw slams shut, so hard a tooth flies across the garage, careening off a hubcap and clattering to parts unknown.

I'm actually glad it does because after deciding not to find out where it comes to rest, I look up and away and spot a wall full of keys! I grab one and race from truck to truck, car to car, seeing which one it might open. I'm sure any minute an army of Sentinels, Tasers blaring, will burst through the garage door and pound me straight into the concrete. No escape, no rescue, no future.

What's more, the Sentinels in here could come to at any minute. That is, if Dane hasn't snitched already! The key hasn't fit in any cars yet, and I'm running out of doors when, at last, it slides into the lock of an SUV.

It's an SUV but still as big as a Greyhound bus. I slide behind the wheel and waste 90 seconds trying to find the move-the-seat-up button so I can reach the steering wheel thingy. I never do, so I'll just have to sit on the edge of my seat for the next five hours.

I turn the key in the ignition, and it fires right up, sounding like a jet plane. One of the Sentinels rises, shaking his head, with both colossal hands on his ears. He's just to my left, and slightly ahead, and so help me I gun the car in drive, crunching his left leg in the process. He'll be able to tell somebody sometime but not anytime soon. Not with that leg.

But at least he's alive. Or re-alive. Or dead again. Or whatever we zombies are calling it these days.

And as I head for the hills, that's more than I can say for Stamp.

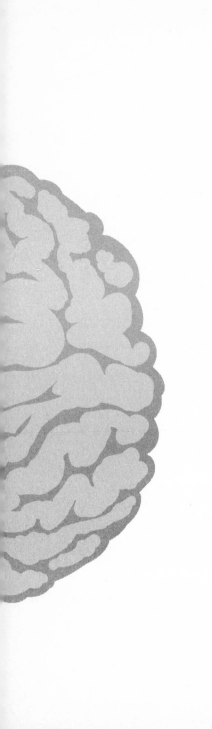

24
Cat Food to Go

I pull off the highway the first chance I get. It's dark. I hadn't expected it to be dark. I thought it was daytime. It felt like daytime, back in the garage, with the bright lights and surrounded by Sentinels. It's not. Not even a little.

The clock on the SUV's dashboard says it's 4:39, and that must be a.m. unless there's a solar eclipse or nuclear winter or something. I'm at some backwoods exit with nothing but gas stations and souvenir stands, both specializing in something known as a pecan log. (Don't. Just don't.)

I was hoping for a used car lot with really bad security or, you know, a running car just sitting there at some fast-food restaurant, but no such luck. At four in the afternoon? Maybe. Four in the morning? Nothing doing.

But I have to get out of this SUV. I don't know if the

Sentinels have tracking beacons or little electronic beeping chips in each tire, but in every movie I've ever seen where someone's on the lam, they ditch the car the first chance they get.

So, car? Prepare to be ditched.

Only one of the gas stations at my exit is still open, and two are service stations where they move the cars they haven't finished yet into the garage and shut the grimy glass doors until the next morning. So that'll work.

I drive the SUV behind one and leave the key in the ignition. I pop the back hatch and scout for anything of value. Nothing. Nothing but tire-changing tools and a roadside emergency kit. I take the kit because if I'm stealing a car that hasn't been fixed yet, it could break down anytime.

But as far as some huge Taser stash or giant Zerker-killing ray gun that might come in handy when I finally catch up with Val? Yeah, no dice.

I stop for a minute to listen for cars speeding along the nearby freeway, the one I just exited, but there's not much traffic this time of night. Or morning. Or whatever.

I creep toward the front of the gas station, keeping an eye out for Sentinels on patrol or locals with banjos or inbred serial killers with hockey masks and machetes, but I don't see any.

Instead I walk to the front of the convenience store part of the gas station and crack the glass with my thumb. A big section falls out and lands with a smash, but no alarm sounds and nobody comes running out of the bushes sparking Tasers at me either.

So that's good, right?

I dunno. It sucks being on the run without Dane. I'm trying not to be all damsel in distress about this, but he was always so much better at this stuff than I was. Being on my own is harder than I thought, and now that I'm free of the center, I'm feeling major guilt about leaving Dane behind.

What if they take all their Sentinel rage out on him? What if they blame him for my escape? Or even think he helped me? I cringe to think what he might be going through right now, but deep down I know I would have never made it if I tried to break Dane out with me. He was too well guarded, and I wasn't. Those are the facts, and here I am. I got what I wanted.

But at what cost?

I can't.

Really.

I can't go there right now.

Concentrate. Guilt trip later.

I find the dead bolt and click it open and creep inside, locking it back, just in case. Yes, there is glass all over the floor, but my dad always taught me to lock a door, even a screen door. And four months on the run with Dane's many house rules has me even more hyper-sensitive about door locking than ever.

Come to think of it, with those house rules, Dad

and Dane have a lot more in common than they think. Remind me to tell Dad that, if Val hasn't yanked off my jaw by the time I find him.

I pause inside, wondering if maybe the fat, smelly gas station owner (don't judge: you know it's what you're thinking) may be asleep on a greasy cot in the back, an empty jug of moonshine tipped over on the floor. But nothing stirs. Not even a mouse.

I stand in front of the row of beer and soda coolers, suddenly parched. I reach for a cold soda, something sugary to perk me up, and chug a bottle of Gargantuan Grape in 10 seconds flat before returning it, empty, to the case. I spot myself in the reflection of the glass door and see a galloping blue nightmare. I'm still wearing Vera's castoffs, right down to the baby-blue beret. I can only imagine what I'll look like to the Normals in a few minutes, tearing off in a stolen car.

"No, Officer, nothing wrong here. Just tooling around in my blue beret and pocket pants at 5:00 a.m., grape soda all over my lips. Why? Am I speeding? Tail-light out? What gives?"

I check out the rack of souvenir T-shirts. I brush the dust off the shoulders of one and read the front: My Other Car Is a Double-Wide. Perfect. There are no shorts, but the shirt is pink with blue writing, so presumably (you know, if this was 1987), it would, could, should match my baggy blue pocket pants.

I slip out of Vera's top and into the shirt. It's big, so I tie it around my waist *Baywatch* style. I grab some white sunglasses to accessorize and a pink fanny pack for the electric pen. I look around the aisles to see if I'm missing something. You know, like maybe this is the type of redneck joint that sells hunting knives and crossbows and cold-seeking bazookas next to the suntan lotion and pickled eggs. But, of course, no luck.

Although there *is* a stack of pet food cans, and I squint in the dim emergency exit lighting to read the list of ingredients on a can of Zippy Cat Chow. Sweet! There, just after liver and before tongue, is the ingredient I've been longing to find: brain. I grab the four cans off the shelf and shove them in the fanny pack. They barely fit.

I hate stealing things, especially as I slip behind the sales counter, yank out the cash drawer, and pocket all $84.59 from the till. But then I figure I'm leaving them an SUV worth at least 10 or 15 grand behind the garage. If they're any kind of savvy gas station owners at all, they'll be way ahead of the game by sundown tomorrow.

I slip into the garage through a side door and find a Peg-Board with four sets of keys. There are cars in two of the four service bays. One set of keys opens the giant garage doors, which I do before sliding the third set into a beat-up pickup truck that no self-respecting state trooper, let alone Sentinel, would look at twice.

It fires up on the fourth try and has at least enough gas to get me back into Cobia County, if not quite to Barracuda Bay. I chug outside, knocking leftover tools and crunching over a leftover can of beer on my way.

I take it slow, lights on, until I reach the on-ramp back to the freeway. I take that slow out of necessity, since the truck is a beast and not exactly a sports car. Still, after about 10 minutes I'm back in the left lane doing a steady 74 miles per hour and heading home.

I feel lightheaded and know why: brain hunger. I unzip my fanny pack and grab the cans of cat food, tossing them onto the dashboard one by one like a Las Vegas blackjack dealer. I save the last one and peel off the lid with my free hand, using two fingers to scoop up the brown and gray gloop inside.

Oh, is it nasty. Really, it's just as wretched as you imagine it might be, but immediately I can sense the brain on my tongue as my body digests the pure cranium electricity. It is sinfully good. I switch to driving with my knees so I can gorge, cavewoman style, scraping every last bit of tongue, liver, and brain goodness from the corners of the can.

I slow to a steady 60 mph without a headlight in sight and finish all four cans in less than five minutes, feeling the brain—preserved, dead, and disgusting as it is—bring me back to life.

I'll need the real stuff to take on Val. No doubt

she's been feasting on live humans all the way to Barracuda Bay. For now this will get me home to Dad, who can hopefully score me some of the good stuff from the morgue.

You know, for saving his life and all . . .

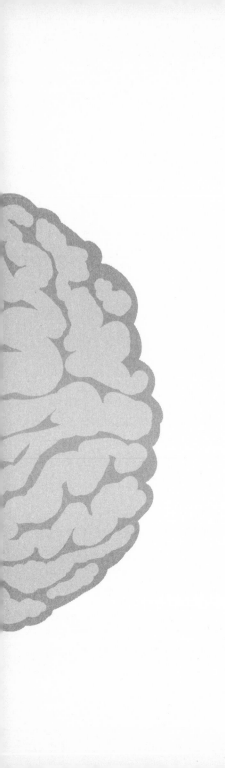

25
Back in Barracuda Bay

Barracuda Bay has changed. All of it. Every last inch. Bathed in the streetlights of what might prove to be the last evening of my Afterlife, I drive by the Barracuda Bay High yard in the broken-down truck I stole back in Bum Suck Somewhereville. It's gasping on its last legs as I cruise by mostly blue and gray portable classrooms. The town's struggling to rebuild the gym and everything else attached. The place looks clean and efficient and logical, but mostly it just looks . . . sad.

But it's more than just the burned-down gym and the rusty cranes still littering the football field. It's the gloom over the tiny little beach town.

A football team. A cheerleading squad. Half the faculty. Dane. Chloe. Bones. Dahlia. Hazel. Me. Stamp. All gone.

In one fiery night.

At first, the papers called it a tragic accident. But that wasn't sexy enough, I suppose, so it became known as the Barracuda Bay Blaze for the duration. Locals just called it a tragedy. All these months later, that tragic air still hangs, like a haze, everywhere I drive.

It hangs over Stamp's house, where a rusty For Sale sign sits crookedly in the dead lawn, Stamp's parents long since gone. Vegas, I think, Stamp said they moved to, or about as far from Florida as you can get without literally leaving the country.

Our house is empty too, though a tan van full of Sentinels—I can tell from the way the tires look nearly flat—sits in the driveway of the old Meyers' place, the house up the street that's been abandoned ever since it fell into foreclosure years ago.

I cruise by slowly, pink trucker cap low over my white sunglasses and my T-shirt collar tugged nearly up to my chin. The house looks grim and empty inside, with just the oven light on to fight the darkness. It's the one we left on all the time, day or night, just in case.

I can only crane my neck so far and, besides, if I linger too long the Sentinels will get suspicious. I speed up but not too much and only relax my shoulders when the van doesn't follow me up the street.

I avoid cruising by any of my other old haunts— Dane and Chloe's trailer, Barracuda Bay Galleria, Greenbriers Grocers, Hazel's house, or even the Sable

Palms Cemetery where I did most of my best grave rubbings—and park the truck in front of the Better Days Boutique downtown.

My pink and blue nightmare of a disguise might work on the Sentinels, but I'm not here for them, and there's no way to beat a Zerker if you're constantly tucking in your souvenir T-shirt or readjusting your shades.

Classical music plays softly in the background as I enter the vintage thrift store that always smells like licorice and white wine. (Don't ask.)

An old woman behind the counter looks up from some paperwork and eyes my unsightly garb. "We're closing in a few minutes, dear."

I nod and disappear into the aisles.

The Better Days Boutique was a favorite of Hazel's and mine over the last few weeks of summer every year, when our back-to-school shopping funds were always at their lowest.

I picture my best friend as she was back then, before Bones turned her Zerker: red-haired and adorable—if completely obnoxious—trying on every old-lady hat in the store while I reminded her about a little thing called "head lice."

She never cared. Making sure everyone in the store knew she was there and full of fun was worth it to her. And, hey, if she had to shave that lovely mane of red hair and get more attention, even better!

The store, my life, my future—I feel lonely without her.

I get busy choosing an outfit. All black. Leggings for kicking range. A hoodie for stealth. A tank top for when it comes time to take off my hoodie. Socks to cover my whitish-gray ankles. Sneakers for running, jumping, and hopefully escaping. And new shades just . . . because.

The older woman behind the counter rings it all up, her nose slightly upturned at the selections. "You do know this is a vintage store, don't you, dear? Wouldn't you prefer something a little more sophisticated?"

"Hey, don't stock it if you don't want to sell it, lady." I can't help it. I'm getting bitchier the longer I'm a zombie.

She blinks twice. "That will be $22.75."

Ouch. I only have $20 left after stopping for gas every few exits on the way down. But I don't want to put anything back, not even the shades.

"Can I get credit for what I'm wearing?" I step away from the sales counter so she can see the glory of my blue and pink nightmare.

She starts to wrinkle her nose.

I point to the pants. "Hey, these are worth $10 on their own. I mean, look at all those pockets."

When she doesn't bite, I throw a Hail Mary in quiet desperation. "You say this is a vintage store? These pants come straight from the '80s! And check out these boots. That is some *Private Benjamin* action right there! They're worth $10 alone, 'cause I know you can sell 'em for $30."

I get plenty of eye roll but also this: "Leave it all in

the dressing room, dear, and I'll figure something out while you change."

I grab the new gear and head to the fitting room to change. Nothing really fits right, but the only other black things in the store are frilly flapper gowns and beaded skirts and ruffled blouses, so I just double-lace the shoes and stretch out the leggings and the tank, and it's okay. Kind of. Sorta.

I check my look in the full-length mirror and roll my own damn eyes. How many black hoodies can one chick own, you know? If only I owned stock in Hanes or some such, I'd be one rich zombie right now. Real Housewives of the Living Dead? That's me!

The old woman eyes me on my way to the counter. "Fifteen dollars, dear, and not a penny less."

Jackpot! I was expecting her not to budge so much. That whole "these pants are so '80s retro" thing was a real stretch.

I smile and give her the $20, anxiously waiting for the $5 in change.

She hands it over reluctantly before turning her back on me and attending to some important BS behind the counter. I shrug and walk out, the pink fanny pack—and the electric pen—snug under my hoodie I got for a steal. (Take that, vintage thrift shop snooty old lady biotch!)

It's getting dark now, the air salty with the nearby sea, smelling as always of home. I'd been hoping to be in Barracuda Bay while the sun was still shining, but a flat tire just outside of Tallahassee and a dead battery just before Miami took up all of my time—and most of my stash.

Now it's nightfall and I can feel Val in the air, out there lurking somewhere not so far away. I leave the truck where it is and walk into the dollar store next to the thrift shop.

Jangly Irish music plays over the sound system as I walk past the cheesy green plastic beer mugs on Aisle 2 and giant bubble gum gold coins at the end of Aisle 4. I find what I'm looking for in Aisle 9 and buy it with three of my precious remaining dollars. I leave the coins behind on the counter because they'll make too much noise where I'm going.

Then I walk hungrily into the dense patch of woods behind the strip mall. It's pitch black, but I don't mind. In fact, it's better that way. The deeper and darker the woods get, the more intense my zombie yellow vision becomes.

Trees take shape, then leaves, then bugs crawling on the leaves. The ground is not just ground but twigs to walk over and stumps to walk around and broken bottles to avoid. I watch birds settled in for the night on branches high above: some big, some small.

They're all too small for what I'm looking for.

Not if I'm going to best Val anytime soon. And the

cat food? In the end, it did more harm than good, with more chemicals than brains and more sick than energy.

I need living brains, full of electricity, if I'm going to stomp Val into Zerker dust. I stop creeping forward into the woods and find a clearing with a stump I can sit on peacefully. I take the treats from the dollar store out of my hoodie pockets and spread them around; caramel squares in one pile, chocolate-covered peanuts in another, candy corns in the last.

Say what you want about candy corn, but forest rodents straight trip over it. I know because Dane taught me this trick the first week in Orlando, before we hooked up with Iceman. We sat there, Dane, Stamp, and I, in front of our own piles of gooey, chewy treats and had our fill of big, fat, juicy rodent brains.

Gross? Yes.

Survival? Necessary.

I sit back and wait. It doesn't take long. The forest kind of erupts, if you know what to listen for.

The squirrels come first. Fast little nutters, sniffing out the chocolate-covered peanuts with their beady noses and reaching with their tiny little hands as I sit, stock-still, waiting.

Then I erupt, hands blitzing their little necks as they squirm and squeal. Their brains aren't much bigger than marbles—tight, pink, chewy little marbles—but they do the trick. If only in small doses. Still, it's like making a whole meal of beer nuts. Good for awhile but hardly Thanksgiving dinner.

It's the raccoons who love the candy corn so much. One by one, silently stalking the forest, brave unlike the skittish squirrels or even the much shyer possums. The raccoons' courage is their undoing, at least on this night.

The first goes down easy, perhaps lulled by the surprise of strong, cold hands snapping her neck in two seconds flat. The second is a little more skittish, possibly more wary from the scent of her brother's blood spilled in great, gushing glugs behind my splattered tree trunk.

But it's the third that goes to town, hissing and spitting and scratching at my wrists until, at last, I ignore its neck and simply crack open its still ranting skull, sucking deep the golf ball–sized brain and chewing it until its live, electric juices make me whole once again.

I put the carcasses, all seven of them, into the plastic bag from the dollar store. I feel guilt-ridden but wired. I use the yellow light of my zombie vision to find a puddle of standing water and wipe the gunk from my hands, noting the dull raccoon scratches and timid squirrel bites on my palms.

I wipe gore from my mouth and chin. And then I walk from the woods to find the strip mall closed. I stand in the parking lot and spy the bank sign across the street. It's already 11:00 p.m., but just to make sure everyone's gone home I walk past each store in the strip mall.

Thrift shop.

Dollar store.

Hardware store.

Pawnshop.

Used record store.

All empty.

Even the check cashing place and the take-out pizza parlor are deserted. It's like a ghost town, but that's no surprise. Barracuda Bay always did roll up its sidewalks around 9:00 p.m. (And yes, that *is* my dad's expression, thanks very much.)

But tonight, I'm glad for the Bay's reputation as a sleepy little beach town. In fact, ever since I found out I wasn't going to make it by sunset and hatched Plan B, I've been counting on it. I yank open the truck door (it tends to stick) and push in the old-fashioned cigarette lighter in the dashboard. I dump the brainless carcasses all over the front seat, on the floorboard, even in the glove box. (The squirrels fit perfectly.)

Then I reach for the five gallons of gas in the backseat and douse it all: carcasses, upholstery, steering wheel, brake pedal, even the yellowed owner's manual. When the cigarette lighter pops out, I toss the gas tank in the truck bed and shove the red-hot lighter into the glistening wet upholstery.

It ignites immediately, and I drop the lighter on the floor, slamming the door and stepping back but staying close enough to rinse, lather, and repeat if the fire goes out. It doesn't.

Just the opposite, in fact. In seconds, the entire interior of the truck is engulfed in flames. We're talking nine-alarm, movie-stunt-gone-haywire fire. In minutes, the whole truck is ablaze, the crackling and hissing of fur and leather and drying bones and breaking glass piercing the night.

I shield my eyes from the flames and heat.

Just to make sure the right people come at the right time, I use the pay phone next to the check cashing place. I dial 9-1-1, and once someone answers, I drop it and just let it hang there.

Now I sit back and wait.

After a minute of dead air, they'll trace the call.

Operation Avenge Stamp is well under way.

I just wish Stamp was here to see it.

26
Daddy's Girl

Two cop cars at first, requesting backup.

Two fire trucks, one big, the other not quite as.

One ambulance, then two.

More cops filter in, four or five after awhile, the cars scattered around the parking lot. Firefighters hose down the truck till the fire turns the gushing water into hot, white steam.

It's still smoldering when, splashing around in thick black puddles, the firemen pick at the remains with axes.

I stand, dressed in black, behind one of the strip mall columns, unseen and ignored, all according to plan.

At first I think the firefighters will miss it, but then one calls out, "Hey, I got something here."

I can imagine him, spotting a raccoon jaw or a gnarly, pointy tooth or a burned-beyond-recognition

271

paw that might be a toe or a pinky finger. It will be enough. It has to be enough.

It is.

The first fireman calls another one over, then one more, and together they huddle, quietly picking around the steaming hunk of smoldering truck with their hatchets and thick, gray gloves.

Finally, one tells a cop, the cops come check it out, they confer with the EMTs, and that's when I hear it: "This is definitely human. Somebody needs to call the coroner."

The coroner: Dad. My dad will be here. And soon.

Sentinels or no, nothing or nobody—living or dead—is going to keep my dad from a dead body. I stand and wait for 5 minutes. Then 10. Then 15. Then 20. The cops get restless. I mean, there's only so many times you can wind and unwind crime scene tape from around a smoldering truck, you know.

At last I see the tan station wagon barreling down the street, little red siren stuck on top and blaring weakly in the middle of the night.

Dad. My dad! I can see him clearly through the window, balding head gleaming in the light of a passing street lamp, his moustache going gray now, his eyes open and alert behind thick bifocals, his face grim.

God, I never thought I'd see him again. And he's alive, with both his hands on the wheel and, I assume, both legs in working order. And . . . he's not alone.

Beside him sits a grim zombie, a Sentinel without the uniform. He's dressed instead as an orderly or assistant or something, down to the face mask and surgical cap, to hide his gray skin and thin, liver-colored lips.

But I can see his dead, black eyes glint in the same street lamp that makes my dad's bald spot shine. The assistant's dead dead, all right, the Living Dead. So maybe Vera was right. The Sentinels have found a way to stick with Dad 24/7, even if it means taking off their trademark berets and dressing as a coroner's assistant to get the job done. Maybe I misjudged the old Keeper.

I watch the station wagon turn in to the shopping center parking lot on two wheels.

I carefully scan the street beyond it. Sure enough, a minute or two later a tan van eases past with flattened wheels from the weight of up to four giant Sentinels. It circles around before parking in the deserted fast-food restaurant lot across the street from the cop-covered strip mall.

I scan the road for any other signs of Sentinels and see none.

And I nearly crumple to the ground. One team. One? Team? Vera told me two, three, even more teams were on their way to catch Val, to protect Dad.

Screw Val. She lied to me. That witch!

But it doesn't matter. In fact, it's even better this way. Fewer Sentinels on the ground in Barracuda Bay mean fewer Sentinels to mess with my plan. I keep my eyes on the road, watching carefully, until I see what I've been waiting for all along: one lonely car going slow, then slower, as it spots Dad rushing to the smoking truck.

The car turns around in the bank down the street and cruises past under the nearest streetlight. And that's when I see her in profile. Val's spiky hair. She's turned to watch the scene, cruel yellow eyes focused on my dad.

The car she's driving is a small black import, tinted windows, fancy rims on the tires. Knowing Val she probably stole it from the school parking lot just to look cool. Before she can spot me, I slip into the phone booth. The phone is one of those heavy, metal boxes, screwed to the metal part of the booth. I grab it on both sides and yank on it once, twice, until it pulls free.

The cops are still milling about, the light bars atop their cars flashing, the firemen putting their tools back, eager to get to the station so they can beat each other on *Halo 16* or something. It's now or never. If I don't cause a ruckus, they'll be gone before I know it.

I hoist the heavy phone unit onto my shoulder and walk unseen until I'm in front of the check cashing place. There's a sign over the door: Premises Monitored 24/7. I hope so. I really, really do. I raise the phone high, then launch it through the plate glass window in the front.

It's loud but not loud enough. But that's not the diversion I was looking for anyway. It comes in a split second: an alarm that has me running for the nearest column. And now the cops and even the firefighters come sprinting from their cars and trucks, passing the column where I cling and flooding into the store.

Once they're all inside, guns drawn, backs to me, I run to the nearest cop car. It's still idling, door wide open, lights flashing—and it's mine. All mine.

I get behind the wheel, strap myself in, and slam it into drive. It bucks like a wild bronco, leaps forward, and nearly pins Dad against the smoldering pickup truck as he continues sifting through the ashes, trying to identify a body that never was.

The Sentinel senses trouble, but he's still in the station wagon, eager to retain his anonymity.

I pull up more gracefully, until my open window faces Dad.

He turns, perturbed until he sees me. Really sees me. "Maddy?" he gushes.

"Get in," I shout. "In the back, and don't ask questions."

He gets in and doesn't ask a single question.

"Buckle up," I say, and the minute he does, I drive right past the Sentinel still struggling to get out of Dad's station wagon with his surgical mask half on, half off, his liver lips frozen in a silent scream.

Inside her little car, Val obviously hears me before she sees me and speeds up as I slam over the curb and into the street.

But her little import is slow, and my cop car is big

and bad and fast. God knows how many horses are stampeding under this shimmery black hood. I nail her car sideways, smashing her right taillight, spinning her around so that she's facing the parking lot.

Her expression is both shocked and evil, and that's before she sees it's me behind the wheel. When she does, she morphs to downright apocalyptic: yellow eyes burning, gray teeth gritting, mouth cursing.

Her slurs drown in our dueling revving.

She guns it. Smoke spews from the friction of one of her tires on the dented undercarriage.

"Maddy," Dad scolds.

But I ignore him, bearing down on Val's little stolen car as it flees into the night.

27
Cabana Charly's and the Eternal Tan

My teeth grind as I stay on Val's tail no problem, turn after turn, her one working brake light winking with each clamp on the brakes as she tries desperately and fails to shake me.

A few turns into the chase, Dad says calmly, "Lights."

The flicker of a smile crosses my face. Of course the first thing he says—the first real thing—is a reminder.

Still, I ignore him (uh, a little busy at the moment) until he says it again: "Lights."

"Dad, what?"

I check him in the rearview, and he's actually grinning. "I don't know who you're chasing or what they did to you or what you intend on doing to them, but if you don't want the rest of Barracuda Bay's finest to spot you in a stolen police car, you need to turn off your lights."

I snort. "Good thinking."

Have you ever tried finding the button to turn off the police lights while speeding down an empty street in the middle of the night at 80 miles per hour, trying to keep up with an angry, panicked Zerker who wants nothing more than to trick you into driving straight into a light pole? Then you know it's not so easy.

I finally find the switch a few minutes later, just as Val's turning toward the wrong side of town and down an old, dusty road I've never been on before. And I know, somehow I know, where she's going to take me: someplace big, someplace deserted, someplace private. Someplace befitting a violent, possibly re-deadly, show-down where the cops and certainly the Sentinels won't know to follow.

"Cabana Charly's," Dad croaks from the back, holding on to his seat belt for dear life. As we take another turn on two wheels, his face goes from hospital sheet white to zombie white.

"Dad, seriously, what? I'm trying to concentrate here."

His voice is eternally patient. "Whoever it is, probably going to the old Cabana Charly's factory. It's the only thing this far out in the boonies."

"The sunscreen place?" I say, killing my headlights to further confuse Val. I stay locked in on her winking taillight as a building looms in the moonlit distance.

"Yeah, it went out of business a few years ago, but I

still have to come out here every few months or so when a homeless person reports a dead body. Usually another homeless person's."

Sunscreen factory. Giant parking lot. Abandoned. Lots of space to kick my teeth in and torture my dad while she's at it. Why wouldn't Val like it?

It's downright Zerker-frickin'-rific!

I slam the brakes, and Val flies ahead through the rusty, open gate of Cabana Charly's. Once I can no longer see her taillights, I creep the car forward into the high brush of the lot just outside the gate. We're like a tractor moving through cornstalks, the weeds are so high. A few feet in, I can't see anything behind me. It's like the car has been buried by dandelions and saw grass.

I slip out of the car, open the back door for Dad, and hand him the keys. "Get lost," I tell him, only half-jokingly.

Before I can say, "No, really, I'm serious, head for the hills," he pulls me in for a gigantic bear hug. With all that's happening, I let him, sinking desperately into his fatherly smell of Old Spice cologne and the hand sanitizer he buys by the gallon for his desk in the coroner's office.

"I miss you, Maddy. Promise me that no matter what happens this time, we'll be together."

"I can't do that, Dad," I groan, shoving him away. "As much as I want to be with you, this isn't the kind of life you want."

"It's *my* life, and I want to be around to watch you grow up."

"This is it," I bark, reminding him. "I won't grow up."

He smiles placidly, too old and wise to get sucked into my eternally teenage drama. "Then I want to be around to watch you get older. Don't play semantics with me, young woman. You know what I mean."

Ugh. I look over my shoulder, imagining what Val has in store for me when I finally catch up with her.

"Will you leave if I promise?"

He nods. "I will pretend to leave if you promise, but I have no intention of running away from my daughter's fight."

Ugh, this guy. "Okay, all right, Dad, but stay here, okay?"

He nods, leaning against the car.

"No, really. Stay here. Don't fake stay here like in some cheesy movie where you come running in at the last minute to save the day. Really stay here."

He nods, but I can't stick around to find out if he's shining me on or not.

After all, I have a Zerker to kill.

At the last minute, just to be sure, I open the back door fast and shove him inside even faster.

He rocks the car and howls to be let out, but I feel better now.

Win or lose, live or die, at least Dad will be safe,

locked in the back of a police cruiser, buried in weeds higher than the top of most school buses. He might die from starvation when nobody finds him, but better that than be gnawed on by some Zerker witch.

And hopefully, when all is said and done, I'll be able to run or walk or even limp out of Cabana Charly's and come find him, let him out. Even if it's the last thing I ever do.

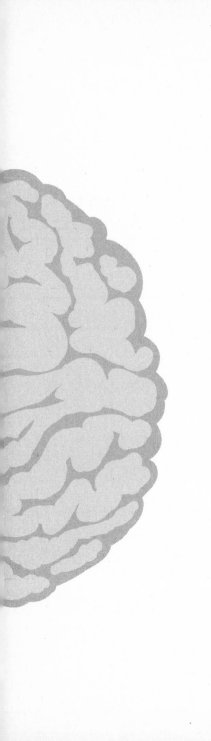

28
Bad to the Bone

The gate's open and Val's car is still running in front of a giant warehouse door. It's cracked open, and a sliver of light pours through. They still pay the power bills after being out of business a few years? Then I hear the long, slow whine of a generator running at Mach 10 somewhere out back. It sounds like every generator on our street when the power's out after a hurricane, a sound I know well.

I crouch on the other side of the door and slip the electric pen from my fanny pack to hide it. If I know Val, she'll have company and she'll frisk me—or worse. I think of hiding it in my shoe, but it might snap in half if I kick her or something, and then where would I be?

I shift on my toes. I feel a pinch at my chest. Bra strap! I work the seam at the underside of my bra until there is a hole just big enough for the pen to slip into. I wriggle it in until it's comfortable and doesn't look quite so obvious under my left breast, but without a full-length mirror and a little better lighting, what do I know?

Then I zip the fanny pack and straighten up. I'm going for stealth mode. But when I slink in the door, there she is: all 5'4" of Val standing right there, hands on hips, crooked smile on her face.

"Where you been?" she says knowingly, making me think she has her own satellite overhead or something and has been watching me with infrared vision this entire time. "We've been waiting for you."

"We?" I should have known better than to think—

Whoa! Who the hell are they?

In a storage cage, among old, dusty boxes of sunscreen and pressing against rusty wire mesh, a Sentinel extraction team is grunting. Five Sentinels, highly trained, highly equipped, all in trademark black. Only something's wrong.

Their eyes are yellow, and not just from the dingy generator lights blinking high overhead. Their skin is less gray, more green, their teeth wet with spittle, their jaws chomping with rage.

"Zerkers?" I spit, walking toward her. "You turned a team of Sentinels into Zerkers?"

So Vera didn't lie after all. She sent more than one measly team to protect Dad. Unfortunately, Val got to them first.

That.

Wily.

Little.

Bitch!

"Why?" I already know the answer. I just figure, the longer I keep her talking, the less likely she is to release the Zerkers.

Val shrugs. "I just wanted to see what would happen."

"And?"

"And," she snaps humorlessly, "you're looking at it."

"I've never seen a Sentinel turned into a Zerker before," I say, stepping slightly back. "I didn't even know it was poss—"

"Quit stalling." She yawns, running a gloved hand through her spiky hair.

Only, it's not a full glove. It's one of those fingerless ones like the BMX dudes wear for whatever reason. She's wearing red leather pants and a black concert T-shirt for some poser rock band she's probably never even listened to and a red vest over that, with a choker chain like some textbook wannabe punk-rock chick. Every stupid accessory just makes me want to smash her head in with a vacant building.

But she's the one with the cageful of Zerkers. All I have is an electric pen pinching the squeeze out of my left nip. So she still sucks.

Her thick black boots give her an inch or two, but

I still look down on her as I approach cautiously. I'm watching her. I'm watching the Zerker-Sentinels as they rattle their cage. And I'm watching for any quick exits. It's not that easy with only two eyeballs.

The warehouse is tall and wide, with lots of black squares where machinery has been moved over the years, revealing the original floor coloring buried below.

Big windows with bars on the other side are broken, letting in moonlight in little slivers or big swaths, depending on the size of the crack. Broken glass litters the warehouse floor. I step on shards, but it's hard to hear them being crushed the closer I get to the Zerkers in the cage.

"Leave them out of it, Val." I choke, failing to hide my nervousness. "I'm here. You're here. Don't be such a chicken."

"Me? Chicken?" Her voice is gravelly, her white skin leathery, her deep yellow eyes aflame with hatred. "Hardly."

"Really?" I snap, because it's been bottled up so long, it had to come out sometime. "That's why you hid up in the control booth while Dane and I tried to save Stamp? That's why you're standing here now, with a cageful of Zerker Sentinels ready to destroy me? 'Cause you're a chicken, that's why!"

She shoves me. Hard. Like, across-the-room hard. I've never been shoved so hard in my life. Not by Dahlia, not by Bones, not by anybody—live or dead—ever. I crash land against the cage, bending it in from the force.

The. Zerkers. Go. Nuts! They try to shove their fat fingers through the openings of the little wire squares. They rattle the cage until I'm sure the hinges will break. And, in fact, a big shard of metal dislodges in the tussle and bounces offs one of my shoes.

It's just out of reach until I sit up and turn over, my body tight from the fall, even though I can't feel anything other than maybe a harsher numbness than usual. That, and the certain reality that I am way out of my league. I reach out with one hand, my back to Val, making groaning noises to cover the scrape of metal as the shard leaves the concrete floor.

The Zerkers see it, but they either can't speak or don't care. They just rattle the cage some more. I turn just in time to see Val advancing on me, boot raised to crush my face. I jab the shard through her knee until the pointy end pops out the underside of her leg.

She howls from shock, not pain, flailing to yank it out.

The Zerkers are howling now too, turned on by the violence, I guess. They're slamming and banging the cage.

How long can that little cage hold against all that rage?

Val limps away backward, smiling as she reaches into her vest pocket.

I stand at last, my body trembling from the force of her last hit.

She holds a small red box with a long black button in the middle. She points it at the cage.

I flinch, imagining what's going to happen when the door swings open and those Zerkers fly out—straight at me, no doubt.

But the door doesn't open. Instead, a light flickers to my right, just behind Val.

She turns to me. "Not there, Maddy. Here!" She waves and walks dramatically toward something out of sight.

I scoot around the cage, around a stack of barrels and old broken slats of wood to find two large tanks standing next to each other. I can't tell what's inside because there's a black sheet covering each one, but they're glass and boxy. I can see that much. Like maybe elevators or those boxes where the lucky winner steps in and a giant fan starts blowing dollar bills around his head.

Hoses and dials stick out of each one. When I'm standing as close to her as I dare and facing both boxes, she yanks the black sheet off the first one.

Inside is a Sentinel. No, wait. A Zerker Sentinel. I can tell by the way he drools and chomps and his yellow eyes beg for mercy at the same time they long for my brain on a silver platter. Or, hell, a paper plate for that matter.

"Wh-wh-who is he?"

The Zerker pounds against the Plexiglas door of his giant box with huge, gray fists.

"And why should I care?" I add.

"You shouldn't care about the Zerker in this box." She caresses the little red clicker in her hand. "But you should care about what happens to him when I . . . do . . . this."

She pushes the black button, and the vague sounds of a vacuum start somewhere in the guts of the big glass box directly in front of me. The Zerker hears them, turning around, then back around, losing his black beret in the process and slamming into the Plexiglas door as it rattles and moans. His clumsiness, the human fear sunk deep in his human DNA, makes his plight all the more pathetic. Then the hoses on each side and on top of the box begin quivering, bulging, and hissing as something starts spraying inside the box.

Now I know what the big glass box is. I know exactly what it is. There used to be one in the Barracuda Bay Galleria: a Cabana Charly's spray tan box. You wore your bikini under your clothes; you paid $10 instead of $30 like they'd charge you for the same thing at the local tanning salon; and if you weren't shy about middle-aged men ogling you for 15 minutes, you got an automatic spray tan for like two-thirds off the going price. You know, just with a live audience.

Val must have found a few old ones on the warehouse floor and thought it would be funny to spray tan a Zerker. But no, that can't be all there is to it. Because the Zerker is going, well, berserk.

He claws desperately at the nozzles as something

white and bubbly coats him from head to toe. In seconds, maybe less, every item of black Sentinel clothing he owns is covered in greasy foam. It clings to everything: his hair, his eyes, his collar, his pockets, his boots, his fingers.

He snarls and wipes it off, but it only makes it worse. He's screaming now, then howling, as smoke begins to fill the box. I watch as the Zerker's clothes melt off, turning a powdery white before falling away. Bright red pustules rush to cover his arms, his neck, his chin, his thighs, his belly.

His white hair burns away to ash, and his skin begins to melt, dripping off his skull. His howls are muzzled now as oozing flesh fills his throat, at least until his lungs burst and leak down his rib cage like giblet gravy. Flesh puddles at his feet, his knotty, skeletal feet. All that's holding him up now is the box as his skeleton leans against the door, ribs and shoulder blades and finger bones clattering to the floor.

"What was that?" I say, mourning the boy, the human, the Sentinel that Zerker once was.

"Did you know there are 17 potentially deadly chemicals in each tube of sunscreen, Maddy?" Val paces in front of the second live spray tanning booth. "But the sunscreen companies, like Cabana Charly's, get away with it because they only use microscopic amounts in each batch. Well, I did some online research recently and discovered that if you use enough of it, there's one ingredient—avotoxia—that will actually eat human flesh.

"So I thought to myself, 'Val, how much avotoxia would it take to deflesh a grown man?' And I discovered, after going through a team or two of Sentinels over the last few days, that if you apply enough undiluted avotoxia, it will strip a man—even a Sentinel—to bone in less than 60 seconds."

"That's what you've been doing with your spare time?" I say, just stalling now, because I'm pretty sure I know who's going in that second box.

"Well, I knew it wouldn't take you too long to get here once you found out who I was and, of course, what I'd done to poor Stamp. So I thought I'd be ready for you, just in case."

And with that, she yanks the black sheet from the second tanning booth.

But it isn't for me after all.

In fact, it's already occupied.

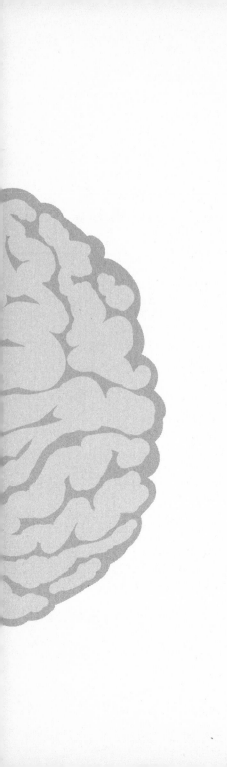

29
After the Afterlife

"Stamp! Stamp? B-b-but . . . how?"

I rush to the Plexiglas door and slam my palms against it.

Surprisingly, Val doesn't stop me.

Stamp's lips are moving, but I can't hear what he's saying. His big yellow eyes are pleading, his big gray hands pressed wide against the door. But they don't reach for mine to trace my fingertips with his own, the way they do in all those prison movies. One is too far up, the other too far down, and he can't quite seem to match them up so good.

He looks lost and helpless, kind of the same way he did after I first brought him back to life in Barracuda Bay. Dane and I kind of baby-stepped him into the Afterlife, but Dane's not here now, and I'm too tired, too weak, to do anything but stand here in awe that he's actually . . . re-alive.

I think of the sweet boy I bumped into, literally, in the hall his first day of school. How beautiful he was and how he didn't quite seem to know it. How eager he was for someone to be his friend, how valuable that friendship was to him, how cherished he became to me.

He was always happy to see me, even when we were fighting. He was like one of those baby ducks who imprint on the first thing they see: a mother duck, a rubber duck, a rooster, whatever. It was like he didn't know I wasn't special, like he believed I was someone worth getting to know.

And the look in his eyes made me believe it as well.

But now? Now his eyes don't look at me but through me.

"Funny thing about zombies," Val whispers close to my ear. "When you bite them, they lose a little too much of themselves. They're still re-alive, but not quite all there, you know? Kind of like our Zerker friends in that cage over there. I guess two zombie bites is just one bite too many, huh, Maddy?"

And just then Stamp moves his head for a better view, and I can see. At that angle, I can see his yellow eyes glinting. And I know, he may be re-alive, but he's already gone.

She saved him once, only to kill him twice.

"I'm sorry, but—"

Before she can finish her apology, I slam the back of my head into her face, smiling at the satisfying crunch of her nose breaking.

She tumbles into a heap, but when I turn to find the clicker it's still clutched firmly in her hand.

She sits, knees up, hands on knees, and shakes her head. Black goo dribbles out of her broken nose. Not too much. She quickly wipes it off with the back of one hand, her clicker hand.

"I guess I deserved that," she says. "I mean, after all I've put you through."

"I saw Stamp's body," I spit, advancing on her once more. "Back at the Splash Zone, in the shark pit. I saw his foot, his hand, his—"

"Did you ever see his face, Maddy?" she says, still on her rump, knees up in front of her.

"But he was there, at the bottom of the tank, looking up at me—"

"His face?" she says gleefully, as if I should be happy she saved Stamp from the shark tank only to turn him into a Zerker. "Did you ever actually see it?"

"I-I-I stopped looking, I guess, after awhile."

"Of course you did. In fact, I was counting on it. That's why it was so easy for me to turn one of those dopey nightclub kids into a Zerker, slip him into Stamp's black-and-white-striped hoodie, and chain him to the bottom of the shark pit. All those sharks, all those waves, the moonlight, the floating chunks of human flesh? I added those to get the sharks excited. Your emotions clouded your judgment. It could have been anybody down there. Anyone at all. But not Stamp. No, I had bigger plans for him, as you see. And plans for you as well."

"Like what?"

"Help me up, and you'll find out."

She dares me with those flickering yellow eyes, and I want to kick in that cocky grin with my thrift shop sneakers. I shake my head, and she waves the clicker in front of her face. I groan and yank her up like a sack of wet cement.

"I'll give you a choice, Maddy, which is more than you gave Bones before you and Dane ripped him apart that night."

"How would you know? You weren't there, and nobody who was survived."

"You mean except for you and Dane? And Stamp, of course? You think you killed every football Zerker or cheerleader Zerker or teacher Zerker that night? Think again. One got out, re-alive. Broken, bent, beaten, but still one of the Living Dead. You might even remember her . . ."

Val's tone is teasing, her eyes provocative. She's enjoying this. Even so, my heart can't help but try to leap at the news.

"Her?" I say, unable to hide the quiver in my voice.

Hopefully, helplessly, ridiculously, somehow I'm imagining Hazel limping from the burning embers of the smoldering gym. Or Chloe. Or, hell, even Dahlia would be a relief at this point.

Val seems to read my mind, shaking her head dolefully. "Mrs. Witherspoon. Art class. She still had her big red glasses clutched in her cold, undead hand."

I shake my head. So many people, so many victims. All because of me. I don't give her the satisfaction of seeing me smile at the mention of Mrs. Witherspoon's name.

"After I got to Barracuda Bay to avenge my brother, well, she wasn't too hard to find. Or break. She was all too eager to let me know what you did to her and the rest of the Zerkers, including my dear brother. Of course, I couldn't let her live with what she knew, but what does it matter, right? I mean, it's not like she wasn't already dead."

She pauses dramatically.

I grieve for poor Mrs. Witherspoon—again. I don't blame her for telling Val. After all, she was a Zerker, and I did copper stake the life out of the old witch!

"When I heard what happened, when I heard what you did, I made it my life's mission to get you back. For months, I stalked you. And when I found you, I saw how much Stamp meant to you. And I knew hurting you wouldn't be enough to make up for what you took from me. At least not at first. But like I said, I'll give you a choice. I can sunscreen Stamp to death, or you can take his place in the box. Your choice—"

My voice is resolute, demanding. "Me. Fine. What-ever. Get him out of there."

Choice? That's a choice? Like there is a choice. What does she think I'm here for? To save myself?

Val cocks one eyebrow, as if maybe she's surprised. "You sure? You saw what happened to the dude behind Door Number 1, right?"

"Val, whatever. I didn't expect to survive a tussle with you anyway, so—"

"Ah," she says, hand on her chest. "That's so sweet. And you're right. You're a dead girl walking, so you're making the right choice. At least this way Stamp gets to live. I mean, it probably won't be much of a life, but—" She shoves me out of the way while she pushes a four-number code on the side of the Plexiglas door. The min-ute she does, it hisses open and Stamp tumbles out, growling, looking confused.

I hug him quickly. I cling to him desperately. I don't care that Val is pounding on my back, that Stamp can't hug me back, doesn't know how to hug me back. Hell, that he doesn't even know me. I know, and I squeeze him hard. Taking in the smell of him, the feel of him, knowing in my cold, dead heart that this will be the last time. I don't care what kind of electronic volt therapy or whatever Dane called it that they're working on in the bowels of the rehabilitation center; there's no coming back from an avotoxia shower. That much I do know.

Stamp's body is a live wire of tension, like the Zerker electricity is surging through him up and down, back and forth. No wonder he can't think straight, can't even line up his hands or remember his ex. Is this how it might have felt to hug Bones? Or Dahlia?

Or even Val?

Val yanks me away from him and literally kicks me into the tanning booth before sliding the door shut. I gasp. I can already smell the chemicals hiding in the hoses and the tubes hooked up to the Spray Tan Death Ray Booth from Hell. Stamp looks at me from the other side of the Plexiglas door, confusion in his yellow eyes.

Damn, I wish I could cry!

And I wish he could talk!

If he could say just one word to me, one last word, it would all be worth it. I don't mind dying again. But dying with Stamp in limbo, bewildered and hurt and angry, feels worse than dying.

It feels like losing.

Stamp shuffles toward the door, hands outstretched, touching the Plexiglas, leaving big smears, lips moving but not saying anything. His gaze finally reaches mine, flickering with intensity, if not recognition. But instead of looking away or squinting angrily like the Sentinel-Zerkers still pounding against their cage, he looks at me, not through me. The eyes soften, then grow, and he's there. Stamp's there! I know he is. And he sees me, with those Zerker eyes, and I know, if he can see me, then after I'm gone, there will still be hope for Stamp.

At that moment, when I see the human, the boy, even the plain old zombie, in Stamp's yellow Zerker eyes, Val shoves him out of the way. He stands to one side, looking more wounded than if she'd torn off one of his arms.

Val's gloating, smiling, enjoying herself, poising the clicker in her hand.

Suddenly Stamp slams his hands down on either side of her head. His fists are closed, and I see them white and heavy as they crack the bones of each of her shoulders with a decisive snap.

She drops like a sack of Zerker, and the clicker skitters to the floor. I watch it tumbling end over end and wonder if it will land on the button and start the avotoxia and turn me into meat soup and dry bones despite all Stamp has done to save me.

It doesn't. For now.

Val's yellow eyes are full of rage as Stamp kicks her into a stack of barrels that barely move. I'd love nothing more than to watch him tear her apart, but I don't have time for that. I rip off my hoodie and reach under my tank top, turning delicately away in case Stamp sees. (Don't ask me why. It makes no sense. For one, he's seen it before. And for another, he's too busy breaking the rest of Val's bones.)

I slip the electric pen out and zap the combination

lock from the inside, trying to find a circuit where—

Hiss, click, it finally opens. I step out quickly, just in case she booby-trapped the sucker to start spraying if the lock is picked from inside.

She didn't. It doesn't.

Val is gurgling with Stamp's foot on her throat. Her wrist is at an odd angle and one foot is twisted badly, but she's still alive. I can tell she's alive from the blaze in her yellow eyes and the hum of bitter electricity shimmering off her in waves. She sees me emerge from the tanning booth and looks almost . . . hopeful.

Stamp is heaving, if not quite breathing, from the effort.

I walk toward him gingerly and reach out a hand.

"Stamp—" is all I get to say before he turns on me, a chunk of Val's thigh in his mouth.

His chin is covered with her black Zerker goo, and his eyes are more yellow than a blinking traffic light. His forehead is thick and lined with anger, and his gory clawlike fingers reach for me.

I bat them away harshly. "Stop it, Stamp," I shout, trying to reason as I stumble backward.

I click the top of Vera's electric pen, trying to get his attention, screaming with each flick: "Stop! Stamp. You. Stop. That. Right. Now!"

He lunges and I duck, trying to jam the pen into his knee. But he follows me, crouching too, his face centimeters away and his rage and fear and confusion in hi-def before he punches me squarely in the forehead.

Not expecting it, I tumble backward before I get really, really pissed. Stamp never trained with Dane and me. Not once. He called it a waste of time and preferred to go clubbing. Maybe he figured the Zerkers would want a dance-off or something when they finally caught up with him. Who knows?

My point is, now he's big and angry but still kind of, I dunno . . . stupid?

And angry. And maybe a little hungry? Whatever we shared back there in the booth, or I thought we shared, is gone. For now, forever, I can't tell, but this much I do know: I came here to avenge Stamp, not get eaten by him!

I approach him, pen in hand, and he looks at that hand, not my other one. So I smack him. Hard. I hear something snap, and it's not just his head. His eyes glow even brighter, and he looks at that hand, so I go to jab the electric pen in his neck and finish this once and for all, when he jukes just in time.

Okay, okay, so maybe he's not so dumb after—

"Umph!" I stumble back.

He advances, catching me off guard with another swift kick to the side. Being a Zerker has made him more limber? And not as dumb as I thought. The warehouse is getting smaller as he keeps pushing me back, back, almost to the vibrating cage of Sentinel Zerkers.

They are howling now, jamming on their cage, and suddenly I see. I see what Stamp is doing. He's leading me to them. He'll corner me, kick open their cage, or break the lock. Or, hell, maybe this sleeper mastermind Zerker yanked the key away from Val and he'll open it and unleash them on me.

On me!

This? This is how it ends? Stamp is alive, and now he's going to kill me? I've heard of jilted lovers, but this is pretty extreme even for a Zerker!

I fight frantically, kicking and jabbing and yanking, and get nowhere.

His left thumb is bent and he's limping. One eye looks wonky, and something brown and green oozes from his nose.

I'm no farther from the Zerker cage, and he's lots closer!

"Stamp," I plead, if only to lull him with my voice.

It doesn't work. He's gurgling at the other Zerkers in the cage, and they're frickin' gurgling back. They're almost like apes talking.

And I wonder, not for the first time, why zombies are so much like us and zombies who've been bitten by Zerkers are so much like animals.

Stamp reaches for the cage, and I kick him in the elbow.

He turns and growls, upper lip covered with Zerker slime, drool running down. And then something catches his eye just to the left.

I turn because I'm figuring it's Val.

It's not. Not even close.

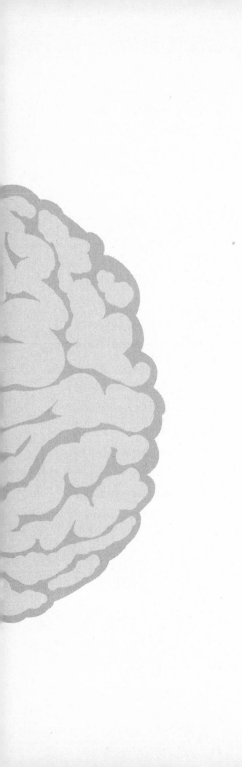

30
Rescue Me

"Umph," Dane groans, shoving his cane through Stamp's arm so hard it gets stuck in the corrugated tin wall of the abandoned warehouse. Stamp goes limp immediately, almost like the cane was made out of . . .

"Copper!" Dane says proudly, clapping like you do when you've done something thoroughly amazifying. Which he has! "I had the Sentinels build me a new one made all out of copper. With a rubber handle, of course."

I crush him in a hug. "Why on earth would the Sentinels build you a new cane? I mean, last I checked you were in handcuffs!"

"Yeah, well, that was before you escaped and I told them I knew exactly where you were going. Sentinels tend to like things like that. Got me a few brownie points and this shiny copper cane. Oh, and a ride here."

"How did you find me?"

He shrugs, trying in vain to pull his copper cane out of Stamp's arm. It's stuck not just through Stamp's bicep but deep into the wall behind him.

Dane grunts and gives up. "Well, I didn't think I would. I just lied to the Sentinels to get out of there and come after you, but they have this police scanner in their vans. So when we found out about the fire in the dollar store parking lot—nice touch, by the way—and then heard the cops squawking about one of their cars being stolen, well, I put two and two together and started looking for you."

"But the weeds," I cry. "I thought I hid myself pretty well."

"You did, only you gave your dad the keys before you locked him in the backseat. He let himself into the front seat and turned the cruiser's lights on."

"Dork," I say, but I don't really mean it. I don't even really know what I'm saying. I'm just . . . wiped out. It's too much, with the Stamp dying and the Stamp living and the Zerker Stamp trying to kill me and Dane—*Dane!* Too much.

"But how can you be here? Smiling? Saving me? When I betrayed you like that, back there at the center?"

He sighs. "Maddy, I knew you would break out of there the minute you didn't turn back to say good-bye when they first split us up. I don't blame you. I just wish I could have gotten here sooner."

I turn, dead heart 10 degrees warmer, and watch as a team of Sentinels—real Sentinels this time, not yellow-eyed Zerker ones—flood the building. They look severe and ignore us as they open up the cage and make quick work of the Zerkers, zapping them in the necks so they fall like cordwood to the factory floor.

I turn, looking for Val, and see her trying to limp out a side window but cursing the thick, steel bars that even she can't break.

Another team of Sentinels catch her and shackle her wrists, then her ankles, then chain all four together, bending her at the waist.

I walk toward them.

Dane says, "Maddy, we're done here. Give it up."

"Look at Stamp. Look at what she did to him."

He does. He stops and looks, his eyes big and admiring to see his old friend still alive. "At least she didn't kill him," he says gently. "Whatever he is, he's alive. That's more than we had before we came back to Barracuda Bay."

"I almost wish she had," I spit, seeing Stamp's greenish-gray skin and the Zerker muck on his chin.

"You don't mean that."

"Okay, but still . . ."

We look at each other, months of knowing one another inside and out shared in a single glance.

"Look, Maddy."

"I see him, all right?"

He smirks that smirk and holds up his left hand.

"No, really look."

"Your pinky!" It's back. His pinky. Is back. Well, I mean, most of it. It's gross and a little gnarly and too pink for his dead white flesh, but it wasn't there a few days ago and now it is! "How did that happen?"

"The Sentinels. I told you, they were experimenting with electricity to repair some of the damage from the sharks. Vera says if I keep up the therapy, my pinky will be—"

"Vera? What does she have to do with your pinky?"

"Maddy, the Keepers are in charge of my therapy. They're in charge of everything at the center. Even . . ." He looks at Stamp, then at me, and smiles. "Even in charge of rehabilitating Zerkers."

"You mean—"

"He means," says a familiar voice from behind, as Vera drags my father into the warehouse, "that there's hope for Stamp yet."

I turn to Dane, then Dad, then Vera. "But how—?"

"Vera organized all of this," Dane says, as if he's Vera's biggest fan or something. "She brought us here immediately."

I turn to Vera. "Even after what I did to you?"

Vera looks spiffy in her new Keeper uniform—even if one arm is in a sling. "I broke my own rule. I crossed the yellow line. I paid the price. My pen?" She holds out a hand.

I give it up reluctantly, somehow certain all this is some dream and the Zerkers are going to break free any minute and rip into us.

"Maddy," Vera says, "I'd like to talk to you when we get back about joining us. About joining the Keepers."

I shake my head, but Dane moves in. "Maddy, listen to her first. Please. For me."

"Why? You said yourself it's better to be free."

Vera says, "I know you two enjoy your freedom. Maddy, joining us at the center isn't a second death sentence. Besides, I think you would make a good Second Afterlife counselor for Stamp."

"Second Afterlife?"

She has her usual calm demeanor on and says logically, as if we're not standing in a warehouse full of Zerker bones and Spray Tan Death Ray Booths from Hell and I didn't, you know, break her arm in half. "When a Zerker comes back from the dark side, Maddy, we call it a Second Afterlife."

"You mean you've done this before?"

I see Stamp, still stuck to the wall with Dane's cane.

I peer up just in time to find Vera and Dane sharing a conspiratorial glance.

I look at Dane. "Well?"

"Yes, Maddy. We have. I have. I—well, this is *my* Second Afterlife."

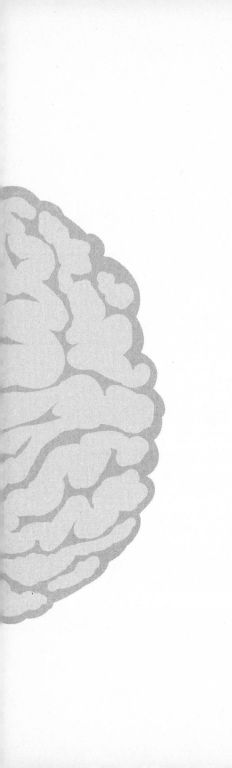

Epilogue
All in the Family

"No, Stamp, I told you already: that's all the brains you get this week."

Stamp huffs in his cell, statuesque but still clumsy in his green Second Afterlife jumpsuit.

His movements are a little jerky, and he still bumps into things, even though there's not that far to go and not too many things to bump into.

"This stucks," he says, shaking his shaved head.

I snort.

He grunts. "You're doing it again, Maddy. You're marking me."

"Mocking you, Stamp. And no, I'm not, but the word is either *stinks* or *sucks*. I think you're getting them confused."

"No," he whines. "I just wasn't sure which one I wanted to use, so I said both."

311

"Oh." I nod, feeling bad now. "Actually, that makes perfect sense."

"See?" He humphs and crosses his arms. He looks clean, healthy. The rehab is working. Slowly but surely.

I tick some boxes off on my clipboard and leave the cell.

"Where are you going?" he says, pacing just in front of the door the way I used to when it was me in the cell and Vera on the outside.

"I have to monitor some tests in the lab, Stamp. You know that."

I try to keep the impatience out of my voice, but it's clear from his expression that I don't succeed. Not entirely anyway.

He does this crumple-face thing he's been doing lately. "But, but . . . I miss you."

I stop and clutch my clipboard to my chest. Yes, I know. It sounds all gooey and like an ultimate awww moment, but sometimes Stamp is like a three-year-old in a toy store. *Stamp wants this. Stamp wants that. Stamp eat now? Stamp laugh now? Stamp miss you. Stamp love you. You let Stamp out now?* And then, just as you're falling for it, he'll notice some bug crawling in the corner or that his shoelaces aren't tied right and he'll immediately drop you like a hot potato.

So, yes, he misses me, but he also misses Dane and Vera and the Sentinel who brings him brains twice a week and the guy who drove him here and the janitor

Sentinel who never gives him the time of day.

"I miss you too, Stamp, but . . . Maddy has more work to do."

"That's all you do is work." He pouts, turning his back to me.

And I have to admit, he's kind of right. Ever since returning to the center, I've made it *my* Afterlife's mission to give Stamp a second one. I think he knows this, which is why he's not really mad. Just pouty.

He's been like that a lot lately, but it's better than when he first came here, all gross-eyed and Zerkery. Vera kept me away from him for the first week, during what she calls rehab but Stamp always calls The Empty Time.

From the sounds of it, I'm glad she did. He stayed in the lab, mostly, while I hung around with Dane in the medical suite, replacing his bandages and timing him on the treadmill as he trained so he could rely less and less on his cane.

"I still think I'll keep it," he tells me as he joins me at the end of the hallway, out of Stamp's hearing range.

"Why?" I say.

He twirls his copper cane with the rubber handle Charlie Chaplin style as we nod to Birch, the Sentinel on duty. "It's cool, don't you think?" Dane says.

"Not really," I say.

He shrugs.

I reach for the elevator button.

Dane pokes it with the rubber tip of his cane instead. "Comes in handy, though, doesn't it?"

"Okay, yes," I admit.

He pulls me to his side for a hug.

The doors ding open, and we both step back, spotting a familiar powder-blue uniform.

"Here to check on your patient?" I ask Vera as we cluster in the alcove outside the elevator.

She has some coloring books and a vocabulary workbook in her hand—the hand attached to the arm I broke. Vera gushes, "He's been combining his words lately. Have you noticed?"

I nod. "His latest is *stucks*, which I believe stands for *stinks* and *sucks*."

Vera smiles. "See, that's why it's so great that you agreed to be his Second Afterlife counselor. It would have taken me weeks to figure out that Stamp word."

"And your arm?" I say, avoiding her gaze as the guilt floods my voice.

"It's fine now." Vera pats my shoulder. "Thanks to your dad, that is."

The doors open, we say our good-byes, and Vera races toward Stamp's cell, eager to explore his growing vocabulary.

"Stamp word." Dane chuckles in the elevator. "I like that. He will, too, once he's back to his old self."

"You think he'll ever get there?" I say, nuzzling him

in the 2.7 seconds we have left before the elevator reaches the ground floor.

"He'll get there." Dane raises his new finger. "Just like Mr. Pinky here! And look at Vera's arm. If he's going to get help anywhere, he's in the right spot."

I bite my lip as we exit the elevator.

We weave through a dozen thuggish Sentinels who all seem to know Dane's name by now.

"Wow, that didn't take you long," I say, admiring Dane in his sleek, new black Sentinel uniform.

"What's that?" he says, after high-fiving a Sentinel so big he nearly has to stoop to enter the elevator.

"Winning over your sworn enemies, the Sentinels?" I say.

"I never called them sworn enemies, did I?"

"Yeah. About 1,000 times. At school, in your trailer, on the way to school, on the way to your trailer, in Orlando, at—"

"All right, all right." He grins as we head toward a door marked with this notice: Keep Out! Approved Personnel Only.

They are double doors, black (though most are red), and guarded by a special six-key entry code. I punch it in—785439, if you're wondering—and wait for the doors to hiss open. I can hear Dad's voice even before signing in at the guard station, where a Sentinel named Clive— yes, yes, I've finally learned some of their names—does a weird handshake thing with Dane.

I arch my eyebrows about it while waiting for Clive to key us in to the second set of hissing double doors.

Dane straightens his beret. "It's a Sentinel thing. You Keepers just wouldn't understand."

I straighten the cuff of my new powder-blue Keeper uniform and walk through the door, smirking.

"Listen, Hector," Dad is saying in his exasperated voice. "You can't just zap these guys anywhere and expect the therapy to work. You have to address the affected wound directly, like this."

Dad puts his surgical mask over the lower half of his face—he always takes it off to berate interns, zombies, whoever—and passes what looks like a bar code scanner over the divot in a young Sentinel's arm.

A kind of rosy-pink glow illuminates the wound. Even from across the room I can smell the skin and muscle healing. It's not like the rotting smell of death but more like . . . hamburger cooking.

Hector nods.

Dad hands the wand over, watching patiently, completely ignoring Dane and me.

The Sentinel waves the wand carefully over the wound. He looks pro in the medical scrubs, apron, and mask Dad made them special order for him last week.

"Fine, yes, like that," Dad says, winking at me. "Just for the next 10 minutes."

"What are you going to be doing?" Hector says.

"Talking to my daughter, that's what!"

Dad motions for us to follow him into the office he's set up in the next room.

As I sit in one of the two chairs on the other side of his desk, I'm struck by how much this office looks like his old coroner's office back home.

"How are you kids today?" His rosy cheeks glow on either side of his new, if graying, goatee.

"Forget us. What's with you scolding a real, live Sentinel like that? You do know Hector could rip you into little pieces that would fit inside one of your desk drawers, right?"

Dad waves dismissively. "Listen, Maddy, the Sentinels asked me for help with their electric therapy program, okay? If they want to do it right, then techs like Hector need to know how to do it right. It's in their own best interest to learn, right?"

I sigh. "Yes, it is, of course, but just remember you're human, okay?"

"How could I forget?" He pours coffee from his new two-cup coffeemaker. I smile to see him adding cream and sugar in the old, cracked Christmas mug he brought from home. "It took them five days to install a toilet, for Pete's sake! It's barbaric to make a grown man go in the woods, Maddy!"

"Well, Dr. Swift, you know zombies don't actually need toilets, right?" Dane smirks, fiddling with one of the pockets on his legs.

"Yes, Dane, I know that perfectly well, but couldn't

they have installed just one toilet when they built this place? I mean, just in case?"

"I can't imagine they were ever planning on inviting humans inside, Dad."

"Yes, well, as the first human to ever become a Sentinel, I hope to make a few more changes around here before I'm done."

"Okay, Dad." I groan, rolling my eyes at Dane. "We just stopped by to see how you were doing." I start to get up.

Dad motions me back down. To Dane he says, "Son, could you go check on Hector for me, please? Make sure he's not starting a fire with the bedsheets again?"

Dane chuckles and winks at me. The doors hiss behind him as he walks back into the lab.

"Dad, obvious much?"

Another dismissive wave. "Dane doesn't care. Besides, how much can you two see of each other anyway? Twenty-four hours a day isn't enough? He can spare your old man a few minutes, can't he?"

I shrug. I really do need to spend more time with Dad. Ever since we dragged him back to the center, we're both knee-deep in work during the day. And since he still has to sleep, he's always zonked out by the time I actually have an hour or two to hang out with him around, say, three in the morning.

I smile.

"So how are you, really, Maddy?"

"I'm good, but I'm used to all this. How are you doing?"

"I'm still working with dead bodies. Only, these ones are walking around."

"I'm sorry it turned out this way. I tried to keep you out of it. Really, I did."

He shrugs. "I got tired of you keeping me out of it. Frankly, I'd rather have a zombie for a daughter than no daughter at all."

"Ah." I crack a joke, if only to not choke up. "That's the nicest thing a human ever said to me."

We chuckle.

"You talk to many humans lately, Maddy?"

We make small talk for a minute or two, just like back home. He looks so comfortable with his rumpled lab coat and his coffee mug. I can't help but be happy to see him here. Time will tell if he'll ever be happy, but . . . was he ever?

Even back home, with his house rules and his concerned face, the only time he seemed really happy was when he was reminding me how scary, creepy, and unhappy the real world is. Now he knows there's a real world beyond the real world, and that's given him even more reasons to be happily unhappy.

Jingling a key chain from the top of his desk, he says, "Do you want to see how Val is doing?"

I shrug.

He stands and leads me through the lab, motioning for Dane to follow. "Hector?" he shouts, pausing before the double doors.

"Going strong, sir."

Dad shoots him a frown.

Hector shakes his head. "Sorry. Going strong, Doctor."

"Better," Dad says, mostly to himself.

Dane and I follow dutifully as Dad leads us down the hall toward a green door marked Keep Out.

"Ignore that," Dad says, sliding in his single key. It's about the same size and heft of the one I stole from Vera to escape to Barracuda Bay.

Inside are two doors. One is a cell, the other clear Plexiglas. Val is in the cell, strapped to a bed. She turns her head toward us, blonde hair no longer spiky but extra greasy instead. Though her eyes blaze a healthy, angry yellow, her mouth is covered by a thin leather strap locked tight at the back of her head.

"We had to muzzle her," Dad explains. "I can't imagine why, but she kept trying to bite me."

"She didn't, did she, Doc?" Dane says with a mock-worried expression.

Dad slaps his shoulder.

I roll my eyes, though it's nice to see them getting along. Dad was always Team Stamp, after all.

"How is she doing?" I say. "I mean, really doing?"

Dad frowns. "She's not taking to the therapy as well as Stamp, obviously. Frankly, I'm not sure she'll ever be completely Zerker-free."

"Is that what this is for?" I turn to the second door, the Plexiglas one that fronts the second mobile spray tanning booth from the Cabana Charly's warehouse.

Dad looks at it regretfully. "I suppose so. I was against the Sentinels moving it here when we left Barracuda Bay, but apparently they're trying to isolate the avotoxia chemical and use it in some kind of anti-Zerker weapon."

Dane nods toward Val, who's suddenly gone quiet. "Are you sure you should be sharing trade secrets in front of her, Doc?"

Dad smirks as he hustles us both from the room. "Val? Look where she is. She's not getting out anytime soon."

Coming April 2014
Book 3 in the
Living Dead Love Story Series

ZOMBIES
Don't Surrender

Rusty Fischer

Also from Rusty Fischer

VAMPLAYERS

At the Afterlife Academy of Exceptionally Dark Arts, the vampires in training follow one of two tracks: they become either Sisters or Saviors. Of course, everyone wants to be a Savior, swooping into infested high schools in matching red leather jumpsuits and wielding crossbows, putting down swarming vampires with deadly efficiency.

But Lily Fielding is just a Sister—a Third Sister at that, a measly trainee. When Lily and her two Sisters, Alice and Cara, are called out to their latest assignment, she figures it's just another run-of-the-mill gig: spot the Vamplayer (part vampire, part player), identify the predictably hot, trampy girl he's set his eyes on, and befriend her before the Vamplayer can turn her to do his bidding.

Finding the sleek and sexy Vamplayer, Tristan, and his equally beautiful and popular target, Bianca, is easy. And when Lily meets the adorably geeky Zander, she too falls under a lover's spell. But this assignment turns out to be trickier than most when the Third Sister must battle the baddest vampire of all.

ISBN# 978-160542449-1
Trade Paperback
US $9.95
AVAILABLE NOW
zombiesdontblog.blogspot.com

MEDALLION

P R E S S

Be in the know on the latest
Medallion Press news by becoming a
Medallion Press Insider!

<u>As an Insider you'll receive:</u>

• Our FREE expanded monthly newsletter,
giving you more insight into Medallion Press

• Advanced press releases and breaking news

• Greater access to all of your favorite
Medallion authors

Joining is easy. Just visit our website at
<u>www.medallionmediagroup.com</u> and click on
the Medallion Press Insider tab.

m e d a l l i o n m e d i a g r o u p . c o m